Chris Kassel's

Black Tongue Speaks

...

Paperback Edition
First Printing October 2016

Cover Art by Monika Ekiert Jezusek

ISBN-13:978-1539408680
ISBN-10:153940868X
BISAC: Short Fiction, Horror

Contents

Foreword

BLACK TONGUE SPEAKS

FOREWORD

FOREWORD: BLOOD IN MASON JARS

Some of us remember childhood as being unbearably sweet; others recall things differently.

I'm in the second group, with the kids who spent inordinate chunks of growing-up time afraid. Not of loving, fawning, tactile reality—one learns early how precious summer sunshine can be. But, perhaps like you, whether or not I wanted to, I saw through the sunshine, beyond the happy birthdays and merry Christmases, to a yawning chasm filled with irrational and incomprehensible things. They were outside my window peering in; they were shuffling and muttering in the basement; they were weeping softly in the attic. Most preposterous of all was when they originated between my own ears, entirely self-induced and self-directed—when nightmares grew so graphic that ultimately, it seemed that there might be more to fear from within than from without.

In adulthood that proved to be precisely the case, didn't it? Just when our boogeymen were chased away, when the demons pulled off their masks and the muttering in the cellar wound up being the sump pump, it turns out that life's genuine horrors are almost always committed by those who are closest to us; by those who—on paper anyway—are supposed to love us.

Random, impersonal fear dissolves with the revelation that you're four times more likely to be murdered by someone you know; when the stranger lurking in the basement is your lover and when the cop says, "We've traced the call and it's coming from inside the house', it's because the call is being made by someone who lives there.

As grownups, it isn't the unknown that takes us down; it's the familiar—

that's when those sunny afternoons grow intolerable and morning is scarier than midnight.

That's when fear becomes omnipotent.

To me, writing horror fiction is like canning evil; the goal is to preserve the essence of the gore and venom in a controlled environment. Codify the nightmares and arrange them in sequence. These seventeens tales are done in the style of the short stories that helped steer me through a creepy childhood—those stories by Blackwood, Bloch, Jackson, Bierce, et al.—of which I really can't find modern examples, at least not in quite this incarnation: Simple and concise with a brain yank or two.

As a kid, reading this sort of fiction helped me process my private creepshow; as an adult, writing it helps me cope with the same creepshow—which, I promise you, hasn't ended yet.

- Chris Kassel, Halloween, 2016

WHERE'S REYNOLDS?

WHERE'S REYNOLDS?

Alexander de Buchan was a singular shopkeeper with a singular personality—when the occasional customer stepped through his creaky doorway and rang the antique brass bell, he emerged from the rear office and was at once gruff and accommodating, polite and terse, cool and ardent, taciturn and verbose—and always on the single subject closest to his heart: Books.

Total mastery of his discipline was why de Buchan was hanging on in a profession that had largely given up the ghost during the previous century.

De Buchan was a dealer in antiquarian volumes specifically, and he operated a dusty old store on the corner of Gautier and Patterson off Massachusetts Avenue in Cambridge. The place might have been a landmark, but the ravages of modernity, from Amazon to eBooks, had sapped most of the serious trade, although the stooped, contrary, well-seasoned proprietor had been on that corner so long that among his few customers were the grandchildren of folks who had frequented his shop in better years.

But 'better years' was strictly a fiscal appraisal. If the truth is told, Alexander de Buchan was perfectly content with his current level of custom—his clique of collectors, his burble of bookworms, his lick of littérateurs. He was notoriously camera-shy and disliked gatherings and superfluous chatter and never promoted his shop.

3

He didn't advertise, and he didn't condescend to be interviewed or do author signings to court a new generation of clientele. He shadowed the shelves of De Buchan Books through the day, a dusty, scholarly ghost, and slept in an apartment attached to the rear. He'd never missed a single rent payment in all the years he'd been there, having outlived a number of landlords and outlasted the rest.

However unique as it might have been, de Buchan's personal history was of little interest to Bruce 'Babycakes' Gunner, a small time hustler who earned his living by scamming local college students. He was 35, but looked a lot younger, and among his favorite cons was posing as a foreign student trying to cash official-looking checks; the unwitting mark, generally a credulous female freshman, deposited the check in her own account, withdrew it in cash and handed it over. Naturally, the check bounced, but by then, not only did Babycakes have the unwitting student's cash, he also had her private banking information.

This and similar scams had seen him through many, many semesters, and would have probably seen him through many more, but in November, a genuine, hustle-free windfall landed on him: His uncle Thornburn died. Thornburn Gunner had been a wealthy, single and relentlessly eccentric octogenarian, one of the city's old-school bluebloods. Thornburn had a family reputation as a pack rat, although someone from the Mayo Clinic might have described him in slightly more favorable terms: As an atypical accumulator of Americana or a quirky connoisseur of curiosities, primarily because the things he hoarded were kept immaculately clean and sat in ordered dignity throughout his vast estate.

The dispensation clauses in his will treated them with the same level of respect. Take his rumpus room model train set, which chugged through a re-creation of 1940s Boston complete with terminals, parks and warehouses. That went to the son of a business subordinate who, thirty years earlier, had expressed interest in his 'choo-choos' and gone on to become an executive at Amtrak. His several hundred Renaissance and Medieval knives, daggers and swords wound up the property of his CFO, the man responsible for reducing the head count when one of his companies absorbed a rival. His thousand *chapeaux,* including an Ecuadorian fireman's hat and an authentic Admiral Nelson bicorn, went to his tailor.

However, among his most prized, most valuable and most secret possessions was an antebellum manuscript that had passed through very few hands before his; a bundle of yellowed stationery consisting of four leaves filled with strong, formal handwriting.

It was the final item in the massive estate with which Thornburn Gunner's trustees now dealt.

Babycakes had not expected any inheritance, of course; Uncle Thorny had been a brutal businessman, a cutthroat CEO, a pitiless proprietor, but he was fundamentally honest. His fortune was above-board and earned the old-fashioned way: By stealing with the blessing of the SEC. At the time of his nephew's first brush with the law, Thornburn had made it known that he had no tolerance for such lifestyles and would oppose this work ethic to his dying day. 'Something for nothing' was Thornburn's professional anathema, but it happened to be Babycakes Gunner's mission statement.

Babycakes was fine with the estrangement, and so the years had gone by, and now he expected that if he was mentioned at all in the will, it would to formally acknowledge his disinheritance.

He was that much more surprised when the estate's executor phoned him the morning following the funeral to let him know that the mysterious manuscript, along with a letter from his late uncle, was awaiting him in a safety deposit box at the attorney's office.

The only stipulation was his adherence to a single basic condition, which was, the lawyer said, explained in detail within the letter.

"Your uncle wanted to find just the right home for all of his heirlooms," said Cormac. He had known the family for decades and was, of course, aware of the reputation of the young man to whom he was speaking.

He went on: "Thornburn treasured this one artifact above all the others, so why the recipient would be you, I couldn't guess in a thousand Sundays. But I'm not paid to speculate, am I? I'm paid to see that Thorny's wishes are carried out to the letter, and so…"

Babycakes shrugged, grinned, pinched himself over his stroke of fortune and picked up the security container at McInerny's tony

Tremont Street law office.

Whereupon, he returned to his duplex and broke the tamper-evident seal and read the letter:

'To my wayward, contumacious and headstrong Nephew:

It will no doubt shock you, as it did old Cormac, that of all my potential heirs I have chosen you to receive my single most cherished possession. As you are about to see, it is a manuscript of astonishing importance. Even more critically, at least to historians, is the fact that it contains the answer to one of the most enduring mysteries in the annals of American letters:

'Who was Reynolds?'

Dear boy, you were chosen not in spite of your particular ethical shortcomings, but because of them. Among my well-meaning and loyal associates, I can't think of a single one who would not be so starry-eyed and giddy simply holding the thing that they wouldn't ultimately mishandle it. Not over money, of course—and it is worth plenty of that—but because they are ethical people, and I firmly believe they'd be swindled by some nefarious grifter uninterested in the genuine worth of the piece, which as I have said, is far more literary than financial.

I chose you, Nephew, because the old expression 'It takes a thief to catch a thief' applies equally to frauds, and at that, you are certainly at the top of your game. I am confident that you will be able to weed out any hustler who would try to exploit what this text represents without truly understanding it...

The manuscript is the final written words of Edgar Allan Poe.

I am certain that this name is a familiar one, even in your netherworld. The document has been fully authenticated; it was composed by Poe at Gunner's Hall on October 3, 1849—the same day he was found unconscious in a Baltimore gutter and transported to the Washington College Hospital, where he died the following Sunday. The pages of which you are now in possession were scooped up by the landlord of Gunner's Hall—your great great great grandfather, it happens—in lieu of the bill owed by Mr. Poe. The landlord died shortly afterward, and the work remained with his wife—your great great great grandmother—who had no idea of its worth, but still kept it among her things—she was, like me, a collector of curiosities. Thus, it managed to slip without much notice through the generations, to me. And now, to you.

As far as I know, its actual significance was never realized. It's not so much that this is the final script composed with the master's quill, but what the text actually reveals.

You see, Poe died without having regained his senses sufficiently to explain how he came by his peculiar predicament in the gutter, but still more mysterious to his fans, then as now, were his dying words, as recorded by the attending physician, Dr. John Joseph Moran.

Preceding his death, Poe cried out a single question repeatedly, and it continued until, as Moran writes, 'the arched heavens encompass'd him':

That query was, 'Where's Reynolds?'

It was a question without an answer—no one present knew to whom Poe was referring. He died unfulfilled, and the mystery has followed Poe's legacy as rabidly as Monsieur C. Auguste Dupin dogging a felon. Despite the best efforts of the academics, Reynold's identity has never been established.

And here you have the genuine value in the thing you now hold within your grasp. These four ocher leaves reveal in full detail, in Poe's own words, the answer to the age-old enigma: Who was Reynolds?

I have read these pages a thousand times of course, but in my lifetime, I chose not to expose them because I have, in my own way, enjoyed the cat-and-mouse pursuits of literary sleuths throughout the ages. But since you are now reading my words, it means that my own skin in the game no longer matters because 'the arched heavens hath encompass'd me.'

Knowing Poe's final question—and the name 'Reynolds'—is your charge, Nephew; that is the string I have attached to this bequest. If you sell the manuscript—and sell it you will; I know you that well— it must be to an individual who can repeat Poe's question instantly, without research, without reference, without legwork, because any true Poe fan knows the name Reynolds as well as he knows what the Raven quoth. And this is the individual I would like to be the ultimate caretaker of the prize, to do with it as he or she sees fit.

So now, go on a quest to find a suitable home for our literary treasure. You will use your electronic telephone, which I am told is capable of making films, to record anyone you approach to ask about Poe's dying query.

9

When you find the person who can recite it without hesitation, I urge you to sell the manuscript for whatever that person is willing to offer, a small amount or a large one. He or she will be the right individual, so what they can afford to pay must be acceptable.

Because, upon conclusively proof that you have carried out my single condition, I have left old Cormac a check to be delivered to you in the amount of three million dollars.

In pace requiescat!

Your Uncle Thorny'

Babycakes twisted his face into a pucker of concentration, put his feet up on the Starphire glass of the coffee table he'd rented-to-own under a fictitious identity and poured himself another Glenmorangie Pride from the bottle he'd siphoned at Magill's and replaced with Ballantine. Sheer Mag punk pulsed from the wireless Play-5 speakers he'd lifted from Anne's apartment, a girl he'd dated for a single weekend.

Now he held aloft the brittle, yellowy, lightly ribbed pages and considered the even, spidery hand inked in neat rows across them. As an artifact, it did indeed have a certain authoritarian gravitas, regardless of what it said.

As to that, of course, he couldn't care less. Poe meant nothing more to him than some name on an old Roger Corman flick and Reynolds was the logo on the aluminum foil used to package cocaine. But he was hard-wired to look for exploitable angles in any opportunity, and in this one, they were legion. Obviously, the easiest out was to sell the manuscript to the highest bidder, then knock ten grand off the price if the client would consent to be filmed speaking the secret word, which Babycakes was happy to feed him beforehand. Old Cormac would be none the wiser— and Old Cormac was not paid to speculate.

But something nagged at Babycakes' inner tickings, and he didn't know exactly what it was. So he drank purloined Scotch until he figured it out: It was a vestigial conscience, unused in years, hitherto a remote abstraction. It was sort of like a soul appendix: You didn't know you had one until it started acting up. But he suddenly realized how proud he was that his wealthy uncle had finally damned him with some faint praise and owned up to his carefully honed skill set. His own father had never done so; the old man had been a total killjoy living in a dimension where nothing quite measured up. Had Babycakes discovered a cure for cancer, the old man would have flipped him off because he had emphysema. So the unexpected avuncular pat on the back, even from the dark side of the moon, meant the world to him.

In the end, he decided to take an absolutely unprecedented course of action by playing it by the rules.

For twenty-four hours, anyway. After that, Babycakes figured, he'd have given the straight 'n' narrow his best shot, and if he hadn't found anyone who knew about Reynolds in that time, the gods had spoken and it was back to monkey business as usual.

And that's how Babycakes Gunner came to ring the antique brass bell of De Buchan Books on that gusty, frosty afternoon in late

November.

The old shop on Gautier and Patterson was the final stop on an expedition intended to tamp out any fires that might break out in his nascent sense of ethics. Throughout the day, as Uncle Thorny had intended, he'd grilled a number of bookstore clerks and counter-jockeys, mostly bored senior citizens, bored college students, and a few who were Olympic quality geeks whose brains, like his, inextricably linked Poe with Vincent Price.

As to Poe's final words, not one had the slightest clue. Guesses ranged from 'Nevermore' to 'Do we have any bourbon left?' to one pencil-necked nerd from Cash-4-Books who'd come closest, suggesting, "Where's Annabel Lee?"

He'd been on his way to the Harvard Square Station to catch the train home—in the morning, he intended to call a series of high-powered rare book dealers and squeeze every cent from Poe's last words. In fact, he might not have bothered to stop at De Buchan Books at all; it was late, it was dark, and the shop was without visible sign that it was even open. But in the display case was a set of antiquarian volumes with raised bands and gilt titles: *The Complete Works of Poe.*

A sign from beyond the pale, perhaps? From Uncle Thorny maybe? Just in case, Babycakes Gunner stepped across the threshold and into the labyrinthine cloister of the shop.

Within, the air was chilly and wore the keen perfume of old books—vanilla and must. Forbidding shelves marched into shadows; burnished folios and embossed collections stood in dark, ordered rows; heavy books were displayed in clamshell cases with double-hinged spines. Two mahogany-framed easy chairs huddled in front of a turbulent, roaring fireplace—and as usual, they were unoccupied.

At the sound of the bell, de Buchan stumped from the umbral bowels of the place. He wore a woolen coat with tape trim accents and silk at the lapel and with an alacrity that was striking for a man of advanced years; he peered over pince-nez spectacles at Babycakes, who had his right arm extended, holding his iPhone 6s out.

"How may I serve you, young man? And why in the world are you holding that up ludicrous apparatus?" asked de Buchan candidly.

"Never mind, Pop; just a quick question for you—don't mean to interrupt your busy day…"

De Buchan made a dismissive gesture at the sarcasm, tossing off his tapered fingers in a flick. "Folks said that the paperback novel would be the death knell for the dealer in antiquarian books, yet here I am."

"My bad, Pop, no offense. So the question is this: 'What were Edgar Allan Poe's dying words?'"

De Buchan didn't miss a beat. He pinched the bridge of his spectacles on the top of his long nose and said, "Why, according to the papers of his physician, his last words were, 'God has his decree legibly written upon the frontlets of every created human being, and demons incarnate, their goal will be the seething waves of blank despair.' Although given his condition, the idea of him babbling poetry at such a moment is highly suspect."

De Buchan pointed again to the iPhone and said acidly: "That is not a recording device is it? I never consent to recorded interviews. It's my personal bugbear. I'm like the Lakota who believe that photography steals a portion of their soul…"

Babycakes frowned; he was only half listening. He was a bit crestfallen: An inexplicable part of him had wanted to comply with his uncle's request to the letter. He slid the iPhone into his pocket. "Doesn't matter now," he said wistfully. "'God' isn't the name I was looking for."

Dejected, he turned away while De Buchan cleared his throat and said, "Name? You may, of course, be referring to Reynolds."

Now Babyface's baby face broke into the broad, slow 'gotcha' grin that old women wear when they're the only Bingo player with N-31 and it completes the card. With his back to the shopkeeper, and as surreptitiously as he could, he removed the iPhone, held it under his arm and started recording again. "Repeat that name, would you?" he said, feigning nonchalance.

The shopkeeper shrugged. "Reynolds? Poe is said to have cried out 'Where's Reynolds' many times in his final hours, although no one has ever determined who that mysterious being might have been."

Babycakes nodded and turned around quickly. "Never mind about the camera, my man; let's discuss some business."

Half an hour later, the business had been discussed. The story was told and the four musty leaves of antebellum stationery were being examined by de Buchan, who had slipped a pair of delicate white gloves over his long fingers. Behind his spectacles, his eyes glittered with the light of eternal fires. He had barely read through the first paragraph before he pronounced, "Absolutely authentic. I have no need to establish provenance; the organization, the symmetry in the various aspects of form, space, movement, the large capital letters—this is Poe's hand, without question. Come, let's compare it to the facsimile in the front piece of the set I have displayed in my window…"

"No need," said Babycakes impatiently. "I'm looking to sell, not chit-chat. I trust my uncle, and he said the story is real."

"Oh, that's rich. Real? The story is fantasy, my boy, not real. Did you read it? This is the final piece of fiction the purest tradition of the Tomahawk Man, Eddy Poe. It isn't real, but it is indubitably authentic."

"So Uncle Thorny said. Look, I confess, I didn't read it. I'm not a big bookworm type, you know? The occasional Ludlum from the airport kiosk, graphic novels, that kind of stuff. But, Poe? I need a little scream queen with my classical literature. Less adjectives, more boobage."

"I see, I see. No matter. Men of my ilk are a shrinking breed, as you can see. But, you are looking to sell. By all means, I am interested in buying. Current commercial conditions being somewhat antagonistic to my traditions, as you can see, I can offer the sum of five hundred dollars."

"Five…?" said Babycakes, his face curling into a frown that showed some teeth. "Look, Pops, I said I didn't read books, but I sure the hell can read newspapers. A couple years ago, a signed original Poe poem sold for a quarter million dollars—I did my due diligence. This has to be worth twice that, especially if the details contain what you brainiacs say it does…"

"The Reynolds story? Indeed it does. But I'm not interested in the resale value, of course. The collection in the display window is one thing; it is not in Poe's own hand. An artifact of this magnitude is something I would want for my personal collection."

He pointed to a small, framed picture that hung on the dark wooden wall behind his antique cash register. "That, for example, is Poe's genuine signature. I've had it for years. But alas, as you noticed, firms like this one are passing into the realm of sweet memories. I'm afraid that five hundred dollars is as high as I can go."

It was a conundrum, but Babycakes had a fail-safe built into his psyche when it came to such decisions: A need for instant gratification. The alternative was to look for a higher bid, and risk the three million over a sum that in the grand scheme was fairly paltry.

Plus, the vestigial conscience was infected and beginning to up. "I have my reasons," he said after a minute, shaking his head at his own ludicrosity at leaving money on the table. "But I am willing to let it go for exactly that amount."

"Excellent!" said de Buchan. "I commend your convivial spirit, young man. Will you accept a personal check?"

That, of course, pushed his convivial spirit a bit too far: "I'm on to that game, Pop. Sorry. Cash on the barrel head; those are the terms."

"Very well. I have a safe in the back, and I can pay you in cash, but it will take me a few minutes. Make yourself comfortable by the hearth in the meantime, where it's warmer."

Babycakes nodded and settled into an overstuffed armchair before the fireplace. He had, at de Buchan's request, donned the pair of white gloves provided, and now he fingered the precious document whose ultimate value had just appreciated by the princely sum of five hundred dollars. It wasn't Ludlum, but the words had a certain allure, even to him. Passions were clearly gushing from the pen of a desperate soul, and desperate souls were Babycakes' stock in trade:

"Where is Reynolds? It has been many hours since I sent for him. His apothecary shop is within a mile, and yet, I am no longer in a fit condition to travel, although—thanks to the Heavens—the poetical mode remains intact.

Where is Reynolds? —Cunning-man or witch, it is irrelevant; he is the only individual beneath the blue empyrean who I believe may be capable of wresting my heart, my intellect, or (more generously) my soul from black extinction.

Reynolds, whose name I first heard uttered among the theosophy and the occult intelligentsia, whose elixir I once sought to restore Virginia Eliza, my life and my bride, before she succumbed to the ubiquitous, imperious intruder death. But alas—his elixir, thaumaturgic as it may be, came too late. It works only upon the dying, not upon the dead, and is useless to those who have already crossed over unto that Plutonian shore..."

Fiction or not, the story was more interesting than any spy potboiler in Babycakes' limited library, so he read more.

Poe went on to describe a certain Baltimore apothecary who was rumored to possess a formula drawn from a secret grimoire; it could stave off death, but not cure it, or so he professed— and feeling the approach of his own demise, Poe had sought desperately to make contact with the fellow... a mysterious occultist called Reynolds.

Babycakes read quickly, turning the four friable leaves as carefully as his sudden interest allowed, but the words betrayed few further clues about Reynolds the man—they were merely an impassioned but failing voice howling out the last few sputters of poetry.

It ended with:

"...Now, I feel the press of cold eternity on my neck, the breath of the Black Messenger, angel or demon, upon the inner flame.

Reynolds! For the love of God, where is Reynol..."

There, the manuscript trailed to nothing, and it was at that moment in history, perhaps, that Poe had stumbled, nearly overcome, nearly insensate, into the gutter in which he was found.

Babycakes was briefly overcome with awe; a sense of the magnitude of emotion he believed must have driven Uncle Thorny to such convoluted lengths to see the manuscript handed over to a proper curator.

And that curator now emerged from the vanilla-scented gloom holding five packets of crisp twenty-dollar bills—perfectly authentic twenties, Babycakes noted, just like the Poe papers. Babycakes counted them, and, satisfied—though now a trifle melancholy with the realization that Uncle Thorny had trusted him only to consign these precious pages, not to treasure them in the family tradition—he handed them over.

Whereupon, de Buchan flung them into the blazing fireplace where they instantly ignited and were shortly reduced to ashes.

Babycakes half rose from the cushioned armchair in horror, but de Buchan raised his gloved right hand in a peremptory gesture of authority: "Now, now, young man—you sold me the pages in good faith; they're mine to dispose of as I think best. And the flames of oblivion are best for that; on this you must be my trusted acolyte. The world needs not know who Reynolds was."

"But... *why?* The historical record alone!? And... its value your Poe collection?" Babycakes jerked his hand toward the small, framed words hanging above the cash register.

"Oh, that?" De Buchan's face now twisted into a pout of profound regret, glancing at the relic. "Yes, that summons from Poe came too late, I'm afraid. By the time I arrived, old Gunner at the tavern said he had no idea what had become of him, and the quack Moran had sequestered him in a back room at some distant hospital and was refusing him visitors in any case. So, indeed, as you say, these pages had historical worth to the world, as well as sentimental value to me, but the larger import is this: Of the clandestine world of the necromancer that sad old sot Poe should never have written, because the cornerstone of the transactions I have had with men across the years has been one of total, unbreakable secrecy."

Babycakes' jaw hung open.

"Indeed," Buchan said, nodding his head, pursing a smile and sounding slightly indignant: "I'm Reynolds."

Babycakes rose, peeled off his white gloves and, shell-shocked, dropped them. As he stumbled toward the door, de Buchan sang after him, "I called it fiction, my boy; that was, I regret, a trite white lie. What I should have said was that any speculation as to Reynold's identity must remain the realm of fiction—for speculative minds and the Poes of future generations. And now, of course, it shall be."

Babycakes Gunner slammed through the door, onto the blustery Boston street, ringing the antique bell to the chime of de Buchan final words, which were his Uncle's final words in eerie echo: *"In pace requiescat!"*

In the morning, Babycakes appeared beneath the imposing shingle of Cormac McInerny & Associates with his iPhone, having convinced himself in the night that de Buchan was nothing more than a doddering madman; that no such explanation was possible in today's fast-paced and hyper-connected world.

Yet, as he attempted to display the video to the dour, impatient attorney, he saw that even in today's fast-paced, hyper-connected word, such things were quite possible: On the video, no image of Alexander de Buchan, *née* Reynolds, appeared; no sound of his movements, no hollow cough of his voice—there was only an empty counter with a small, framed Poe signature behind it.

Supernatural men and women of that ilk, of course, do not cast images.

And so, without proof, no check would be forthcoming from the manifestly delighted Cormac McInerny, and neither he nor Babycakes Gunner chose to mention the incident again.

ZUMBY FOREVER!

The thing began with a surprise call from my little sister, which happens so rarely that I was sure she was going to tell me that she'd been diagnosed with a malignant melanoma or something. Maybe some relative I hadn't thought about in decades had croaked, or maybe (a more likely scenario based on the lucky star she seems to have been born under) she'd won the Lotto, which would be icing on the cake of a thriving business, three beautiful children and a stupidly wealthy husband.

So it was all the stranger when she gargled out, in her almost hysterically cheerful warble, "Remember Zumby?"

Not that I have anything against my little sister, of course—I should be charitable up front and point that out. I don't begrudge her any of the string of outsized successes with which adulthood has graced her, and to be fair, several times over the years she's bailed me out of financial fiascos with a timely loan. And most of that money I still owe her—which is one of the reasons I never call and rarely return her voice messages. Not that she's ever pressured me for repayment either, not once—she wouldn't. I doubt she even remembers the sum. It's her Pollyanna Syndrome that I can't cozy up to: She's one of those people so blissfully unbothered by the daily shitstorm of bloopers we all endure that she seems detached from reality, as if she'd numbered each of life's potential hiccups on a scale of one through ten, then managed to erase one through nine. Had she been calling me to tell me about

23

her terminal cancer, I'm sure she'd have found a way to sugarcoat it, like, "Well, at least I don't have to worry about flossing my teeth anymore."

Anyway; Zumby? That was really over the top. That was unabashed whackadoodle. For starters, my sister is four years my junior, which means that she'd only been eight years old when I got it into my delinquent little skull to buy that mail order monkey from the back of *Boy's Life Magazine*, and when all the dust had settled from the resulting quagmire, before my parents had forced me to get rid of it, I'd only owned the thing for one week in total. In all, that seven-day disaster meant $13.95 plus monkey room and board down the ass gasket, which hurt, even though I'd pilfered most of it from the change jar Dad kept in his study along with his illegal Cuban cigars.

My sister's memory must have been like a steel trap: Up until that one berserk outburst a week into the escapade, Zumby had remained in a hamper in my closet, and as far as I could remember, she'd only seen him a couple of times, tops.

"Yeah, sure I remember Zumby, I guess," I answered. "I'm surprised you do."

"Oh, Zumby was cute as all get out; I used to sneak in your room and cuddle the heck out of the little rascal when you weren't around. He was my l'il snuggle bunny!"

"Really?" Actually, I was genuinely flabbergasted. Not that a second grader had managed to scamboozle her big brother, but that anyone—especially a sappy, impressionable kid with a Sesame Street jones—could have found that simian sewer rat anything but repulsive. As I recall, he looked permanently ready to chew your nose off.

"Aw, he was my l'il widdy-biddy stumple-sillykins. My baby-bugga-boo, my lovey lum-lums. Too bad he went insane."

That was, I thought, putting it mildly. The way the story happened was, I sent the cash to some shady PO Box in Hialeah, Florida, to an outfit called Briney Breezes Pets, and for a week afterward I hung around rather pointedly by the front door near time that the UPS truck sailed by, intending to intercept the package before anyone with parental authority could notice. Dad was a loan officer at the bank, so he was out of my hair between eight and five, but Mom had developed a sort of paranormal precognition—what we boys called 'spidey-sense'—when it came to my regular bouts of mischief making. She'd kept me in the corner of her eagle eye for most of that week, waiting for the other shoe to drop while the first one was still on my foot. She knew instinctively that something was up, but I had already honed my body lingo skills into total and complete denial—something that in adulthood has helped me dodge more than one litigious bullet—and she let her guard down long enough to take a dump just as the brown truck pulled up.

Regrettably unavoidable, however, was the fact that at this same moment, my pesty little sister happened to be sitting on our porch swing slobbering over a Pudding Pop like some mongoloid gamine, so she was in on my undercover monkeyshines from the git.

In fact, as I recall, I had to ante up a week of chore-doing and back-rubs simply to keep her mouth shut. So, she was present when I slipped gingerly into my room and unwrapped the box, equipped with a screen-paneled window and a single banana for nourishment.

Inside, a tiny, hairy, emaciated primate with a reptilian knob of blackish flesh poking out its mouth—presumably a tongue—lay heaving and gasping, too weak for fight or flight. There were no pet care instructions in the shipping container; only the banana and a pink card that read, *"I'm Zumby: Love Me Forever!"*

Briney Breezes had provided the beast with no water source, so Zumby had clearly arrived midway through his final countdown. He also hadn't eaten his banana—turns out that this species detests them, and, as I later discovered, has a preference for Vienna Sausages and Cheez Whiz.

What in the world was I thinking? Well, to be fair, I knew exactly what I was thinking. This was a gentle, retro era when *Tarzan of the Jungle* was not viewed as a racist tome about white supremacy, and the idea of leaping through the neighborhood with a personal, attentive Cheetah seemed like the epitome of desirable cool. I saw myself sitting in social studies with my slave-monkey perched obediently on the back slat of my desk chair, prepared to perform small acts of succor for me, like sharpening my pencils or stealing grape juice from Susan Timor's lunchbox.

I was sure that the school had some statute against bringing pets into classrooms, but I was equally confident that my monkey could be grandfathered in. Buddy O'Hanion was allowed to bring his Seeing Eye shepherd to school, wasn't he? All I had to do was find a single thing that my ape could do that I couldn't and *voilà*, in like Flynn. Any issues my teachers had would be an ACLU wet dream.

I fully expected that my $13.95 would buy me a lifelong companion who'd prove both omnipotent and adorable, savagely protective of my interests yet able to charm the peel off an onion. What I saw shriveled up at the bottom of that UPS box that hot August afternoon was anything but, and not by a long shot, and my first thought about school was that my best course might be let nature takes its course and bring Zumby's skeleton in for show-and-tell.

My little sister probably wouldn't have stood for it, of course— she was the type that freaks when someone lights an ant on fire with a magnifying glass. So I filched an eye dropper from the medicine cabinet and squirted some water into the gaping little mouth, and over the next hour, nursed him into some semblance of not-dead.

Somehow recalling all this, my little sister now went on interminably: "Aw, he was a little wubby-fubbles. A pinky-winky, poochie-peachie l'il shoogah-boogah, a..."

"Awright," I interrupted, "I get it, I get it. Why are you even bringing up the subject after all these years?"

27

She probably couldn't have guessed how severely, at the time, the Zumby episode had screwed with my self-esteem. Couldn't have known, because it involved some private shames I've buried as deeply inside my psyche as they can go, and won't even discuss them with a court-ordered shrink. I certainly didn't appreciate some random phone call at ten PM from a near-stranger three thousand miles away dredging the whole thing up again, especially while using terms like 'schmooky pookie-poo'.

See, although that foul little monkey had only been under my charge for a short while, during those few days I learned some unpleasant truths about myself: Primarily, that I was somewhat less than the godlike boon to humankind that I'd always imagined myself, but in fact was a bit of a toady; an abject, mean-spirited prick—feelings I've never entirely been able to shake to this day.

Not that I didn't do my best for my new high-maintenance charge—I did, and far beyond the call of duty. In an ironic twist of fate, I became Zumby's butt-boy instead of the other way around, raiding the pantry for his favorite snacks, which turned out to be those Armour's Original Vienna hotdog abortions and the gooey sludge of OSHA-orange carcinogen called Cheez Whiz. In fact, he'd eat nothing else, so it was back to Dad's change jar and furtive trips to 7-Eleven to stock up on these culinary abominations, because if I didn't provide them, Zumby would begin to make this high-pitched, unmistakably threatening screech that sooner or later was bound to alert my folks.

Other than that, for these first few days, Zumby seemed content to lounge in the clothes hamper where I had him sequestered, and although it had a lid so that no one entering my room unbidden would be the wiser, he defecated and urinated pretty non-stop, so I was forced to become my own valet, laundering everything inside the hamper once a day lest the smell get out of hand. I tried to do it at night, or when mom was at the store, but at least once she saw me trundling up the basement stairs with a basket of clean clothes, and instead of praising me for my sudden domestication, not to mention my filial saintliness at saving her housework, she screwed up her face in a combination of mistrust and bafflement, shook her head and returned to whatever mindless tripe she was reading in *Better Homes & Gardens*.

I was in that proverbial realm between a rock and a hard place, and, with school starting in a few weeks, I recognized the approach of a dilemma to rival the 6:15 Grand Trunk express train with me stuck on the tracks. Like a newborn infant, Zumby demanded feedings every three hours, day and night, and although by the end of the week I was worn to a frazzle and barely able to keep my shit together due to sheer exhaustion, my fear of discovery—and subsequent punishment—outweighed my need for rest, at least for a while. But I knew that once eighth grade kicked in, I was pretty much out of options.

Not only that, but far from becoming the envy of my neighborhood gang, I could suddenly no longer participate in the most rudimentary pastimes of summer, sandlot baseball and pick-up basketball and lighting dumpsters on fire. I told my friends

29

that I had mononucleosis, hinting that I might have contracted it from French-kissing Susan Timor, thus trying to salvage something of my reputation. The entire situation obviously had a shelf life, and sure enough, after a week of these subservient shenanigans, I finally fell asleep and didn't awaken until I heard the blood-curdling shrieks of my mother coming from the living room.

I tore toward the sound, and by the time I got there, I found my father trembling in the foyer with a steel trap he'd bought for the possum that kept eating our garbage, and Zumby with his incisors embedded firmly into my mother's right arm. The look in Zumby's eyes was one of such maddened depravity that Charles Manson might have signed up for an extension course—my mother was in hysterics as blood cascaded onto her prized, ultra-plush Pearlescent White shag and my father stood there mugging like a dolt, too afraid to move despite the unfolding carnage and the fact that the longer he waited, the greater the likelihood that he'd have to replace the entire expensive carpet.

I manned up and seized Zumby by the testicles, which my instincts told me were more valuable to him than any meal that didn't come from a convenience store, and sure enough, he instantly released my mother's arm and bared his incisors toward me, the gonad-squeezer. As terrified as I was, thinking on my feet went along with the adrenalin rush, and in a single heroic move, I managed to jam the crazed creature into to the critter trap and shut it tightly.

So much for Tootsie Wootsy Snicker Doodle Snoogypuss.

At this point, I should relate that at the time of this spectacle, my sister was away at Brownie camp and missed the fireworks. I should also add that before attacking my mother, Zumby had run rampant through the house, ripping a silk-lined, fox-fur stole to pieces and destroying two hundred dollars' worth of my father's smuggled Pinar Del Rio cigars. That alone should have ensured Zumby's death sentence, but by the time they'd returned from the hospital, with my mother full of tetanus shots and Meperidine, my dad was calm enough to hear the whole convoluted tale, which I only marginally embellished with some parts about being coerced into ordering Zumby by the bigger boys. And to his miserly credit, once my Dad found out that the cash for the monkey had actually been his to begin with, he gave me 24 hours to sell my monkey to whichever unsuspecting sap might pony up the fourteen bucks.

"Caveat emptor," he said grandly and wickedly, which I believe is how he looked at the sub-prime loans he made to dopey clients who defaulted on houses he'd subsequently repossess.

And this brings us to the darkest portion of this entire debacle—the albatross of Zumby shame that I'd most like to unburden myself of. You see, I probably could have fobbed off Zumby on one of my credulous, dip-shit buddies—they were, for the most part, nascent hoodlums with sadistic streaks who'd have loved nothing more than a tiny pet to torment, or better yet, to train as an assassin to assault the high school jocks whose asses they were not yet big enough to kick.

But I knew too much about Zumby's alter ego to expose them to injury, and beside, revealing the Zumby story would also have been a tacit admission that I hadn't really sucked Susan Timor's face, and I didn't need that crap following me into eighth grade. So, after I mimeographed a couple dozen 'Live Baby Monkey For Sale' signs at the library, borrowing adjectives from the original *Boy's Life* ad like 'Will Amuse Children and Adults for Hours' and 'Affectionate, Loveable and Safe', I rode my Schwinn to the far side of town, down near the river where the best houses were beat-up bungalows and the worst were shacks made of plywood and corrugated steel, and tacked them up on walls and telephone poles.

Now, I knew the chances of anybody from that side of the tracks actually having a spare fourteen bucks to spring for a random squirrel monkey were slim to none, but by then, quite frankly, I couldn't have cared less if anybody bought the little succubus—if it was up to me, I'd have flipped Zumby my middle finger, called animal control and sent him into la-la land with a phenobarbital cocktail and a snicker. Vienna Sausage this, douchebag. But I needed to show my father that I'd at least made a trouper's effort to get him his fourteen dollars back—that, or I'd risk spending the rest of the summer weeding flowerbeds in front of the bank.

So, imagine my surprise when on the morning after I posted the signs, a kid from school called Rudy Ramocki showed up on my doorstep with his mother. In his left hand, he was clutching one of my flyers.

I say 'his left hand' specifically, because poor Rudy had what was then referred to as a 'withered' right arm—some primary nerve had been severed during childbirth and his arm had atrophied into an ugly, useless hook that he clutched against his chest like a wounded bird.

Kaiser Wilhelm of Prussia had a withered arm, but you'll have to trust me when I tell you that Rudy Ramocki was no Kaiser Wilhelm. He was a mortifyingly shy and wispy waif who at twelve already looked like he was losing his hair. In school we were relentless; we called him 'The Gimpster' and every time we passed him in the hall we shoved him, knocked his books out of his one good arm and guffawed as he scrabbled and scrambled to pick them up again while we encouraged him by laughing, 'Win one for The Gimpster!'

I'm by no means proud of this side of my personality, and as I say, I don't much like to be reminded of it. But there was Rudy, simpering on my front porch, wanting my monkey, and it happened to be a Saturday, so my father was home. Dreadfully afraid that Rudy would spill the beans about my treatment of him, I was ingratiating and fawning, offering to show him my collection of beetles impaled on sewing needles while his mother spoke earnestly to my parents in our screened-in porch.

My bedroom window was open, and I could hear every word his mother said, and I'm afraid that Rudy could too: "Lord knows we can't afford the fourteen dollars, but Hubert and me are so worried about little Rudy. He hasn't made a single friend since we moved here. A lot of the other boys are better situated in life, if you catch my meaning, and they're awfully mean to him in school because of his clothes and, of course… the arm. Not saying your boy is one of them, but the rest of them are regular old bullies. We thought a little pet monkey might be just the thing to perk Rudy up, to get him out of the summer doldrums. If it works, I dare say it will be worth every penny…"

Now, if at that point I had still imagined my parents had any shred of moral superiority, they shortly vanished like cocaine up Keith Richard's nose. Far from relating the potential dangers that Zumby posed, they gushed over his cuteness in terms almost as nauseating as my sister's: "Aw, he's just the most precious little honey bunny—eats lettuce, carrots, apples, darn near anything you eat…!"

"Oh, my Hubert is a meat and potatoes fellow," Rudy's mother answered, reddening. "Doesn't much care for garden truck."

"He'll eat Vienna Sausages like they're going out of style," I volunteered. Trying to spare Rudy any further embarrassment, I'd gone to the garage to fetch the steel critter trap where we'd been keeping Zumby since the attack and I now stood in the porch doorway while behind me, Rudy peered warily into the cage.

No one had fed or watered Zumby since yesterday—doing so would have required us to open the trap, and nobody wanted to do that. By now, he'd reverted back to the moribund, tongue-lagging, air-gasping mess that he'd been when he first arrived.

34

Even so, Mom blanched when she saw him and Dad gripped the arm of the wicker love seat so tightly his knuckles looked like they belonged to an albino.

"Oh, we have cans and cans of those little mini-dogs!" Rudy's mother said cheerily, pronouncing it 'dawgs'. "Cans and cans!"

Meanwhile, Rudy had curled up his nose at the fecal stench rising from the cage. His mother cried out, "Look, Rudolph! Wouldn't you like to give little Buttercupper Bumpkins a new home?"

"Zumby," I corrected her and Rudy looked doubtful, but by then, his mother was peeling single dollar bills off a small roll and counting them carefully onto the coffee table.

I didn't know whether I wanted to cheer loudly or implode into a puddle of disgrace the consistency of Cheese Whiz, but the transaction happened and I handed over the cage, while my Dad—somewhat insensitively, said—"Sure the boy can handle that cage with his dead-weight arm all twisted up like that?"

I was afraid my Dad would force me to carry the damn thing all the way to Rudy's house, but Rudy seized the cage from me violently with his good arm. It was the first time I'd ever seen Rudy show any defiance whatsoever, and I said, weakly, "Love him forever."

Well, for the rest of that day, and all through that night, we hung around the phone, more or less waiting for an enraged call from Hubert the husband, or more likely, from the cops, but it never came, and by the time school started three weeks later, the Zumby incident had been consigned to and locked within that dusty compartment of family history from which items are never, ever withdrawn, not even when one is drunk or on medication. In a fit of guilt, though, I walked over to the library the next afternoon and looked up squirrel monkeys in the *World Book Encyclopedia*, and was somewhat relieved to read that in the wild, they only live a few years and in captivity, less than two. If old Rudy could weather that storm, I told myself, he'd be off the hook by sophomore year.

I had some trepidations about running into him on the first day of school of course, but as it happens, my fears were for nothing. Apparently, the week before school started, the Ramocki family had been evicted for defaulting on their mortgage and had moved on to parts unknown—and that was the last time I even thought much about the Zumby saga.

Until my little sister's unwelcome phone call, that is. As to that, in response to my question about the reason for it, she chortled, "Turns out you weren't the only kid suckered into that Boy's Life ad!"

I never said I was. But out of politeness I replied, "How so?"

"Well, I was surfing the net the other day, looking for information about Zanzibar conversation furniture sets or some such First World nonsense, and I stumbled upon a Zumby site. Can you believe it?—it turns out that there's a whole web page devoted to Zumby aficionados. Apparently, they sold a lot of those little mugwumps when we were kids. And cutest of all, it turns out that they were all named Zumby! That silly pet company must have saved on money by printing out thousands and thousands of 'My Name is Zumby. Love Me Forever!' cards."

"Thousands and thousands?" I asked.

"Oh yes, check out the web site! There are Zumby fans with chapters all over the United States, kind of like a nostalgia club. They have barbecues and potluck dinners and meetings and stuff. I have no idea what they talk about when they get together, but it's probably just a bunch of sappy oldsters like us who like to hang out and chat and reminisce about the good old days, before we had internets and iPhones and Netflixes… And they were good old days, weren't they? Suzie Bake ovens, Barbie's Fashion Bouquet, Spirograph, Saturday morning Scooby Doo cartoons! Remember all the fun we had?!"

Actually, I remember throwing red-hot pennies at stray cats and burning swear words into the neighbor's lawn with lighter fluid, but I sort of wanted to end the call without a fight, so I thanked her for the heads-up about the web site and tried to wedge in a 'goodbye'.

"Oh, now I wish we'd at least taken one photo of Zumby, before… You know, before he went all rogue. When he was still my little Hugs McGee, my cutie-patootie, snoochie-boochie, my yumbalicious l'il …"

"Bye, Sis," I said, and hung up.

But, damn if it didn't get the better of me at around three o'clock that morning, waking me up like a peptic ulcer, and I finally threw in the towel and accessed the web site. There it was, though without a lot of information—just a scarlet screen with white letters that read 'Love Zumby Forever!'

There was, however, a small open dialogue box at the bottom that read 'Enter Zip' and the whole thing seemed a bit creepy, like a big phishing scam unfolding before my eyes, but—call me a fool, call me a sucker, call me a sappy oldster looking to reminisce—I finally did it, pounding in my five digits, and immediately, a second screen appeared displaying a name, a time and a date.

The time was 8:30 PM, the date two days away and the place was a rundown VFW Hall, Post 65 that had stood for 120 years on… the Ramocki side of town. I thought I might have read about Post 65 recently, and since the Zumby page was a bust, I Googled it and found the newspaper article from a few weeks ago about a couple of local punks breaking in and stealing a bunch of cash donations and liquor. They ran photos of the two suspects, and I was struck with how much they looked the kids I used to run with, and I remember shaking my head in disgust— Post 65 veterans do a righteous job of teaching young people about the flag, feeding the homeless, and raising money for the fire department. As I say, I've evolved a bit since the good old days, but even then, we had a sense of patriotism. When we stole money and booze, it was from the sacristy at church.

The more I thought about it—and believe me, I tried not to think about it—the stranger the whole scenario played out. What were the chances that the Zumby shindig would have been happening a mere two days from now? Like, one in a billion? Whatever the odds were, I was sure they were astronomical. Unless, of course, my little sister was playing some sort of perverted prank on me—not her style at all—or else the Zumby Forever! Club had meetings all the time. Maybe—and this did not seem entirely out of realm of possibilities—they were Zumbyholics and this was sort of like a regular A.A. meeting. Come to think of it, my little sister seemed to be a bit Zumby obsessed, even after all these years. Could be she was a candidate for Z.A.

My calls to the VFW Hall rang on into eternity; they obviously hadn't heard of the technological advances we've made in answering machines since World War I. I even pedaled my antique Schwinn over there—one too many DUIs in the grocery getter—and the place looked like it usually did: Completely deserted, like these vets had won the war but lost the peace. I cruised around to the back, and there was a small sign above the rear door by the dumpster. It said, "Zumby Forever!" in white letters against a scarlet background and nothing more.

It was enough to keep me on tenterhooks, though. Why? Who knows why? Let's say I don't have a lot on my plate these days and leave it at that. But gradually, I grew genuinely perturbed. Then a trifle frantic. Memories I hadn't thought of in years bubbled to the surface like scum in a stockpot. Concepts that I had, for the most part, swallowed like backwash in my lifelong, ultimately selfish search for absolution reappeared with a vengeance. I conjured up sins I'd piled up like McDonald's wrappers against a snow fence: Unrepentant and unabsolved, I suppose they were ultimately unforgotten.

Is there something more meaningful to penance than self-flagellation, I asked myself—a deeper reason it was given to us as a Sacrament and not as a suggestion? Is there truth to the idea that the hair shirt is actually a dispensation of divine mercy that imparts grace to the penitent, secures power over consciences and relieves the emotional strain of troubled souls?

Geez, I hope not.

Nevertheless, two days hence, at the appointed time, I fired up my orange Stingray 5-speed, plopped my old heinie on the Mylar glitter banana seat and wended my way through the old familiar streets, feeling almost kid-like again as I pedaled down the well-worn bike paths, across the Grand Trunk tracks we used to tie mice to, and down the dirt road to the VFW Hall.

I arrived at 8:30 exactly. There were a few old hoopties in the lot, wrecks even worse than mine, cars that looked like they'd have their own class in the Demolition Derby, but there weren't many of them, and they were all huddled tightly in the rear near the dumpster, as if the gathering of the Zumby Forever! Club was something either totally covert and mysterious or something irreconcilably obscene.

My mind fluttered, and I was prepared to accept either interpretation as I stepped inside the dark hall. In the vestibule, a man approached—he was about seventy, and painfully thin, almost like a Holocaust survivor. In fact, his blank ogle reminded me of the hollow, haunted faces you see in those monochrome Pathé newsreels of concentration camps being liberated, where the victims look like they are so sick and tired of the whole existence phenomenon that they don't really give a shit if they're saved or not. In any case, he didn't try to block my way or ask me for credentials or otherwise impede my progress; he just stuck his emaciated mug too far into my personal space, as though he was trying to smell me, so I gave him a dirty look and a poke to the solar plexus and moved on inside the hall.

It was, to say the least, a remarkable tableau. Card tables were scattered willy-nilly around the room, while around them slogged a parade of slow, ghastly-looking souls, each with the same Auschwitzy attitude as the doorman, and they all moved with the identical, meandering shamble. The tables were weighed with food, but nobody was taking any, and I shortly saw why: There was nothing available but cans of Armour Brand Original Vienna Sausage and jars of Cheez Whiz. If it was somebody's idea of a clever joke, it was an elaborate one, and mostly wasted since whoever was behind it had failed to provide utensils or plates—even paper ones. If anyone present had wanted to avail themselves of a stone-cold cheesy frank or two, they would have to use their hands. But evidently, nobody did, and the food containers simply sat untouched, as gaping and stupid looking as the mouths of the club members.

As conspicuous as the lack of tableware was, I quickly noticed the absence of anything even vaguely Zumby related—no banners, no Zumby memorabilia for sale, no Zumby posters on the wall, no vintage Zumby ads… In fact, beside the sagging buffet tables, there was nothing at all in the hall but a tattered American flag in the corner by the stage and a few cheap plastic lawn chairs. *Love Zumby Forever!* was a cool enough tagline, but I guess even eternity has a sell-by date.

So I sat down in one of the lawn chairs and tried to muster up the energy to make it back home, where I supposed I'd jot the whole experience down to a brief rent in the fabric of sanity, a view into the netherworld of the genuinely messed-up mind. Maybe I'd drop my little sister a nastygram to let her know, but not so nasty that I couldn't later claim I'd just been kidding. That took some sharp compositional skills, and I reckoned that I was just was the guy to handle it.

But just as I had worked up the juice to skedaddle, another old timer approached me—this one so similar in appearance to the first that I thought the coot had tracked me down to get another whiff. I was about to provide him with another poke in the breastbone when I realized it was not the same dude—clutched closely to the chest of this one, like a Biafran woman going through the sad, poignant but useless gesture of cradling a dead infant, was a withered arm.

It took a moment—it had been decades, after all. But the look of despair was the same one I remembered as he staggered off under the weight of Zumby's cage, and I was thus responsible for: If it wasn't bottomless misery, I can say with confidence that it still hadn't found a bottom.

"Rudy?" I wondered.

He pursed his thin lips into a sad frown and pushed out his good arm in a gesture of greeting, but when I rose and attempted to shake it, I saw to my horror that it was a prosthesis.

I had no idea what to say, but only that I ought to say something. I went with, "Oh, man. That is some truly fucked-up luck, brother. You lost the only arm you had?"

His face was briefly lit with a sick, passing twinkle. It was irony indeed, but I suddenly realized that it went deeper than that. My jaw dropped like one of these Zumby zombies. "Zumby?" I asked.

Rudy nodded. "He bit me right through the steel bars on the walk home. I didn't want to tell my mother since she'd spent some of the rent money to buy me the present and I didn't want to disappoint her. So I hid the wound for as long as I could, until an infection set in, and, well..."

He tried to shrug, but without working nerves, his right shoulder had neither mobility nor function.

"You know, it wasn't my idea to sell you the damn thing," I choked out in a somewhat lame apology. "I wanted to have it put down, you know—at the dog pound or somewhere." I made the shooting gesture with my thumb and forefinger. " But Dad insisted—and you know dads..."

43

Again, the ludicrous half shrug: "Not really. Not long after we left town, mine jumped in front of an oncoming train."

"Wow!" It was the sort of revelation that—as much as 'wow' sums it up—really required something more. "That well and truly sucks, Rudy. If it's any consolation, mine met a pretty grisly end too: Emphysema caught up with him on a hunting trip and he died of exposure. Back in '96; he lasted two days out there, apparently. Unable to crawl for help…"

When I saw that this didn't make the slightest bit of difference to Rudy, I asked, "How long did you have to deal with it? With Zumby, I mean."

Now his face swooped in closer, and if it was possible for his countenance to grow even bleaker, it did. The Bible speaks of wailing and the gnashing of teeth, and Rudy's few remaining teeth gnashed.

"Zumby is still alive," he said.

"Why, that's just not possible," I said confidently. "I looked it up for you, honest injun. Two years, max, then *pffft*. *The World Book* said so."

This time, Rudy didn't even bother trying the shrug. He draped his fake hand across my shoulder, and I could feel the cold steel of his fingers through my hoodie. Slowly, almost imperceptivity, but irresistibly, he nudged me toward the front of the hall.

As a pre-pubescent tool, I'd spent a few mandatory years as an altar boy, and although it seemed like the most mortifyingly uncool way one could spend a Sunday morning, I soon figured out ways to make it stomachable. Like, looking up the skirts of girls when they mounted the choir dias, Odd-jobbing my teachers in the Adam's apple with the communion plate when they received the host, filching Gallo Chablis from the sacristy cupboard and lifting dollar bills from the collection basket—sins which I may have revealed during my bi-monthly trips to the Confessional, but probably not.

That was the mind's eye image that appeared before me as Rudy impelled me toward the VFW hall stage stairs, and I mounted them with the same sense of resignation and fatalistic disgust I'd felt when I stepped onto the altar every Sunday in my idiotic little habit. This figures, I thought: With two good shoulders, I could shrug until the cows came home.

I surveyed the room. The clot of tortured losers came to some semblance of attention, some propping themselves up against sausage tables, some finding lawn chairs, others sinking to the floor and bending arthritic limbs into that moronic sitting position that's even hard for kindergarteners to maintain— 'Indian style'.

The stage curtain rustled and two twelve year old boys were thrust forward, and they stood blinking and trembling on either side of me. One looked up at me, desperate but suddenly hopeful, and cried, "You're a fucking grownup. Do something. Get us out of this shit."

But the other hushed him. "Not his problem. I told you that breaking into this place was a retard idea. Told you, and told you, but would you listen? Easy peasy, you said… Now we got to pay the price."

I realized that these boys were the same ones I'd seen in the newspaper clipping—the VFW Hall burglars. I wanted to give them some words of advice since there didn't seem to be many reasons to offer them solace. All that came out of me was, "Don't be too hard on them, boys. They have no idea what they're doing."

Which was true. At least, they had no real say in what they were doing. Problem was, Zumby did. Or rather, Zumbys did.

From the ducts, through the rear door, slithering through the ring of windows that lined the hall's upper walls and from the behind the stage curtain, an army of angry Zumbys suddenly poured in a frenzy of madness. They swarmed the stage, tiny, foul-smelling, bug-eyed and maniacal, teeth bared, flaring with fires of vengeance aimed at sadistic Boy Scouts, savage altar boys, bully boys, bloodthirsty boys, boys who knew what a boy's real life was all about, and it didn't come from the pages of *Boy's Life*.

Except for the Zumby part.

Which Zumby was my Zumby, I was never to learn. What I did learn was a lesson that would have been a lot more valuable had I been given time to apply it, which I wasn't:

I'd wanted penance, and like Captain Willard in *Apocalypse Now*, for my sins, I got it.

46

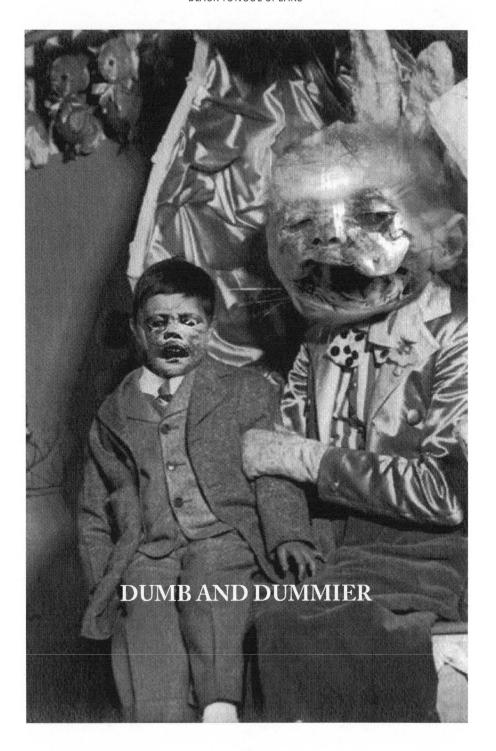

DUMB AND DUMMIER

By executive mandate, in the future, everyone's fifteen minutes of fame will be reduced to five.

It was in this world that Freemantle Cobbs decided to extend his notoriety for an additional five minutes—possibly ten. Cobbs was a comedian. With unruly shocks of ketchup-colored hair poking out at odd angles across his peanut-shaped head and the sort of schnozz that made you chuckle before he even opened his yap, you might say he'd been born to be one.

That's not to say that being born to certain calling is a guarantee of success, and prior to meeting Hugo McHugoface, Freemantle Cobbs struggled through many unpaid open mic gigs, occasionally scoring a semi-paid set if the headliner forgot to pop his humor-enhancing nootropics, which was to that futuristic stand-up comedy what steroids are to bodybuilding.

The problem wasn't that Freemantle Cobbs wasn't particularly funny—even though he wasn't—it was that he insisted on writing his material the old-fashioned way: By noticing the foibles 'n' flaws of modern living and coming up with one-liners to exploit them. Even if you could do that with consummate skill—which he couldn't—you were still competing with the modern wave of yuckster who, in seconds, could process every single news story in the world through multi-core, single-atom computer brains operating with quantum electrodynamics, then filter them

49

through a matrix of every joke ever written by anyone about anything and come up with an array of possible bits. Better still, software then assembled those jokes in the precise order that best suited whatever audience demographic you were expecting at your show, thus narrowing your routine down to the one guaranteed to fire on every cylinder, every time.

This was the modern breed of humorist—streamlined, efficient, trim, ultra-healthy and generally insanely attractive. It was true that a certain amount of physical schtick was still a hit with audiences, but a sculpted model body often could contort in a way that fat old Borscht Belt schlubs couldn't.

As such, that type of comic had been obsolete since the dawn of New Comedy.

Freemantle Cobbs was a bit of schlub, but he certainly wasn't fat. In fact, he looked like he'd escaped from a Siberian gulag and hiked all the way to Moscow in the middle of winter. He had chalk-white, scarecrow limbs and a scrawny, Ichabod Crane neck, and he insisted on slithering them into a silly retro suit decorated with South Park characters. Although the intended effect was one of low-culture shock humor, the days of attracting a following by blowing up watermelons were gone. On the modern stage, where female comedians looked like Aphrodite and male comedians like Adonis, Freemantle Cobbs came across as far more disturbing than funny, and his sets were usually followed by scarcely-audible applause.

Until he met Hugo McHugoface, that is. Hugo was another

old-school comic who wrote his own bits, and who was also a bit of a physical abomination. Hugo was only four gnarled and twisted feet tall, and he had the crusty face of a peeled apple left out on the windowsill for a week. His jokes were meaner than Freemantle's and were often little more than obscenity-laced rants filled with graphic violence and tactless references to recent world tragedies. His audience was generally too horrified to heckle or boo, and when his sets ended, the applause he drew was even sparser than Cobbs'.

After one particularly grueling gig in which a crowd of forty had dwindled to four, the two met and bonded at the club bar over the latest cocktail craze, the Triple V, made with V-8 and 'VV'—Absolut's new gimmick, vulva-flavored vodka—a sort of erotic Clamato Juice for losers.

The club's owner had just informed them that hitherto and henceforth they were both unwelcome to perform on open mic nights, which is perhaps the bottom of a career barrel on par with an Olympic swimmer drowning in a Dixie Cup.

"Know what we should do?" said Freemantle, sucking his fishy cocktail. "We should team up. You and me. Form an Odd Couple act, like Felix and Oscar. Bob and Ray. Abbott & Costello, those guys..."

"Us?" groused the dwarf into his drink. "Who'd we be, the Deadbeat Duo? Dude, that's like failure squared. That's binary bankruptcy. That's..."

A drunken-sounding voice spoke up from the shadows: "I'll tell ya what that is, shall I, boys? Thassa great idea."

It turns out that a member of the audience they thought they'd scared away had had actually found a secluded corner of the bar. He slurred on, pointing to Hugo: "You could climb up inna his lap," he said, pointing to Freemantle, "and make like wunna them ol' time ventriloquist acts, y'know, like Edgar Bergen and Mortimer Snerd. Paul Winchell and Jerry Mahoney. Alone you two are as funny as infected scrotal sores, but together, in an act like that? Could work. Nobody tries that kinda cutting-edge stuff anymore. *The Dumb and Dummier Show.* Plus, it would freak the frig outta the audience at the end if ya started dancing around to show 'em you're not really a dummy—you're really a Oompa-Loompa."

Hugo was not in the least offended by being called an Oompa-Loompa. In fact, after many decades of being referred to by the humiliating and degrading term 'Little People', future folks suffering dwarfism welcomed the less derogatory reference to Roald Dahl's charming, loyal, hard-working and highly literate race of orange slaves. Hugo was a proud member of the Oompa-Loompans of America (OLA) and, in any case, he saw the genius in the idea immediately.

And so did Freemantle. "Wow! You know what they say about drunks and children?!" he laughed.

"Easy to seduce?" Hugo responded—the kind of humor that tended to get him barred from performing.

So they made a pact over Triple Vs at the bar of Kasey's Komedy Klub. Freemantle's spindly fingers wrapped around Hugo's stubby, canned-wiener digits and 'The Dumb and Dummier Show' was born, then and there, as a phoenix rising from the ashes of humiliation, as victory snatched from the jaws of defeat.

And an unprecedented victory it proved to be, unmatched in the annals of New Comedy's short history. Despite a few rough edges, honing their material proved to be a snap. Hugo agreed to jettison most of his racist and misogynistic jokes and Freemantle agreed to run his script through a state-of-the-art Yackov Yuxvec Comedy Translator, which accepted Freemantle's unfunny text as input and, by using electrical activity from the brainwaves of an array of volunteer audiences, produced a user-specific joke vector file as output.

The beautiful thing about the Yuxvec system was that you could dial in a detailed audience spec based on the people who had purchased tickets for various shows. The GICs— Globally Implanted Chip—installed in their brains would then instantaneously spit out a comedy routine suited to that particular group, based on their racial makeup, level of education, allergies, recent deaths in the family, phobias and propensity to heckle or become belligerent after a categorical number of cocktails.

The act hit heights almost as soon as they took it on the road. Grist for their humor mill could be topical or nostalgic, biting or gentle, silly or intellectual—each routine was custom designed and unique, hastily committed to memory in the fifteen minutes before curtain time or read from the surgically installed teleprompters within their optic nerves. The freshness of the material, the lack of rehearsing, the impromptu feel, it all added to the magic. In fact, the comedy *je ne sais quoi* was not the strength of zingers, but the synergy of the interplay. Like the great duos of yore, alone, neither one of them was conspicuously clever or uncommonly witty or even vaguely likeable, but together they were a hoot. Their international success was something for which no vaudevillian chef could write a recipe, no theatrical alchemist could produce an elixir; no magician's magic could pull out of his hat.

It just 'was'.

Part of it, of course, was the sheer novelty of the concept. As the drunk in the bar had sagely noted, ventriloquist shows had grown so passé they were new again; they were as outdated as automobiles and airplanes, and so, turned out to be a breath of fresh laughing gas in the global atmosphere of formula guffaws. Anyway, the art of voice-throwing was as lost as making gold from lead and cursive writing, so key to the whole act was that all Freemantle had to do was pretend to go through the motions of working a dummy's mechanisms, from fake control rods to the brass eye sticks with which little Hugo was fitted; his dummy make-up, quite realistic, did the rest.

The actual jokes were generated from the billions of other historical skits recorded verbatim in the database, and though by no means side-splittingly clever in any rational comedic sense;

they were laser-beam focused to tickle the funny bones in sold-out rooms. If the crowd contained a number of embryologists or blastocyst implant surgeons or chicken farmers, they told egg jokes: In one skit, Hugo McHugoface, the self-described 'Stradivarius of Dummies', put too much salt on his scrambled eggs, earning a chiding from Freemantle, to which Hugo promptly replied, "You should know all about eggs—you lay enough of 'em!"

The audience roared.

If they were entertaining macho groups like Bioguys of Columbus or Androphiliacs Anonymous, this one was sure to bring down the house: "Sure ventriloquism is a great hobby for women! Ventriloquists always get the last word!"

They used plenty of one-time one-liners that fit a lone occasion, and that was fine—the Yackov Yuxvec Comedy Translator had a million of 'em. One such joke was delivered to a convention filled with plastic surgeons specializing in the new fad of face transplanting, wherein everyone was becoming the fashion model of their dreams: Hugo made some particularly insensitive remark to his 'human dummy', which is how he referred to Freemantle throughout the act, and Freemantle responded by slapping him. "Is that your face or are you just ad-libbing until Halloween?"

Along the way, little Hugo developed his signature laugh—a hysterical cackle that sounded so demented that children all over the globe began to mimic it—and it soon became famous as the 'Hugo Haw Haw'.

The climax of the stage show, of course, was the finale, when little shrunken Hugo suddenly leaped merrily from Freemantle's lap, tore off all of his clothing down to a Speedo thong decorated with Family Guy characters, and cavorted about the stage like a deranged chimpanzee, proving that he was not a wooden ventriloquist's prop after all, but like a metamorphosed Pinocchio, a real boy.

As suited the hyper-progressive era in which this story unfolds, the global phenomenon that was The Dumb and Dummier Show, in which billions of chuckle-starved minions within the vast, insensitive empire of U.A. (Universal Agendia) rediscovered the simple, wholesome pleasures of vaudeville, lasted two whole weeks. Then, the act's reception began wear thin around the edges, seats began to go empty in stadiums, audiences began to dwindle and no hoo-doo from the Yackov Yuxvec Comedy Translator could win them back—they'd moved on to another Flavor of the Picosecond.

Behind the scenes, things had never gone smoothly anyway— each assumed, and loudly maintained, that his individual talent carried the duo's triumphs and that the other one was merely along for the ride. It was the nasty little showbiz secret, of course, but it had been endemic to comedy teams of the past. Dean Martin preferred golf and booze to Jerry Lewis; Abbott thought Costello was a Grade-A jerk, and it's common knowledge in Hollywood that in a fit of alcohol-fueled lust, Paul Winchell once put Jerry Mahoney in a wood lathe, whittled him into the shape of a phallus and sent him to Lucille Ball.

Naturally, when their popularity began to wane, each blamed the other. Hugo had flubbed this line or that one, Freemantle had screwed up the timing in this skit or that one; Hugo accused Freemantle of becoming insufferably vain about his appearance, combing down his arrant hair with metrosexual gel, even toning down the idiotic red color with dye: "If the audience wanted to see a beefcake supermodel funnyman, they have literally millions to choose from!"

For his part, Freemantle thought that Hugo's madcap gesticulations as he did the act's closing segment as a real human being, albeit a disgustingly tiny one, crossed the bonds of what was acceptable in a G-rated show. "If the audience wanted to see an inch worm they'd go to an entomology museum!"

Tish bang.

As their ratings tanked further, it did not look likely that the ending would be happy. Especially since, among the rare occasions in which they'd shared a room during their international tours, Freemantle had learned something remarkable about Hugo McHugoface—something so scandalous and flagrant that if revealed, it truly threatened to turn the world upside down. Or, depending on your perspective, right side up.

At the very least, revealing the secret on an international stage, with all its ghastly implications, would catapult Freemantle's own fame over the five-minute bar, no doubt for the extra five he was after.

The Oppez Walton Show was the very forum he was looking for.

Oppez Walton was a galactic phenomenon that far outstripped the meager multi-national renown of *The Dumb and Dummier Show*. Her neurovision program was syndicated through the colonized solar system, and her fan base included the floating cities of Venus, the homesteads on Enceladus and Trans-Neptunia. She was so popular in the Jovian system that Europa had been renamed 'Opezza'. An orbiting spacecraft filled with aliens from the 224th Quadrant of the Magellanic Cloud never missed an episode, and thanks to the development of the Yackov Yuxvec Literally Universal Language Translator, they understood all the quips and witticism of the guests, and learned to filter celebrity opinions through the Yackov Yuxvec Oh, Come On Now! Translator, which made stupid concepts sound intelligent.

The most remarkable part of *The Oppez Walton Show* was that it was the exception to prove the five-minutes-of-fame rule. Her variety hour had been at the top of the ratings game for more than a month, thanks primarily to her warm, funny, smart, charming and curious persona. More than that, perhaps, it was because, after an initial, opening show about her weight problem, she had undergone a total and very public body makeover, removing the stigma previously attached to face-transplants, melanin suctioning and having one's stomach removed and transplanted with the stomach of an anorexic. She was 'Everywoman', and fittingly, every woman, every man, every transwoman, every intersexual hermaphrodite, every bioguy and every androphiliac adored her.

When Freemantle Cobbs approached her show's producers about an exclusive opportunity to have the genuine skeleton in the Hugo McHugoface closet revealed, live in studio, there was some initial resistance, but they knew that even Oppez's star-power had a shelf life, and such a rating-generating episode might be exactly what she needed to maintain her position as 'The Most Influential Woman on Neurovision'.

They'd finally agreed, and that was exactly where Freemantle Cobbs was headed on the crisp, beautiful morning—typical of New Yopolis in the autumn—of Octember 32, 20—.

He'd decided to walk the twenty-two blocks between The Crystal Intifada—the ritzy, nature-infused residential complex where he lived—and the vast OBC Studios where *The Oppez Walton Show* was brain-machine interfaced. He had options beyond walking, of course—he could have taken the Evacuated Tube, the Superconducting Maglev Train, the Terraspread Tunnel Bus or a Yellow SolarBullet Taxi, but unfortunately, he couldn't take his own trusty personal mobility pod. The night before, a rogue woolly mammoth had escaped from the Zigeunerfamilienlager Center for Developmental Biology and destroyed the municipal garage where he stored it.

But, Freemantle's foray into the great outdoors was quite wonderful. He'd almost forgotten how refreshing it was, and the sunshine felt warm on his skin despite the inevitable melanoma, and he filled his lung with cool fall air despite it being filled with carcinogenic micro-particulates. In the distance, the Space

Elevator glittered in the morning light: It was now half-finished at the 25,000 miles tall mark, briefly stuck between floors. For the time being, it was a stairway to nowhere, but a marvel of Universal Agendia technology nonetheless.

So invigorating was the walk that he was oblivious to the sad-looking nanofactory rats around him slithering toward their two-hour shifts, each one wearing a robotic suit that kept them company and showed them continuous streams of data by reading digital information from radio frequency identification tags embedded in fire hydrants. Freemantle made a mental note to pick one of these newfangled suits for himself.

At the studio, Freemantle Cobbs was treated as befitted his celebrity-hood. Fawning interns escorted him through the Green Room, the Gold Room, the Platinum Room, the Rare Earth Metal room and seated him with great pomp in the Anti-Matter Room, where he only had to sit through a brief neuromarketing advertisement for the show's sponsors, American Express, who were introducing their new ultra-exclusive Hydrogen Nucleus With Two Additional Neutrons Card, with a spending limit so high that you could use it to buy a planet.

Although the gorgeous and eager young attendants pumped him for some information about the 'big secret' he was about to reveal, Freemantle twisted his thin, freckle-splattered lips into a wry grin. "Soon enough…" he said, "…you, Oppez Walton, and the entire contiguous solar system, including those chartreuse-colored freaks up in the orbiting Span can, shall know Hugo

McHugoface's dastardly truth…"

The suspense was nearly unbearable; instant gratification was such an ingrained requirement in this future Moirai-land that bulimics sometimes puked even before they ate. Fortunately, Oppez Walton herself was hemorrhaging curiosity juice, and with minutes, he was hustled onto the expansive set and seated in the identical chair where Thumkol, Lord of Phobos had just sat. In fact, there was still a little fuchsia-colored body fluid on the cushion, which he quickly wiped away.

Some folks who'd seen Oppez in person described her as being so outlandishly beautiful that it was hard to catch your breath upon first gazing at her. Freemantle had prepared himself in the Anti-Matter Room once the commercial ended, repeating to himself, "She's only human, she's only human…"

But now that he was actually facing her, he wasn't so sure: What human could exist in such anatomical perfection? Each pore looked like it had been designed by master craftsmen; every eyelash was the painstaking work of an artisan. Her lips were like precision-milled gemstones—a priceless ruby without the visible traces of iron oxide that can sometimes reduce the value. Her eyes? The clearest, most pristine Himalayan lakes, only again, without the microbial parasites. But it was her skin that was her most striking feature—no color chart could describe it. It was as if photographs of all the world's most attractive women had been superimposed and translated into one shimmering, flawless individual—which is essentially the orders she'd given her plastic surgeons during her face transplant.

"Well?" she cried eagerly as the magnetic resonance neuroimaging camera beamed the encounter live, directly into the brains of her voluminous viewership. "This is the moment the entire solar system, from Mercury to the Kuiper Belt, has been waiting for, Mr. Cobbs! End the suspense, put us out of our misery, quench our fires of desire! What is Hugo McHugoface's big secret…?"

Freemantle Cobb's played the pause well. He knew, of course, that he would never again perform as part of *The Dumb and Dummier Show*—that his revelation would be the end of that partnership forever—no sucking face like Martin and Lewis on some future telethon. But according to Nielsen ratings/shares, it was nearly over anyway, so he adjusted his Bob's Burgers tie leisurely, stretched his lanky limbs, put a twig-like finger against his beak nose and with a dramatic stage flourish announced:

"Hugo McHugoface really is a ventriloquist dummy!"

He reaped a comic's greatest reward: Laughter. It rang from the honeycomb-inspired hexagonal alumina rafters of the OBC mega-studio, it flooded from viewers in the space stations above Haumea and Makemake, it retched out of the one-eyed, one-horned flying purple aliens orbiting the earth, it dumped from domiciles on Deimos, and most of all, it erupted from the unblemished chromium-colored lips of Oppez Walton.

Alas, however, as gratifying as unrestrained snorts and belly laughs were, and despite the inevitable endorphin rush that went along with them, today, chortles were not what Freemantle was after. Now he drew forth from an inner pocket of a series of plasmon-generated Röntgen radiation images he had taken with a high-tech version of those X-Ray specs comic books used to sell for a dollar, but which never really worked. The R-Waves specs he had purchased from the back of *Spontaneous Parametric Down-Conversion Quarterly* magazine did, and through them, he'd hoped to scan his audiences and see chicks' underwear right through their clothes.

He ha experimented on Hugo as soon as the delivery drone dropped them off, surreptitiously of course, in case the foul little troll might think he was turning homo. He could scarcely contain his horror when, through the postage-stamp-sized viewer, he realized he could see through Hugo's polyurethane skin, all the way to his innards, and instead of having guts and bones, Hugo was made of proprioceptive sensors and accelerometers, servo motors, actuators, gyros and infra-red range finders.

Tales of humanoid robots ran in the rumor mills, of course, but with cloning as routine as pedicures, it hardly seemed worth anybody's trouble. Yet here it was, in front of his own R-ray eyes. Freemantle used the 5-yottapixel camera to snap a few pictures, then lay back in bed to figure out how to proceed.

In the end, and for the time being anyway, he'd opted to do nothing. The act was just beginning to ignite, and in the days that followed, as the offers from comedy showcases across the globe began pouring in, he saw no reason to make waves. He knew that he held an ultimate ace up his sleeve—the sleeve with Inspector Gadget on it—and until Freemantle Mania crested, he'd keep his annoying little dummy's secret to himself. And throughout that time, of course, he had enjoyed not only the sight of girl's underwear, but of their uteri and ovaries too, right through their clothes.

But now the time had come, and he leaned back with self-satisfied harrumph, folding his scrawny meat hooks over his chest and watched as, incredulously, Oppez picked up one of the images and held it up to her face to examine it.

She examined it for a long time. A long, long time. Finally, her silence became awkward, especially after he asked, "So? What do ya think about them apples?" and she did not respond.

"Hello, anybody home?" he said, mugging like a comic before a tough crowd. "You want impressions? How about I'll be the guest and you pretend to be the host? Nothing? Have we let the terrorists win?"

Suddenly, as he watched, the photo slipped from her fingers and fluttered to the floor. Freemantle could see that her eyes were unblinking, fixed upon the very spot she'd been looking at, even though her hands were now empty.

"What the…?" said Freemantle, turning to address the guy operating the photon detector, and discovered that he too was perfectly motionless, staring into oblivion. Behind him, the crew, the producers, even the juicy little interns—nobody was moving;

they all stood still as if frozen, midway through whatever they had been doing.

In fact, there was no sound in the vast warehouse studio at all.

Freemantle started to rise, then heard the buzz of a remote-control field robot. A cute little mini-rover rolled up on a six-wheel rocker-bogie, extended a mechanical arm, picked up the R-Ray image of Hugo McHugoface's runty little android bowels that Oppez had dropped and set it on fire. The arm reached for the other images still spread across the podium, and when Freemantle tried to intervene, he found that he too was utterly paralyzed and unable to move so much as a little finger or blink an eyelid.

The last thing he saw was the robot igniting the other pictures in a brilliant, multi-color burst of flames—then his vision faded to black.

Ten miles away, atop the metal skeleton of the space elevator, in a control center made of meshes of carbon nanotubes, a shrunken little hobgoblin who looked exactly like Hugo McHugoface sat at a vast bank of interactive 3D tabletop displays and haptic touchscreens.

His name was Cornelius Beauregard; he was a maverick roboticist who pretty much controlled the cyber-side of Universal Agendia on behalf of the Master Plutocracy. Hugo McHugoface had been one of his early android failures, built in his own image, since he was a bit narcissistic. The robotic doppelganger had escaped, much like his woolly mammoths, although he'd only admit to the FUBAR under the influence of extreme torture or copious amounts of clitoris-flavored Cognac. He had no idea that his little avatar had recently made it big on the stand-up circuit—he didn't pay much attention to comedy news, and beside, Hugo McHugoface's stage persona had required him to wear a lot of dummy makeup.

In any case, he'd been busy working on the space elevator when one of his current line of androids suggested he tune into the morning braincast of one of his most successful gynoids—the lovely Oppez Walton. He now picked up the signal midway through the show and was equally surprised to see Freemantle Cobbs, a zany, goofball, funny-faced droid he'd once made to amuse his niece, then, like Hugo McHugoface, lost track of. He occasionally regretted having outfitted his synthetic cyborgs with artificial intelligence algorithms that came complete with invented histories, but what was done was done.

With a simian lope, the imp swung over to the planar board and dispatched one of the rover bots he had installed throughout New Yopolis, directing it destroy the images Freemantle had taken of Hugo's half-assed piezoelectric essence—nobody likes to be reminded of a faux pas like Hugo McHugoface. After that, he erased the memory banks of all the androids involved, and with a flip of a switch, of that portion of the global population's brain chips that had ever watched or could even remember *The Oppez Walton Show.*

In the end, he figured, screw it: What was done could be undone.

The whole cleansing operation took less than two minutes, and back in the OBC studio, when Freemantle Cobb's vision and hearing returned, he found himself looking across a strange podium at a lovely woman with lips like luscious jewels and eyes like meltwater lakes. She peered back at him, blinked a few times and looked puzzled.

Neither had the slightest idea who the other one was, or for that matter, who they were themselves.

GREEN LIGHT

Jeni's mother had been missing for six years—on that point, nobody disagreed. The point on which people disagreed was whether or not Jeni's mother was still alive, living under an assumed name, perhaps with a new identity and a new family, or whether she was decaying at the bottom of one of the dozens of lakes around Taborville.

If the latter scenario was true, Jeni's mother was certainly put there—the grisly speculation went—by Jeni's father.

Jeni had considered both, life or lake, but she held a third possibility tightly inside her. For reasons she could neither explain nor fully accept, she pictured her mother trapped somewhere, helpless, in some warp, some wormhole, and every time she saw the image, the entire thing was suffused in a wash of greenish light. It was not a pleasant image—being trapped was only marginally better than being dead and far worse than being with a new and loving husband somewhere far away—a better fate than her own loveless, rigid father had offered—but the tragedy was Jeni's to process as she could, to cling to any image that allowed her cope.

And yet, this picture of her mother did not help her cope in any positive way. It terrified her. Even so, it had lodged so tightly within her conscience that she couldn't shake it loose.

She may not have understood it, but Jeni knew the precise

moment when the vision had first occurred to her: Four years earlier, when she was ten years old. Two years to the day after her mother vanished, her father had announced that she was old enough to know the truth, and thereupon launched a yearly ritual on the anniversary of the June disappearance, where he'd take her down to the sheriff's office under the guise of having her learn first-hand the progress of the missing persons investigation. Jeni had seen through that scam right away, since by then the case was already two years old, and as far as she could tell, nobody had made any progress at all.

Sheriff August Denny had a hard-edged office attached to the courthouse. He was a politician more than a lawman, and he never stopped campaigning. His subordinates were not only his campaign staff, they were his kin: The chief deputy was his cousin, the dispatcher was his daughter and the county's lone drug agent was his son-in-law. Jeni had only seen Sheriff Denny a couple of times in her life—the jurisdiction was wide and he spent a lot of time in the sparse office or playing golf with the town's few business elites—but he'd seemed at first like a potent, powerful overlord who would shortly find her mother.

Now, with her mother still unfound, with Denny's torso pushing against brown shirt like a 4-H sow, so big that his belly hairs protruded from the space between the buttons, drifting into a trance with his hands folded over his slovenly gut, slack-jawed and eyelids droopy, what had once seemed like introspective wisdom now seemed like nothing more slovenly disinterest. His bulk, which had once seemed imposing, now made it look like he

70

couldn't stand to support himself.

During that first trip to the sheriff's office, and on every trip since, Sheriff Denny had the daughter-dispatcher, who was also the property room manager, bring out the meager manila file of evidence. It included a letter, typed and printed at the local library, which her father maintained had been left on the kitchen counter by her mother.

That first year, the fat sheriff read it aloud, his thick voice seeping like black ooze from the rim of the shower spigot, and from the first sentence, Jeni knew it didn't sound the least bit like her mother. It was filled with phrases like '…been restless for years…' and '…met someone else…' and ended with the saccharine plea that '…my daughter Jeni and my husband especially find it in their hearts to forgive me.'

In the first place, Jeni would swear on stacks of Bible that her mother had been rationally content with her lot and radiated an almost childlike optimism that allowed her to make good of anything in life–she made tea from the bumblebee weed that grew along the edge of the driveway, for example. As for meeting someone else, there was no one else in the mean, stagnant, oppressive clutches of Taborville to meet. And apologizing was something she'd never heard her mother do, not once. She'd been a forgiving person capable of excusing poor behavior with a fatalistic, almost zen-like shrug—Jeni's behavior, that of her compulsive, tic-prone husband, and especially, her own.

As Denny read from the evidence folder, his flaccid, florid

face sagged like corn leaves in a summer drought; he looked vulnerable and weak, like he was putting himself to sleep.

Behind him on his desk lay his telephone, and there was a single green light on it that indicated his answering machine was on. As he read from the letter, Jeni fixated on the light, and seemed to slip into a sort of surreal state where everything began to expand and contract in waves, and she was suddenly able to see her mother's face, wincing at the forged words and the invented excuses as the sheriff drawled them out, while behind her, as a beacon, the green light blew up to unimaginable proportions.

From that moment, memories of her mother and the ominous glow of the small, square green light on Denny's phone became inseparably fused in her mind's images

On the ride home, her father had said, curtly and smugly, "Satisfied now? Do you finally get it?"

Jeni nodded—in some ways, she did.

In Taborville, her father was considered an outlier—as an adult, he'd been assimilated into town life, but not particularly appreciated. He'd grown up on a nearby hog farm eating nothing but salt pork and boiled potatoes, and he'd spent his teenage years slaughtering swine, slitting their throats and collecting the blood to sell to butchers for sausage. He'd soon realized that he didn't want to work sunup to sundown while relying on fickle weather, so he'd gone to work as a quality inspector at a pork processing plant in Wellston. He still spent his hours around bleeding hogs, but now with some authority and while wearing a tie.

He led an extraordinarily regulated life, and it baffled Jeni that he'd retained nothing from the beauty of outdoor work—the sounds of morning unfolding, the sunlight filtering through a network of branches, the field's fierce perfumes as things sprouted and composted at the same time—but only the regimentation. She knew that a lot of the folks in Taborville believed that if her mother had left him, it stood to reason—who'd want to live with such a tightly wound, OCD mess? If he hadn't killed her, they hoped she'd found some beefcake cowboy who'd squired her off to somewhere warm and sunny and overflowing with exotic drinks.

Had her mother been the type? Jeni doubted it, but then again, people rarely wore on the outside the face of who they were on the inside. She had a handful of photographs, though none that showed them together as mother and daughter. By his own admission, after she vanished, her father had thrown out everything she owned. These were snapshots sent to her by her aunt, her mother's only sister, who lived three states away, and they showed her mother before she was married. Jeni's favorite had been taken when her mother was around fourteen, Jeni's age. She was on the beach at Saugatuck wearing sunglasses, a lacy top and cut-off jeans: Her form had the exquisite willowiness of a boy's, yet tingled with the dazzle of a woman's grace.

Jeni had inherited her figure, but she knew she was working it wrong. She was constricted and contained, unable to find poetry in her coltish limbs, still gangly and awkward when she shifted inside them.

She was a guarded girl—that's what her teachers said. Her shirtwaist dresses, limp, straw-colored hair, wan freckle-spackled face floating through the hard halls of Taborville High made her a plain and dusty-dull nobody whose family had somehow, for some reason, undergone a convulsion of such outlandish size that she'd become a somebody.

Nobody at school or in town really wanted to make eye contact with her, to ingest her emptiness, because even after all this time—long after the gossip had faded like skunk smell in the morning—Jeni remained suspended in unique isolation. It would have been easier on everyone had she grown into a violent delinquent or a chattery tramp, because people could handle a personality grown as large as a tragedy. But as ghostly waif haunted by an endless sense of something akin to homesickness even though she was at home, sidling through their lives without a sound? They couldn't know the incessant volume inside her head, of course, and to see her was to feel a lump grow in their throats, and because they were simple people whose mothers and daughters and aunts and wives never went missing, the sight of her was perpetually disconcerting.

But Jeni felt exactly the same. Even to herself, she was an agitation in the atmosphere, an emotional enigma: She couldn't cry because her mother was dead—she didn't know. She couldn't cry because her mother had abandoned her—she didn't know. So she trembled in an interminable, excruciating limbo where her mother remained trapped somewhere, suffused with sick green light like the one on the sheriff's phone.

She took solace in the bumblebee weed growing in the half-shade by the driveway, and like her mother, sometimes she picked it, dried it and steeped it in tea. The plant was vigorous and would persist long after the tea-makers were gone—it was mint without a scent, and since it flowered unevenly, it bore spikes that were always half-covered in ghost-colored blossoms, giving it the perpetual appearance of being unfinished.

This year in June, following the anniversary trip to Denny's office, she'd had a profoundly disturbing conversation with her father. At first, she thought it was his attempt to deliver the requisite birds and bees lecture, but midway through it he'd drifted off into some private torment, talking about the need to 'cube' things in life, to move beyond the trouble moments, to pack your most awful memories into compartments, then sequester those compartments in what he called 'your hidey-holes'.

It had sounded so nearly like a confession that it had affected her for days afterward—so much that she'd finally screwed up the courage to approach the only other lawman in the county. Lee Lofland was Taborville's police chief, which meant he was a police sergeant who operated from a desk in the rear room of his father's shot-and-beer bar on Market Street. The municipal board had sprung for the cost of a uniform and a patrol car with a quarter million miles on it and nothing more, and included in his job description reading the town's water meters once a month.

But Lofland was not beholden to the sheriff's department, and in fact, he was the one who generally responded to family fistfights calls during the first and third week of every month after someone spent the assistance check on drugs or booze, and again at the end of the month when more fights broke out because there was neither money nor drugs left.

Jeni approached him during the relative quiet of the second week, and he nodded and seemed to digest what the tremulous young girl had to tell him. He knew about the case, of course, but it had been under the sheriff's jurisdiction before he'd even taken his job. He'd seen the alleged bye-bye note, and although he recognized the level of corruption that existed in the county cop shop, he could find no evidence of criminal wrongdoing in the disappearance of Jeni's mother.

"But do you believe she wrote the letter?" Jeni asked.

Lofland weighed his words carefully, measuring precisely how to reveal intangible truths to a girl who was nearly a woman, but not quite. Behind him stood a shelf stocked with pickled eggs and pig's feet: " Forgive my French, but sometimes my job requires me to work on intuition—what field training calls 'the asshole alarm'. I know your father; how tightly wound up he is. With people like that, things can go from zero to totally wrong in a fraction of a second. But he's smart. If I was in court and you were a prosecutor, I'd admit that I have no idea who wrote that letter. On the street, I'd bet my badge that it wasn't her."

76

"Do you think she's alive?"

"Again, I'm not in court—I'm sorry, honey, but I think your mother is probably not alive."

She nodded without showing emotion. On an impulse, she told the story about the sheriff's office, the insensitive recitations and the image of her mother's face behind the ominous green light that had dominated her thoughts for the last four years. Lofland said, "What else does a green light mean to you? When you see one on the corner of Market and High Street?"

"It means to go," she said flatly, pinching the pleat in her skirt.

"Maybe it's your mother's way of telling you to move on with your life, Jeni. I don't think she'd ever want to you let her go, but I think you'd agree that she wouldn't want you stuck at a red light indefinitely."

He was right, of course, and those words saw her through another few weeks, until early August, when everything was stale and still and the clouds on the horizon gathered but never arrived. There were no breezes or rain and the temperature flirted with one hundred degrees. In Jeni's window, in her bedroom, a three-foot square window fan moved around the hot air like effluvia in a swamp.

It would be another year before the court could declare her mother legally dead, at which point her father said he'd equip the place with air conditioning from the insurance payout, but for now, the fan would have to do. The rest of the grid had their units running full tilt, however, and at 10:35 in the evening, with her father working the midnight shift at the packing plant, the power failed.

Alone in the dark, she was paralyzed with fear. The crickets in the yard sounded berserk. A dog screeched in the neighbor's yard and somebody threw gears in a car as it peeled away into the distance. She used her phone to call her father's job, as much to determine that he was actually there as to ask advice.

He offered it anyway, and without equivocating: "It's probably a fuse. Probably nothing but a fuse. You have to go down in the cellar and throw the breaker. The top one, the one that controls all the others. Go get a flashlight from the drawer under the toaster oven…"

"I can't," she said. "I hate it down there. I don't know how to throw breakers."

"No, you got to do it, Jeni. There's no other option. Listen to me. The fuse box is over in the corner by the sump pump, on the wall. Black box. Throw the top switch from right to left."

"I can't."

His voice took on an angry edge that was near hysteria. "Stop saying that, damn it. If you don't do it, the sump will overflow and the whole house will flood. And the longer you wait, the longer you'll sit there moping around in the dark. Do it now, and in the meantime, I'll call the power company. Call me immediately when the lights come back on. We can't risk an outage."

He hung up, and she sat there for a moment, sucking in the oily air. As the light on her phone dimmed, the darkness and the oppressive weight of heat pulled in closer. In fact, she'd been honest with her father: She had an encompassing fear of basements in any house under any circumstance—she'd descend into hers only a couple times a year, and then, only furtively and under the direst of needs. Now, the idea of taking those stairs alone, with nothing but a flashlight, assaulted her night terrors to their very core.

In time, though, rationality wore through. This was, if nothing else, a dire need, and the idea of a flooded house and a frantic father to whom things might go from zero to insanity in the blink of an eye, and even more than that, perhaps, her inevitable life in a world where she would shortly have to assume the duties of adulthood—it all kicked in simultaneously and she forced herself up and slowly to the kitchen, where she found the flashlight and picked her way, step by step, into the yawning cellar.

It was a great cavern of shadows and furtive things that leaped and swung around as she threw light across the spread of darkness and over to the sump pump corner. There, on the wall, was a steel box with several rows of black breaker knobs, and, just as her father had said, with a bigger, central switch on top. But she was supposed to flip it from right to left, and it was already to the left as far as it would go. So she threw it the other way and waited to hear if the fan in her upstairs window kicked on, and when it didn't, she threw the switch the opposite way, then back again, and again and again, and when she had done it a ridiculous number of times and was about to call her father in a full-blown panic, she saw through the dirty pane of the basement window above her head that a light suddenly winked on in a house across the street. And then, she heard the distant whirr of her fan starting up.

Relieved to a level beyond what was purely rational, she spun around, and there, off in a corner where plastic storage totes were stacked, behind useless furniture and cast-off appliances, beneath several tiers of dusty boxes, she recognized the tiny, angry, insolent, insistent green light on the face of a chest freezer.

So then, of course, she knew. The hidey-hole. She knew before she knocked aside the cobwebbed chairs and dust-crusted totes; she knew before she tore the duct tape sealing the freezer shut; she knew before she threw open the freezer lid and shone the flashlight across sad limbs wrapped tightly around the cold white torso, and immediately afterward, she knew why her father couldn't risk a power outage nor have a daughter too afraid to throw a breaker switch.

Her father: She heard his truck crunching the gravel by the bumblebee weed; she heard the slamming kitchen door and she heard the savage voice as it began to howl for her from the head of the basement stairs.

THE SCRUTING

From the diary of Moses Irby Westbrook, titled 'A Lone Scene and Single Incident in the Great Rebellion':

'The Scruting failed me at some point during the night of April 10, 1862, and for that sweet dispensation, I must presently thank or curse all the hosts of Heaven.

Herein, I give an epitomized sketch of the Scruting in general and the Scruting's final glorious failure in particular, along with an account of the remarkable conflict that followed, from which I, along with my brother Loftin, emerged unscathed.

As introduction, I am Moses Irby Westbrook, born in in Frakesville, Tennessee on December 3, 1840, son of John Westbrook and his wife Olive Irby of Kinloch Laggan, Scotland, now deceased. I am the seventh of fifteen children, three of whom died in infancy, four in childhood and five of whom, beside me, are alive at the time of this writing.

Most recently, our beloved brother Calvin, scarcely seventeen, was killed in the Battle of Fishing Creek this January 19.

In September of the previous year, we three Westbrooks had signed aboard Captain John C. Heitherout's Sumpter Grays, succumbing to the excitement and adventure of going off to war. Calvin, the youngest of us, was most vocal and persuasive in his passionate dedication to the Southern creed and his willingness to stay with it until death, which it sadly happens, he did. Though perhaps not so eager as Calvin, Loftin and I were at least certain that we were on the right side of the question, the most sacred cause—as we then saw it—that ever called a man to arms.

Six months in, Calvin is gone, yet Loftin and I live still, and though God's glory has so far cared over us, I can surely state that our eyes have been opened to hardships of life, standing guard in military camps far from our feather beds, broke of rest, weeping bitterly as our brother and companions die around us and have endured such horrors of war as having slept in a field among the mangled dead as though it were nothing more ghastly than an apple orchard and their brains upon the ground were fruit.

The battle about which I am reporting occurred today, and it is now past midnight, making it the following day, or April 14. I am writing these notes by the light of a fire which I have stirred up, much to the grumbling of Loftin, who lies beside me on blankets, clearly exhausted from the exertions of our hard-fought battle.

Though I am dreadfully tired myself, further sleep remains for me elusive—a hare in the underbrush. My thoughts are burdened with images of the day's furious contest, most especially of the initial charge across the bluff when we were driven in by three or four thousand of the enemy with fixed bayonets, swarming like a hive of bees, who forced us into a ravine beneath a hail of shell and musketry.

I replay this lone scene and single incident over and over because it was during this first great assault of the battle that I had fully anticipated, and readily awaited Loftin's death, and then, within a space of five more minutes, my own.

Our deaths were ordained to be in the most gallant style, of course, with clear consciences and strong arms: I knew it would happen in this precise fashion because the Scruting told me so.

So now I offer an account of the peculiar gift of Scruting.

My grandmother Gaira Irby assured me that the two sights, called by her people in the Grampians *taibhsearchd*, is fairly common there, where as much as 10% of the population is thus affected. Here in the New World, it is perhaps only one individual in several generation who might possess the ability: A species of involuntary prophetic vision, whether direct or symbolical. Mine was of the direct type, as was first evidenced by my clairvoyant seeing, at five years old, of an awful and destructive storm of violence passing over our neighboring town of Carmichael, wherein I predicted ten souls killed outright and four more mortally wounded who would yield to injuries within two days.

I even foretold damages in the exact amount of fifty thousand dollars.

I cannot explain the occurrence beyond to say that I saw it in a dream that was more real than waking life: In that dream, I heard plainly as I now hear tree crickets the tremendous roar of a tornado afar off and making its advance with irresistible impetuosity toward Carmichael, and in a few minutes it was upon them, wreaking vengeance with lavish hands. I watched as clearly as I now see this page by firelight as the atmosphere darkened; I saw fence rails, treetops and timbers of enormous size sent whirling through the air and houses tossed about like marbles in the fingers of a giant. I even named the casualties: Alexander Gathercole, one child killed, himself and baby badly hurt. Mr. Rayback, severely injured, wife and one child killed, and another not expected to live. Rev. Erasmus Duncan, himself not at home, lady and servant slightly injured. James Parker, severely injured. C. C. Baltzell, severely injured; child's skill fractured, not expected to live. And so on.

Three days hence, on March 18, 1845, it all happened exactly as I had described, with those I named as killed or dying being identical to the newspaper account. And it so frightened my parents, thinking that I must be possessed by demons to have the future presented to my view, that they hauled me before our fine Methodist Episcopal preacher, Samuel Atmore. Atmore was a sober and thoughtful fellow dedicated to a more-or-less rigorous empiricism, and he assured my parents that such a thing as they described could not have happened, as—the family story goes— he reassured them, "Only the divine hand of Providence can unveil events before they happen; among mortal men, the future must always remain inscrutable."

My Grandmother, who put more credit in the deep-seated traditions of her people than in Methodist ministers, replied, "The boy appears to be scruting the future nonetheless."

From that moment forth, the Westbrook family chose to worship at home and always referred to my phenomenal talent of two sights as 'The Scruting'.

The Scruting came again the in '48 when I divined myself aboard a steamboat above Memphis, watching another steamer burning. Its starboard wheelhouse was ablaze and all that I could make out of the name of the boat were the last four letters , b-o-r-a. As the craft ran aground, I saw that people were leaping off and of them one hundred forty drowned. I reported every detail of this to my Grandmother, avoiding further trouble with my parents, and she had no doubt as to the reality of my prognostic vision and so was not surprised when two days later the newspapers held a story of the identical tragedy occurring to the steamship Tambora when two of her four boilers exploded.

The most usual of these extra-normal events occurs to me after dusk when a sudden or violent death is about to occur, since the impending event is to make a deep impression upon my mind. It was by this means that I predicted my mother's death of puerperal fever after birthing her final child Edme, and later, the death of my own dear Grandmother who had maintained with such conviction that the world was as full of preternatural events as it was of natural forces, and who had believed in my Scruting with perhaps more faith than she believed in God.

As you can imagine, many times I tried to stave off the unhappy events I had scruted with every device at my disposal, but these attempts always failed, and I came gradually to understand that they were ordained to happen exactly as I saw them happen, and that—whether gift or curse—my Scruting could see the future but could not change it. Following the death of my Grandmother, I would not share my captivating visions with anyone, for any reason, and I only write this now because it seems that the Scruting has finally failed me, and of that I am truly grateful, since I may, perhaps, be blessed with a long life with many children of my own.

Although, it should now be clear that when, four days ago, I saw the initial portion of today's battle in finest detail, with sound and smell and violent action—a vision ending upon the death of Loftin by a Yankee shell and my own, a short time later by a Yankee bayonet—I had not the slightest reason to doubt that the events would happen precisely like that. I told no one, since the burden was better borne alone, but over the intervening days I made my peace as best I could, and carried through my hourly duties to the cause with all due circumspection and attention.

And yesterday morning, it commenced at 6 AM exactly as I saw that it would, hearing the firing of musketry coming from the advance guards and us called to muster and standing in formation while General Whitaker Dixon, second-in-command, rode among us singing out, "I have put you in motion to offer battle to the invaders of your country, boys—fire low, fire low," as we waited in breathless anticipation for the climactic charge. There were those among us who needed to be restrained from driving forward—we cheered and raised a huzzah as the firing grew awful grand, and as we were ordered to march, we cried out, "The enemy has seen our Battle Flag."

We made a line below the brow of a hill nearest the fighting, intending to flank the Yanks should they retreat, as this would be their only path if they were cut off from the river. We remained cool and alert and the sun shone like a copper penny upon the fields and the smoke rose in great clouds, and as the day passed its apex, the pitch of battle beyond the hill increased until the roar of musketry and the grape became incessant and the enemy crested the hill and descended upon us in a great wave of blue with bayonets sparkling in the sunlight.

This is the very moment that I expected Loftin to die, and myself soon afterward—expected it so matter of factly that I briefly lay down my Springfield and closed my eyes and waited, murmuring a final supplication for our souls to be delivered.

Yet when I opened them again, I was still in the Land of the Living and the bayonet charge had passed me by without inflicting a scratch and Loftin, along with the rest of the Sumpter Grays, had reformed in some other place, so I fetched my weapon up and charged away with another Regiment without thinking— in the midst of such turmoil, thinking is not a priority.

We made a furious and desperate charge against the Union batteries, and the enemy fell back in many directions. We kept up manfully and advanced in the face of galling fire, running over piles of dead and wounded, and continued until the Yanks were routed and we were so exhausted that the commander thought it prudent that we retire. I left the awful field, somewhat sickened as our noble Southerners polished off the wounded enemy with saber and pistol, and went in search of my unit, finally quartering beneath a tarpaulin I found suspended over two low-hanging branches on a tree on a rise above the tracks of the Mobile and Ohio railroad.

When I awoke, I was pleased beyond reckoning to find Loftin beside me, and though I cannot seem to find further sleep tonight, I would just as soon get these words down on paper while they remain keen in my mind, for whomever may one day read them.

Yet now, I hear strange sounds in the darkness—surely it is the sound of the pickets shooting, as though Grant's routed Federal forces have returned from the grave to fight again. And now, as I write these words, Loftin is jerked away by the gun-play, and we hear the call to muster in the road once again—and as he pulls his clothing tight again and checks his musket I ask him what we'd done the day before and he replies, 'We stood for most of it awaiting a ferry to transport us across the Buffalo River, swollen due to the heavy rains, which is why we didn't attack last night,' and looks queerly at me, asking me if I am fully in myself and imploring me to step lively because the moment of truth is upon us.

Thus I am forced to reckon another truth: It is still the morning before the battle and I last night I Scruted the entire thing beyond the time of my death, owing, no doubt, to the magnitude of the carnage that will follow.

I see now, as I could not have seen otherwise, what the final toll will be:

Of the Confederates, of 10,490 total, 2.067 will be killed and 4,408 wounded; of the Union side, of 13,904 total there will be 1,715 killed and 7,621 wounded.

Given time, I could no doubt list them, one by one, and I now am in unshakeable confidence that my name and Loftin's name will be among them. Of this, as God is my witness, I am presently as certain as I am that in fact my Scruting has not failed me after all, and that this horrific battle has not yet happened.'

The diary of Moses Irby Westbrook has passed through my family for seven generations. How many of us have read it, I can't say, but I can state with some certainty that most of those who read must not have believed it.

However, I have no real doubt of it, since the casualty figures he lists for the Battle of Buffalo River, which occurred on April 13, 1862, during which he—along with his brother Loftin—died, are accurate to the man.

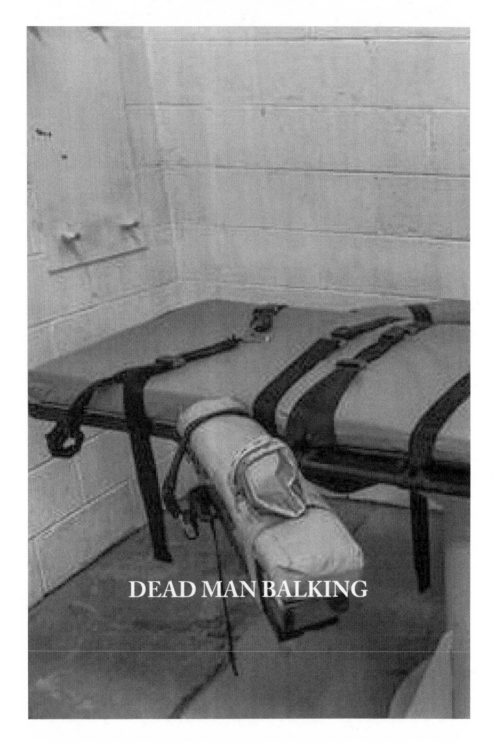

DEAD MAN BALKING

When you first met Bennie Lou Waggaman, you'd find that there was one thing he liked to think about even more than cheating the executioner: His Grandmomma Lurietta's down-home cooking.

For as long as you'd listen, he'd tell you that he missed her crawfish soup more than he missed the ladies, more than he missed bellowing hallelujah in the little wooden church house by Cypress Creek, more than he missed the smell of the angry green water in Biloxi Bay before a storm.

He'd tell you about Grandmomma Lurietta's chicken fried steak, made with cheap, pounded, tenderized beef and eggs from the henhouse in back of her camelback shotgun hut in rural Perigal County where he was raised along with seven brothers and four sisters; he'd tell you about her cornbread, pronouncing cornbread like it had four syllables—*co-wurn bray-yit*—and he'd go on and on about her mud pie, a regional favorite: "Niggas useta come from aw across the county fo a slice o Grandmomma Lurietta's Mississippi Mud Pie, tell you what. An they wouldn't leave till they et some of her shrimp gumbo neither. Said it was granny-slappin good…"

Then he'd throw back his bald head and loose a big horselaugh at the odd, ironic Southern expression, showing far too much ease for someone awaiting execution in Unit 22 of the State Prison at

Moreauville.

The one thing he wouldn't tell you much about was the crime that landed him there, and for me, it was just as well. At the time, I was a young journalist on my first major assignment at the *Metro Voice*, an urban tabloid renowned for its investigative work—I think the reason I was given the Bennie Lou Waggaman interview was that he was, even to the most rabid activists at the paper, although another black dude railroaded through the system, so clearly guilty of a crime so horrific that his race didn't even matter—they'd have fried Brad Pitt if he'd done what Bennie Lou Waggaman did.

That is, break into an isolated house on Highway 609, tie up a family of three—a young woman and her two school-aged children—rape the mother then slit all their throats. DNA analysis was inconclusive, and Waggaman might have gotten away with the crime. But he'd left a living witness: By the grace of someone or something on high, one of the little girls had survived the throat-slitting and had identified him without hesitation.

The crime editor of *Metro Voice* was a grossly overweight college drop-out in his mid-thirties, and I often wondered if one of the reasons he'd tossed me that assignment was that I represented his antithesis: I was a thin, eager twenty-two-year-old with a journalism degree from Emerson. I assumed there was something inherently sadistic about him, and it seemed likely that sending a petite, pretty—fact, not ego—Caucasian chick from Boston into the belly of the Deep South beast to confront a psychopathic black mass murderer probably, on some level, got his rocks off.

As far as the astronomically low odds that Bennie Lou Waggaman might actually be innocent; that he'd share some vital tidbit of information during out interview that would allow me to turn the case on its head in the few days he had left to live and save him from execution?

I confess, that's what got my rocks off.

As it turned out, I might as well have been interviewing Paula Deen. After I'd done meticulous research to see if the investigation had left any stone unturned, after I'd analyzed the trial notes to see any question had been unasked—after I'd gone through the trouble of renting a Subaru, driving the hundred miles to the prison, dealing with red tape paperwork forced on by leering corrections officers—men and women—undergone a humiliating strip search by the latter, only to be informed that the clothes I'd put back on were all I'd be allowed to take into the interview room; no pens, no video recorder, no paper—all Waggaman wanted to talk about was recipes.

At least I got him to allow me quote him from memory, so, as anti-journalistic as it is, anything I transcribe here is as I remember it, although I must say, I impressed myself with my instant-recall skills—I didn't know I had them. Obviously, I was used to the reporter's usual toolbox, including cameras, notepads and a couple of spare Sharpies, but the prison couldn't care less.

As I say, Waggaman went on for a ridiculously long time about his grandmother's cooking, but before we got that far, I did ask manage to wedge in a question: Since, barring the sort of miracle that had saved the life of his nine year old victim, he was facing state-sanctioned execution in less than a week. I wondered how he could present such a calm—almost beatific—front. His expression made him seem disarmingly happy.

"Cause it ain't gonna happen," he said with perfect confidence.

I reminded him that he'd exhausted all his appeals; that the initial judge had rejected them along with the District Court; the State Court had upheld the conviction and the Supreme Court had refused to hear it. And although Governor Dabney had the option of granting him clemency, not only had he scoffed at the idea, he'd publicly, (and rather unprofessionally, I thought) suggested that not only would he perform the execution himself, he'd do it three times in a row to cover all the victims.

Bennie Lou Waggaman was not fazed in the slightest by the hourglass suspended in front of him. Again, he insisted that the execution would never happen. "King Jesus gonna deliver me from that hangman's noose, sure as He stilled the waters and healed the cripples. He maybe gonna wait till the cock crows the final time before He do, but mark my words, the hangman gonna be cheated outa this nigga's neck."

Whatever. I didn't want to remind him that he was slated to die of lethal injection, not hanging, but I did press him for some details regarding the crime. Since he claimed to have been twenty miles away at the time, he maintained that he could not provide them.

That's when he switched into his cascade of culinary reminiscences from his childhood.

And that's when I hit upon a story idea that might actually have some angles I could sink my eager young pearly whites into. Something with the brutal edge of hard truth tempered by some nostalgia. I could show a human side of a ruthless baby killer: Touchstones from his own childhood.

So, I asked him the obvious lead-in question—what did he intend to order for his last meal?

The sluice gate was thus raised; the fire hydrant busted open, and from it flooded gulf shrimp and flounder, cornpone and stewed okra, drop cookies and marshmallows. It became clear by the broad and artless grin I saw through the shatterproof plastic that separated me from Bennie Lou Waggaman, and the joyful abandon I heard through the cheap plastic phone through which we were communicating, that he had spent the last eleven years not moping, not penitent, not making his peace with his creator, but thinking about Grandmomma Lurietta's crawfish soup.

"I grew up at Grandmomma's knee," he gushed. "Watched her measure that flour and cut in that margareen; I helped her peel them shrimps and shuck them oystas. Dif'rent time, dif'rent circumstance, I coulda run circles around Commander's Palace and K Paul chefs. Hell, coulda run them kitchens single handed, I knows cookery that well."

Briefly, his eyes closed and when his lips retracted, they reminded me of panther lips. A huge set of teeth emerged. He shook his head and let fly the first of many deep, sonorous laughs I was to hear that afternoon. It was eerie, because I believed that in his mind's eye he was seeing Grandmomma's knee, probably wrapped in a dress worn from years of country washings, dusty with corn flour, sticky with molasses, smelling like ham hocks, and not what you and I would be seeing, eternally and inescapably—the hot blood of a four-year-old spurting through our fingers.

The deal with last meals for death row inmates, as I subsequently learned on-line, is this: Every state has different rules, but in this one, an inmate can request whatever he wants, and the prison chef, who is another inmate, usually tries to accommodate, albeit with the ingredients available, so long as the total expenditure is less than forty dollars. A dude in Texas, for example, requested 50 tacos and got five, while in most prisons, the common request for filet mignon winds up being hamburger, since that's what they already have in the kitchen.

Waggaman ticked off the last meal items he had ordered and it was a list indeed. Everything previously mentioned, plus potato salad, black bean dip, chicken and waffles, fried okra and barbecued pigs feet. It was a wish list of a child with an edible Toys R Us catalog who still sort of believes it all comes from an elf factory on the North Pole. But he described every item in such meticulous detail, including prep times and oven temperatures, that I sort of got lost inside the maze of his obsessive compulsions. As I say, it was my first major interview and I didn't yet have a handle on how to steer things when they went off the rail. But in the end, he admitted that the warden had sent the list back and told him to pick three items, because that's all the ball the state was willing to play.

Another horsey guffaw: "I like to went out o my mind tryin to decide! In the end I made a dart out o a Bic pen and threw it."

"And?" I asked.

He pantomimed as if he was opening an envelope in an awards ceremony and read off the invisible winners, grinning, "Crawfish soup, shrimp gumbo and Mississippi mud pie. Done. Like to starve me to death, know what I'm sayin? No seconds, and no doggie bags. I know cuz I axed."

He was making jokes, this rapist toddler-killing throat-slitter, and I—cub reporter for a somewhat less-than-great metropolitan newspaper—was laughing.

And then, zip, like that, my interview was over. We were out of time, and essentially all I had gotten out of him was when to fold the whipped cream into the cream cheese. If I was going to convince my slovenly, misanthropic boss that I had an interesting last meal story, it was going to take some foo-foo dust.

In the end, the killer provided the dust. As I thanked him for his time—an awkward nod to how little of it he had left—I said, rather shallowly, that if there was anything I could do for him to help him through his final days on earth, I'd try. He dropped

99

his voice down a couple decibels and said that, as a matter of fact, there was. He asked me if I remembered the key ingredient that made Grandmomma Lurietta's mud pie famous throughout Perigal County.

"Almonds!" I said brightly, proud of my newly discovered phonographic memory.

Waggaman frowned. "Not jest any almonds, missy—on'y the wild almonds grow in the woods by Cypress Creek. That's all Grandmomma would use. They called Amara almonds."

I blushed at my error. "Amara almonds. I will remember that," I vowed.

"Well, missy. If y'all could find it inside yo'self, I really need you to do more than remember it. I need you to get me some. See, prison cook be a righteous cat, eager to do me right, but he incarcerated, like me. He got no access to Amara almonds. If there's any way you could bring up a l'il ol' bag o Amara almonds from Cypress Creek, you'd be doing a poor old nigga a solid, cuz it jest ain't Grandmomma Lurietta's mud pie usin state-issued almonds..."

"Well, I..." I stammered. "I mean... How...?

"Easy as... pie. You all go down to Cypress Creek downtown and behind the colored folks theater be Grady Dunn Lane, and you all follow that all the way to the gully, and there at the end is a little wooden juke wit my big brother Tiger-T behind the bar. He gon set you up with a bag o Amara almonds, then you all come on back up heah—I been on Death Row these eleven year and ever'body I met didn't become an enemy. You bring them Amara almonds back in a day or two; the right folk'll get 'em to the prison cook."

My face must have gone all Suzy Creamcheese, because Waggaman's panther grin widened until his bald black head looked like a skull wrapped in electrical tape. "You wanna be a newspaper gyal?" he said. "This all gon make a helluva story."

Actually, it would. And it did. It was crazy, and although I didn't understand exactly how crazy until I got home. As it happened, this was the stuff I thought I wanted; this was The Seymour Hersh-Woodward/Bernstein-Daniel Ellsberg muckraking career path I'd been envisioning for myself.

How crazy was it? Well, first thing the next morning, I brought a written version of my mental notes into my editor's cluttered shoebox office in the rear of Campus Books, where Metro Voice is published. He had his feet on the desk, with a pile of police blotters on one side and empty Arby's bags on the other. He did appear to be listening to me with undistracted interest, although I confess, his bloated gut, partially exposed beneath his 'Booty Pirate' t-shirt, was to me pretty distracting. I was running through the specifics of the interview, including the detailed culinary methodology behind Waggaman's detailed last meal requests, when suddenly he interrupted and sniffed, "That's preposterous!"

"What is?" I asked.

"A quarter cup of margarine? Why would you use all those authentic, fresh, heirloom ingredients and then rely on margarine? That shit's Satan's spread."

I allowed my notepad to sag; I raised the left half of my upper lip and made eye contact. "Seriously?"

"Yeah," he shrugged, making even more of his gut protrude. "All I'm saying is margarine is filled with trans-fat and synthetic carcinogenic chemicals and stuff."

"You think roast beef sliders aren't?"

Another shrug: "Margarine's worse. Especially for, like, nursing mothers."

The proximity of his moobs to the mental image of primates lactating made a little puke back up in my drainpipe. "Look, with respect, that's hardly germane to the story."

"Okay," he frowned. "Continue."

I took the wise course, leapfrogged the rest and went directly to the Mississippi Mud Pie, telling a small white ingredient lie when I rattle off one-and-a-half cups of fresh creamery butter, but told the absolute truth when I mentioned the 'secret' ingredient, sixteen ounces of crushed, lightly toasted Amara almonds.

"So," I spouted eagerly, "I went home and Googled 'Amara almonds', and it turns out they do grow wild in Perigal County. *Prunus amygdalus amara.* There are two kinds of almonds the world, sweet ones and bitter ones, and this is the bitter kind. Now the kicker: Amara almonds are totally toxic; they are loaded with naturally occurring cyanide and a handful of them can kill you. Waggaman asked for a whole frickin' bag. I think that's his end game! He kept going on and on about how he is going to 'cheat the hangman' and I think that's exactly what he's trying to do: I think he wants to commit suicide before they can execute him!"

My editor spent a moment with his fat brain in overdrive, then said, "That's a stretch, I gotta say. How was he going to get the poison almonds if you didn't happen to score the interview?"

"I don't know. If not me, then someone from *ProPublica* maybe. Possibly a relative. Who knows? He's resourceful, obviously. And you have to admit, it's pretty diabolical. Lucky I was on my A-game, huh? I might have done it, too—fetched the almonds and delivered them. There is something unaccountably… charming about the dude."

"Really," said the uncharming editor, sniffing, a trifle piqued. "So you aren't gonna do it?"

"Are you on crack?" I laughed. "What do you suppose the legal penalty is for smuggling lethal contraband into death row? I don't want to be Christiane Amanpour that bad."

He removed his legs from the table and folded his fat arms over his fat torso. "So, to summarize then: All that work and we still have no story. Hip hip hooray. You don't even have a video of the nut asking you for the nuts. Groovy. Say, there's a new nightclub opening up on North Central. Maybe I should send you out to review it. Maybe you could be our entertainment editor."

"Maybe I could go back to school and get a marketing degree," I said wistfully. "But, hear me out. I won't give Waggaman enough almonds to hang himself, but I do have the address of the place I was supposed to pick them up… Some old dive bar down in Cypress Creek where his brother works. On the night of the execution, I could show up there and do a piece on the family's reaction, before and after he's put to death."

"Won't the family be at the prison?"

"I doubt it—he comes from one of those whackadoodle rural families with twenty-five children. I'm sure they don't execute people in stadiums. Besides, Waggaman is absolutely, unshakably convinced that he won't be executed. It's like his mantra. I think he's just looking at the whole last meal thing as a cheap excuse to get some of Grandmomma Lurietta soul food."

Now I saw a glitter of lasciviousness light up behind my editor's thick glasses as he painted himself a portrait of a trim (I'm a vegan obsessed with yoga) pretty (so sue me) little blond cheerleader-type sitting in a seedy backwater honkytonk and trying to pry private information from poor black people. "That might get squirrely…" he warned, leering. "It isn't all moonlight and magnolias down there."

"Ye of little faith!" I p'shawed—as my senior thesis at Emerson I'd done an exposé of functional heroin addicts in the Ron Brown

Scholarship program. The key, I found, is respect, understanding and Mace.

"If you're willing do it," he said at last. "And provided it's halfway decent, I'd be willing to run it as a lead."

That decided it for me: 'Halfway decent' this, Lives-In-Mom's-Basement Boy.

Bennie Lou Waggaman was scheduled to die on Friday night at 12:01, which, of course, would technically make it Saturday. The reason for this is that specific dates appear on death warrants, but not times; they schedule them as early as possible so if there are any execution snafus, they have the rest of the day to fix them. If they can't and it dragged on to the following day, they have to start over with a whole new court order.

Following capital punishment rules to the letter, the legal mechanics hour-by-hour—even minute-by minute—is vital to officials involved in the process. It's probably what allows them to deal with the oxymoronic hypocrisy of murdering people to teach people it's wrong to murder people.

On Friday afternoon, I rented another Subaru and made the trek down Highway 609 to the swamps of Perigal County, excited and full of spunk, vinegar and pepper spray. The fog was thick where the rich bottom land of the gulf plain gave over to hardwood forest, and still thicker where it united with dense thickets of briars and cane and formed a nearly solid sub-tropical jungle, broken only by a handful of fields and derelict towns like Cyprus

Creek.

My research had shown that this had once been a thriving, hustling epicenter for the timber industry; L, NO & T Railroad agents had come for crossties and wagon makers for stave-bolts and spoke material. At one time, there had been a sawmill and an apparel factory, a post office, five churches, a bank and several public and private schools and the community had proudly produced most of its own cotton and corn.

Then, inevitably, reality reared its head and the fledgling, mostly-black colony of Cyprus Creek felt the triple whammy of mechanized agriculture, natural disasters and hostile race relations. The factories closed, the bank failed, Main Street died, and finally, even the Sister Workers of the Baptist Church of Perigal County, whose dormitory had proved accommodations to pupils from the surrounding farms, had given up the ghost.

Today, Cypress Creek existed as the poorest of the poor—evident by the downtown I wended through, where the two remaining anchors, Burkett Feed & Seed and Taylor Sheet Metal Work, looked like they hadn't been painted in decades. The movie house, which was actually called 'Rex Colored People Theater', still had a marquee with the letters 'T WZ' remaining from the last film they'd shown—'The Wiz'.

Behind it, though, was a creepy lane called Grady Dunn, and it dropped away into a neighborhood of shotgun houses, many with boarded windows and doors obscured by untended vines. Some displayed a now-vanished sense of rural enterprise, with faded signs advertising services that likely were not still available: 'CC Pawn & Firearm' yawned next to 'Darius Legal Services'.

At the end of the lane, pushed back against the pine barren, stood Waggaman Catfish House. It was built of rough-hewn boards and roofed with the sort of shingles hand-split with an axe, and unlike the peeling-paint businesses in town, this place looked like it hadn't been painted ever. The lot contained nothing that could have been confused with a working vehicle—only an Oldsmobile on cinder blocks and some rusted farm equipment.

It was open though, and the faint light coming from the only window indicated that contrary to appearance, it was actually wired for electricity. I gathered up my Sony Voice recorder, my spiral scratchpad and my Sabre Red mace, took a few deep breaths of thick swamp air, steeled myself and went inside.

The interior was dimly lit and consisted of a few rickety tables scattered around a sawdust floor, a long pine bar, a pool table and a few posters of Dallas Cowboys' linebacker DeShawn Everett stapled to the wall; Everett was, I'd read the only Cyprus Creeker besides Bennie Lou Waggaman to achieve any sort of national notoriety.

My attention was quickly diverted by the man behind the counter—he looked so much like Bennie himself that I thought I'd been punked—that Bennie had escaped and had simply waited for me to show up for the almonds so he could rape me and slit my throat. The rictus grin was identical, peeling back from shovel-shaped incisors like the dome at Cowboys Stadium;

the bald head was covered with the same thin, glittery black skin. Even the equine chortle and the penchant for referring to me as 'missy' matched: "Well, missy, you a bit late fo the almonds, ain't you? Ain't no time lef now…"

I was flabbergasted. "You look like his… twin," I said.

"Cuz I am. Come into the world ten minutes afo him, but look like I'm gonna leave it a good spell afterward."

"Look, sorry about the almonds— but that wasn't going to happen: Killing a condemned prisoner is a federal crime. But you may know, I'm from Metro Voice; I'd like to ask you a bit about Bennie Lou's life—would you consent to an interview?"

"Not sure much lef to be said that ain't been said. Bennie just born wit meanness inside—all us uns knew it. I mean, ever'body else fled town long since, nobody made no amends, and I think the on'y reason Bennie stuck around for the revenge."

Suddenly, I had a thought: "Do you have a phone?" I interrupted, holding up my iPhone, remembering that I had promised to call my editor when I got here—probably so he could gloat and do other nasty things. "I can't get a signal."

"Naw, nearest phone at the feed sto, and they closed. Got no internet down heah in the holler, missy. Ain't no need. Internet jest a bunch o tubes. And tubes be filled wit cats."

I had to admit, that was the single strangest comment I had ever heard about Wi-Fi, even from inveterate luddites. Flustered, I asked, "You don't like cats?"

"I likes 'em, but Wee-Gyal don't." He pointed and, as my eyes adjusted to the dim light, I saw that there was a full-grown hog in the corner, in the sawdust, sound asleep, snuffling.

It would be an interesting interview, albeit a short one. He told me his name was Lennie Lou Waggaman and offered me a plate of fried catfish and a glass of homemade liquor, neither of which I accepted. But I did ask him pointedly about the Amara almonds. "Did you know what they were for, Lennie?"

"Course I knew. Ain't got computers down heah in Cyprus Creek, but we have Grandmomma Lurietta's know-how—taught us ever' herb, ever' leaf, every' flower, every' nut grow round these muck swamps. Knew which uns would cure ya an which uns would kill ya."

"And you were willing to go to that length to see that 'the man' didn't get his pound of flesh?"

I'm not sure if he recognized the Shakespearean idiom, but something sure cracked him up. He did a mirrored replay of his twin's explosive snort, head back, slapping his thighs. He fetched a mason jar from beneath the bar and poured himself a few fingers of clear fluid from a dusty bottle and sucked down half of it, which made his bright black eyes sparkle even more.

"White man done took his pound of flesh five hundred years gone by, missy—chewed it up and spit out the bones. We Waggamans be the bones. Me an Bennie, tryin to go to them

Sister Workers school, county commissioner come by and said, 'Why you tryin to teach them niggers anything, we needs 'em to drive tractors.' School closed and we was spat out. We bones alrighty, but we smart bones nonetheless; Grandmomma Lurietta made damn sho o that. What time you spect it is rightch now?"

"8:37 exactly," I said, a bit smugly since phone clocks still work in anti- technology black holes like Cyprus Creek.

"And when Bennie spected to take his las' walk?"

"12:01."

"He ain't gonna take it, missy. Make no mistake there. He knowd that long afo you come along. All us uns knew it. State decree say last meal got to be served three hours afo the execution, an Lawd knows, white screws likes they rules. Bennie born wit a meanness inside, like I said, and he gon leave with it too, in under half an hour—right after he polish off that damn meal!"

"Oh, my God—somebody else got him the Amara almonds...?"

Lennie Lou went haw-haw, haw-haw, sounding more like a donkey than a horse—as far as I could tell, some guy who thought cats lived inside internet tubes was making fun of me.

"Naw, them nuts was nothin but icin on the cake, missy—o rather, icin on the mud pie. What Bennie request for his las' meal? Lemme guess: Shrimp etouffé? Crawfish boil? All yo internets, all yo research, all you interviews, and nobody thought to ask anybody down heah, did they? All us Waggamans the

110

same, even Grandmomma Lurietta, been that way fo always. We got smart bones all right, but we also deathly allergic to shellfish."

I sat there for a moment, blinking like a stupid little blond vegan cheerleader, then I packed up and ran. But with the nearest phone in the feed store and the feed store closed, of course, I was too late.

Bennie cheated the executioner, just as he had guaranteed me he would, and more than once; I was just too dense to work out the details.

I titled the feature 'Smart Bones' in acquiescence to his smart bones. It made a good story, for sure. My only one, as it happens—I quit the tabloid game right after filing it.

Metro Voice went belly up a few years later, and as far as I know, my editor hasn't worked since—I believe he still lives with his parents. I went back to Emerson and got my marketing degree, and ironically, today I am the public relations ambassador for Fleischmann's, the world's largest producer of margarine.

THE HARD SEASON

Cordelia Quinlan liberated herself from the passenger seat of
her nephew's new Sebring and stood in the stark, early morning
sunlight looking up at her new home. Her eye was forgiving
of the façade, but it was not a building, she thought. It was an
edifice. Even the word 'structure' contained too much poetry to
fit the grim pile—a sheer, ghastly grey high-rise built as a low-
income housing unit five decades before, now re-purposed as
a low-income nursing home for folks with Medicaid waivers.
Having a Medicaid waiver meant that the state picked up
the tab for long-term care instead of the harried children, the
overburdened next of kin, the struggling friends...

...Or the nephews.

The frontage of the nursing home was irrelevant to Cordelia
Quinlan in any case; she stood in the hot sun trying to assess
the spirit. She was eighty-two years old, and with that august
perspective, she realized that the face of anything was as short-
lived as pollen on the corn leaves. The sequestered soul, the
essence of an environment—the piece of architect, the plot of
real estate or even a train full of disparate individuals traveling
together, linked but apart—ran deeper than Portland cement
or cobbly loam or the frowns of passengers. It expanded
and flourished or shriveled into corruption based on the
temperaments of the people within—an amalgamation of their
hearts, blending into one, like their smells.

113

In front of the boxy high-rise, a concrete walkway worked a sterile path the door. An old man in a wheelchair huddled in a waiting area where a few late-season petunias looked wan and thirsty. He cast a lackluster glance toward Cordelia and her pasty nephew, who was unloading her meager possessions and two suitcases, all of which had fit easily inside the Chrysler. Even seated you could see that the wheelchair man was tall, and although wasted with disease and doped into docility by Hadol, it was plain that he'd once been an imposing specimen, a man's man. Cordelia left her nephew to the heavy lifting and approached the man with a confident bearing—a little slower than she'd have liked to, since she'd always been a brisk walker, but with a confidence that increased a little bit with every step. She peered at his face, his ineffably sad eyes and pale skin, thin as an onion peel.

"Why, you're a lawyer, aren't you?" Cordelia said.

Now, the vacancy slipped from his gaze, and his thin lips curled into a near sneer—a very lawyerly expression. "In another life, perhaps I was. Is it still that obvious?"

"It is. Not to some, maybe, but certainly to me. I know a legal eagle when I see one—I used to sit through entire trials, beginning to end. It was better than a sporting event, watching you lawyers clash. It *was* a sporting event—the defendant, the victim, they were second string. It was a contest of wills, of discipline, of wits between the titans—the lawyers. My favorite arena was the old county courthouse in Carlton, I used to spend weeks at a time in just drinking it in."

"Carlton," he said vaguely. "Is that upstate?"

"Yes, in Pawnee County. It's a grand old courthouse, with walls of Indiana limestone, floors of granite and stairways of Vermont marble. Now that was a structure of poetry, not an edifice at all, like this…" She pointed at the nursing home. "…dismal megalith. If you had tried a case in the Pawnee courthouse, I'm sure you'd remember it…"

"I may have. I may not have. Can't say either way—I went in for knee arthroplasty and came out with Alzheimer's."

"Never mind, I shall describe it all to you in detail. We'll have time, see? I'm moving in today. My nephew can no longer bear the burden of me, what with his failing ice cream concessions and so on, so we sold my little house in Carlton and…"

Now the cheerful, mucilaginous nephew came lumbering up the walk, lugging suitcases, looking unburdened despite the weight: Convincing his dotty aunt to cover his debts, buy him a car and go quietly into the good night—the Golden Age Care Center on a Medicaid waiver—had been a brilliant stroke of fortune and finagling. Not that she was leaving much behind—Cordelia had always been an odd egg, he mused—a crotchety loner, an inveterate spinster. He wondered if there was any chance she was gay, or if they even had gay in her generation. In any event, shifting her from her small house on Kiowa Avenue, where she had no one to look after her if she fell in the shower or had a stroke in her azalea garden to Golden Age, where they had safety railings and bathtub trusses and low-pile rugs to prevent tripping, was a logical decision for which she should be commended.

"See that, Aunt Cordy?" called out the nephew, wedging her belongings through the Golden Age door and into the vestibule. "You made a friend here already—that's one more than you had in Carlton. Told you transitioning would be a breeze. Chop-chop. There's a common area for reading here. An activity center for socializing—even a full time dietician on staff and security, 24/7. Safe and fun."

Cordelia bent close to the wheelchair man and said, "This is the hard season of life, when that which is unbearable comes to the surface and defies us to bear it. And we'll surely learn to bear it, counselor. The edifice is hideous, but it scents well."

The expression about life's hard seasons had come from her own aunt, Georgia Quinlan. Cordelia had only heard her use it a few times; it was not a phrase to drop flippantly. The first time was when she was eight years old and her parents were killed in a car wreck along the interstate and she'd ended up the charge of her late father's brother Morrison and his wife Georgia in a small farmhouse on the outskirts of Bucklin: "This is your hard season, Cordelia," her aunt had told her the first night she'd slept in her strange new bed when her life was filled with crazy unknowables. "Morrison and I are here to see you weather it. To help you grow through it and flourish."

The second time was in 1944, when the Western Union telegram

116

arrived, the words painstakingly typed, cut out and pasted by hand to a sheet of paper: 'The Secretary of War desires me to express his deepest regrets that your husband Corporal Morrison B. Quinlan was killed in action on twenty-seven July in France.'

"This is our hard season, Cordelia," she'd said as they wailed and clutched at each other. "We have become a precious twosome now, and it's up to us to rebuke the wild winds and find our stronghold."

The third time was when Cordelia was fifteen, and the city of Bucklin exercised eminent domain to condemn the entire neighborhood where Aunt Georgia and she lived to make room for a municipal expansion project. It was all above board and perfectly legal—these were civil litigators and not at all the sort of firebrand criminal attorneys that Cordelia later admired. Birkin Cemetery, adjacent to the farmhouse, was included in transaction because it was city-owned and had been largely unused since the turn of the century and the requisite two-thirds of plot owners could not be found to raise an objection.

A cemetery is a field of hard seasons, Cordelia thought. The loss of this one was more poignant to her than the house where she'd weathered the death of her parents—her room had overlooked it. She recalled the terror she'd first felt in peeling back the gingham curtains her aunt had hung in an effort to make the room more inviting; she remembered her initial glimpse of the desolate graveyard slumbering behind a rusting iron fence, the markers haphazard, the plots grown to prairie weeds, a few mulberry trees drooping and untended. At night the eeriness grew worse— almost intolerable, when every sough of wind and each creaking branch seemed to her the protest of forgotten people.

With her own parents interred fifty miles to the north and her uncle's cross among the neat white rows of dominos overlooking Normandy Beach in Colleville-sur-Mer, she had no connection with these mysterious and aberrant bones, their names and dates, perhaps their ranks if they were in the Soldiers Lot, possibly some didactic Latin reminders like *Fugit hora* and *Memento mori*, everything decaying into dust, where—without a context—their stories already lay.

She was not the sort of little girl to share her private thoughts, so she kept these nightly terrors to herself, and gradually, as the years passed, she grew to love and trust her aunt as much as if she'd been her birth mother. In time, inevitably, she become used to the cemetery and its proximity. At ten, she began to peer over the iron fence during the day and wonder why no one ever came to mourn their kin, their friends, their children.

Because there were children buried there, for sure. Soon, Cordelia made small, furtive forays beyond the weedy gate, listening to the rustle of grasshoppers as they played among the headstones, oblivious to their import. And, she was forced to reckon, without a mourner to remember the smiles and tears of the deceased, perhaps they had none. Some of the inscriptions had already weathered to illegibility, but she could make out others. And she began to read them, one by one, and, in pronouncing the names out loud, to wonder who these children had been, how they'd died, if anyone had reassured them during their hard seasons or wept when they'd met the one they couldn't outlast.

Among them was Hetty Annunsen, who had died in 1847 at the age of eleven—no other details were given, but the stone read, *'Our Beloved Daughter, Into the Sunshine.'*

Josiah Ambrose Bardeen, despite his laudable name and optimistic epitaph, 'With a Greater Thing to Do' had died at nine in 1870.

Levi Ferry had been 15 years old when, the carving read he'd *'Fallen Asleep in Jesus.'* His sister Alma, died two years later, but in life had *'Walked in Beauty.'*

Many were under five, and Lavinia Seiling's year of birth and year of death, 1887, were the same.

As to the cause of these precious deaths, the Birkin library offered some clues. There'd been a milk fever epidemic in the 1840s and a measles outbreak in the decade following. The Homestead Act had regulated the disposition of millions of acres of federal land in 1862, land that was often the ancestral home of native people, and there were frequent raids of the new settlement farms by the Comanche. Smallpox ravaged the county in 1869 and cholera in '76. Surviving many years beyond birth had been a challenge then, and the ways a child might die were legion. But, as always, Cordelia had a sense of reality that ran through deeper veins that those in her human system—she intuited storylines where none existed, and whether or not they were accurate became immaterial. Certainly, they rang with as much truth as any surviving diary or newspaper clipping. For little Josiah Ambrose Bardeen, she created a complex narrative in which he'd been the son of a tenant farmer in Fairview, destined to be a great botanist, always seen wandering far afield in the tallgrass prairie to collect paperflowers and desert chicory. One day he'd encountered a rogue band of Indians from the Comancheria who filled him with arrows, although he escaped and made it home, he'd died in his mother's arms while she mourned the greater things he'd been destined to achieve.

Alma Ferry had been a selfless nurse, she supposed—the only healthy person in Birkin willing to enter the smallpox camp a mile from town where those infected were quarantined, giving them support and medical assistance until she too was struck down by the disease.

Lavinia Sieling had been stillborn, but in respect, her parents had named another daughter Lavinia, and this one had grown up among the rolling hills and meandering streams then surrounding the growing town.

Hetty Annunsen had loved to read, especially in the porch swing on a summer day when the arc of sunlight over the landscape make everything shimmer in a wash of gold.

There were no girls her age living near the farmhouse in Birkin, so Cordelia formed committed allegiances with the names on the headstones. Where she had once feared that their unquiet, unremembered spirits might step wailing from their graves, she now summoned them forth, one by one. They became her companions, and she comforted them, helped them rediscover the people they'd been and become the people they might have become had the hammer of mortality not intervened. With these resurrected souls, she spend many, many childhood days beneath the ever-changing skies, running through corn and grass fields that stretched away into the horizon, playing Red Light, Green Light and Statues or descending into creek beds to catch frogs and dig for crawfish.

In 1947, in its progressive wisdom, the city of Birkin had condemned these acres and all the people there, treating the living and dead as equals—the moldered bones, the phantom children catching crawfish in Smoky Creek and the genuine girl who cheered them on. Those who breathed were evicted while the graves were exhumed by a low-bid excavating company with a backhoe. The original plan had called for relocation, but in general, the workmen hadn't found anything to relocate; the bodies themselves had long since decayed with their pasteboard caskets, and no remaining relatives really cared.

Now, if nothing else, their reanimated spirits went with Cordelia to her new home in Pawnee County on the other side of the state.

That move to Carlton was the final hard season that Aunt Georgia had endured, and that's where Cordelia had lived with her aunt until Georgia passed away in 1974, and from then on, alone and content with her fictions and her fantasies and her bittersweet memories of her own seasons, hard and soft. When her nephew had come weeping and begging with a portfolio of troubles, it's fair to say that his heart was without the grace and imagination and circumspection of her own.

But, she'd done what was necessary to keep him from bankruptcy, and bought him his new Sebring so that he could look like a businessman, and as a result, Cordelia Quinlan became one of one hundred forty-seven residents in the grim and uninviting Golden Age Care Center, where any care provided was an afterthought—where the nurses spent an inordinate part of the day watching soap operas in the dayroom, where staff turnover was atrocious and understaffing endemic, where cash and hearing aids and family treasures, often held by people suffering acute dementia, frequently disappeared.

Like the abandoned graves in the Birkin cemetery had been, untended and no longer relevant, many of the poor old souls were living entirely on the negligible largesse of the state, and had nobody on the outside to advocate for their interests.

From the day she moved in, however, Cordelia brought some balm to the blistered Golden Age community. It began when she discovered that her wheel chaired lawyer's name was Annunsen—she'd asked him if he'd ever read in family journals or genealogies of a relative named Hetty who'd died in childhood. He couldn't remember, of course, but it made no difference. She assured him that the name was unusual and that there must have been some connection; she helped him think and put some family timelines together, and together they decided that Hetty must have been the daughter of his great grandfather.

The names of other Golden Age seniors had not existed on any stone in the yard, but these stones had been pulverized by digging buckets attached to mechanical arms, so she told them stories of their own family members, who may have been unknown, but who had been no less real. She gave Alma Ferry to Dinah Finney, and regaled her with tales of her grand niece's heroism in bringing comfort to smallpox victims held in tents a mile, and described the rounds in such amazing detail that they could smell the carbolic acid she used to disinfect utensils.

The would-be botanist became Josiah Ambrose Breckenridge, a name no less aristocratic than Bardeen and shared by Gideon Breckenridge who lived on the fifth floor and had microscopic deposits of protein in his brain that prevented him from swearing that his family had all been British and unlikely to have been shot by Comanches. Tabitha Nicholson was overjoyed to learn that she'd had a great grandmother named Lavinia, and a great grand aunt named Lavinia as well; and each person who asked found something about themselves that no one had ever before cared enough to inform them.

In this way, Cordelia Quinlan managed to revive her childhood friends, giving them new identities that took root in new minds and sprouted. When asked how she managed to know so much about so many diverse histories, she smiled and rebuffed critics with a wave of her hand, as noble old women are allowed to do:

"I've archived neglected memories for many years. I am the one who sweeps cobwebs from attics and polishes heirlooms so long ago forgotten that they are suddenly new things, in life's prime again. I am an incubator for forgotten essence."

And over the next two decades at Golden Age, it wasn't merely memories she helped improve. She put a black square of carpet by the stairwell, and those residents with Alzheimer's avoided crossing it and falling down the stairs because they thought it was a hole. She bought an old velvet theater rope from a flea market during one of few excursions Golden Age residents were allowed to enjoy and hung it in front of the exit where those suffering most acutely from confusion tended to flee, convincing them that they were members of an exclusive club. Escapes were nearly eliminated.

Cordelia Quinlan died at the laudable age of 102, but lasted long enough to see Golden Age purchased by a progressive medical group with a more wholesome attitude toward life care homes than their predecessors. They renamed it Brookdale Campus Retirement Community and they were impressed to learn that Cordelia had been instrumental in bringing about many dramatic improvements to the place in the twenty years she'd lived there— the more so when they learned that she had not been paid a single visit by anyone in all that time.

During her residency, many of her fellow Golden Agers had died, but they were replaced by new ones, so she altered and retrofitted her stories to the listener. Those few who realized this did not object, and as a result, her characters—Hetty, and Josiah, and Lavinia and so on—took on new lives with new twists and new sets of relatives.

The Brookdale doctors knew something of the sordid history of Golden Age, and were more surprised when Cordelia, having consented to briefly tell them her story, said that she herself had chosen the place, not her flighty, irresponsible nephew.

To clarify the reason why, she said, "Because I would consent to nowhere else. You see, this is the very plot of land the city council condemned in 1947 and razed to usher in their silly view of progress. This eyesore, this unyielding heap of concrete blocks, this hideous edifice, is built upon the site of Birkin Cemetery."

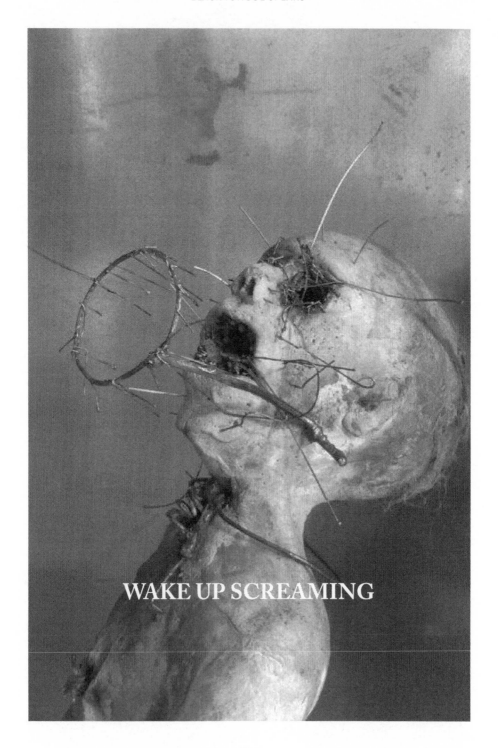

WAKE UP SCREAMING

The morning Robert Edelman woke up screaming, he had a transitional meeting with the Board of Directors at Keway Solutions during which he would officially hand over the corporate reins to his replacement as Chief Executive Officer.

Edelman was retiring at the age agreed upon by the charter; the meeting in the C-suite of the corporate headquarters was protocol and proceeded along as amicably as could be. Edelman himself had spearheaded the search for the new top dog, and with the board's approval, he'd settled on a candidate he knew would make the shareholders happy. Logan Montgomery was an industry superhero, 45 years old and trim as an athlete; a polished industry veteran who had already occupied several executive suites and had even been on the cover of Forbes. Moreover, he was a scratch golfer with fabulous hair.

Montgomery's compensation package was astronomical, of course, but every member of the board had approved it: CEOs were among the most overpaid class on the planet, and, like Edelman, Montgomery's base salary was in the high hundred thousands and his stock options in the millions with bonuses and club memberships tacked on. In part, of course, this was the board's way of covering their asses if anything went haywire. If the resume was impressive, the pay was blood seeking its own level, and if things went south, they'd go south with the 'right' candidate—nobody could blame the board for that.

On the morning Robert Edelman woke up screaming, he'd dressed appropriately, as the bridesmaid, not the bride. These traditions were subtle but fundamental. He wore a dark charcoal suit, a crisp white shirt, and top-drawer accessories, including a gold Ronde Louis Carter watch and a Maxwell Scott attaché. His wife Alma had chosen the tie—a nod to the first time he'd every dressed up for an executive meeting, a year out of Yale, and that day, she'd picked the tie. Then as now, she'd picked the perfect specimen; a subtly patterned blue silk cravat from Ermenegildo Zegna.

The morning that Robert Edelman woke up screaming, Logan Montgomery appeared in the same style of boardroom formal, but with a little more pizazz—a brighter tie, a suit a few shades of gray lighter. He represented the future, and Edelman, along with his mind-blowing golden parachute, the past—of that, the Board of Directors were certain.

Everything moved along swimmingly as members filtered into the open, naturally-lit room overlooking the city's financial district; they were in their element and it was collegiality above everything else. But when Edelman approached Montgomery to shake his hand, instead of congratulating him, he looked him directly and intently into his eyes and said, "What if we're not living in a real world, Logan? What if we're digital beings living in a computer simulation created by our far-future descendants?"

Edelman kept his smile broad and earnest and hardly anybody but Montgomery even made out what he was saying—those closest were either disengaged as a rule or thought they'd misunderstood him Montgomery himself was suitably adept at thinking on his feet, but this time, he was without an adequate retort, even one in the spirit of what he assumed was a jocular, albeit weird, comment.

A moment later, the meeting came to order. Seats were taken, the arrangement reflecting the organizational philosophy of Keway Solutions: Barclay Howe, the chairman, sat at the head of a U-shaped table with Edelman to his right, directly beside him. Next time, this place would belong to Logan Montgomery, but for now, Howe needed the outgoing CEO to provide him tidbits of information and pass him notes regarding other members' comments—Howe liked to sound on top of things. Since regulations and pressure from investors had pushed the Keway to make the board more demographically and professionally diverse, Barclay Howe was not an industry insider. Among the others, there was one black face, one woman and twelve old white cronies.

The agenda was predictably stultifying. Each board member gave a brief personal introduction, even though Montgomery had met them throughout the hiring process and had vetted them as thoroughly as they'd vetted him. These were formalities undertaken according to rules that everyone present understood—most of them were CEOs themselves. There was a brief presentation about Robert Edelman's twenty year legacy with the firm (his three predecessors had only made it six years combined), then there was a bland report from the Strategic

Thinking Committee.

Next, Stuart Kayser, the COO sitting at the Chairman's left, ran through a series of overhead projections showing solid earnings and positive cash flows.

Robert Edelman stared across the chestnut cherry conference table at Kayser. Kayser was a sober, straight-faced little weasel who, in Edelman's opinion, dressed too British and thought too Yiddish, and Edelman knew that, as always, the folks in the room were slogging through complex statistical jargon made intentionally as thick as oil pan sludge. Kayser didn't want to convey information as much as make goulash out it, and it occurred to Edelman that within seconds, he could rise, walk nonchalantly to the window, come up behind Kayser and wrap his fingers around his noodle neck and strangle him to death.

A minute later, Howe nudged Edelman's immaculately tailored, vicuña-clad left shoulder—the rare fabric was an ode to sensitive skin and a desensitized bank account. Howe had a question related to shareholders' equity and retained earnings, and wanted a point cleared up before he asked it. Edelman wrote the response on the pad of paper in front of him and held it so that Howe could see it without making to too obvious. Howe's lips turned up, his ears reddened. Just as quickly, Edelman flipped the pad over and went back to simpering at Kayser's obtuse presentation.

He had written, 'I have a pen in my pocket I could jam directly into your eyeball."

And he did have one—a Chopard fountain pen with a rose-gold finish.

The morning Robert Edelman woke up screaming, soaked in sweat, his wife panicked briefly, then went into soothe mode, like her mother had done when her father had woken screaming. Alma was convinced that her father's regular nocturnal outbursts were residue from the time he'd spent with the 180th Infantry Regiment in Sicily during World War II. Although he'd never shared any details with the family, as an adult Alma Edelman had done some research into the Canicatti massacre, where two dozen civilians were shot to death by the 180th Infantry Regiment. To her, this adequately explained her father's life-long edginess, his guilt-racked depression, his screaming.

It is the nature of soldiers to put emotions aside during the day, Alma told herself, only to have them sneak out at night. Although her husband had never served, she assumed that Post Traumatic Stress might affect survivors of the corporate minefield as easily. In fact, she couldn't imagine how it could be otherwise. Certainly, in Robert's rarified stratosphere, the business world was the social equivalent of warfare, and lopping off the heads of underlings was table stakes. It was natural, she assumed, to feel the combined weight of the genocide sooner or later. The number of family friends who'd somehow underperformed while working for him, whom he'd subsequently, summarily executed, was astonishing: Chad Galloway, Leon Harbauer, Darryl Wesson— they'd attended their children's christenings and later, their children's weddings. Lou Langdon and his pretty young wife and their new home on Wyndcroft—first came foreclosure, then eviction, finally, the ultimate humiliating sale of their personal belongings from a local storage facility. And there was Geoffrey Hudson—Robert had known Geoffrey since they were at St. Bridget Prep; they'd gone to Yale together and played in the same golf league, attended the same church and belonged to the same yacht club. Something Hudson had done late in his career—Alma had no idea what—had caused a catastrophic meltdown between the old friends, and Hudson had been terminated; he'd died a year later of pancreatic cancer, no doubt—Alma believed—brought on by the stress.

You might be able to forget about those beings—those dislodged lives—over morning coffee; you might be able ignore the predatory nature of your ladder climb at power lunches with the mayor, the governor, the state senator. You could, perhaps, even sugarcoat your tradecraft when you ran into one of your professional hits at a subsequent social event, even as the wives were looking elsewhere in awkward embarrassment.

But at three AM, Alma suspected, you could not lock them out entirely; they found chinks in your psyche, rents in your conscience, and seeped into your system while you slept. Churchill had called Sicily the soft underbelly of Nazi Germany—big, powerful words from a big, powerful man—and she suspected that her father's own vulnerable spot was memories of opening fire on unarmed Italian citizens in the Canicatti soap factory in 1943. And she also assumed that in climbing vocational mountains like Robert had, storming emotionless corporation shores and orchestrating mergers was like annexing countries and the subsequent downsizings were like dehumanizing slaughters. Dismissals—even of old friends—had to happen without mercy or compunction, she understood that. And it must have taken the sort of toll on Robert's soul that the orders in Sicily had on her father's.

And when the accumulation of fundamental remorse reached critical mass—and of this, she had no doubt—you woke up screaming.

Robert and Alma Edelman lived in a twin-gabled Victorian house nestled atop Huckleberry Hill and surrounded by hundreds of acres of open space and walking trails. They had one child, a daughter named Daphne who lived in San Francisco. Daphne was an oral surgeon who was also married to an oral surgeon. She lived well, but not as well as she had when she was growing up, and nowhere near as well as her parents did now; the serious money had begun to roll in after Daphne had left for UCLA School of Dentistry. But she would someday, come hell or high water— Alma was certain of that. Daphne thought about the world in different terms than she did. Daphne had written a life syllabus where the categories were mostly greed; she was fiercely ambitious, and didn't seem to have much empathy to hold her back. She was not close to either parent, and although Alma hated to admit it, she was willing to bet that Daphne Edelman never woke up screaming.

But Robert? —the following morning he woke up screaming

again. Alma didn't want to pressure him much, since she thought she knew the source in any case. His brain was defaulting; his nervous system was stuck on overdrive, his mind was undergoing a normal reaction to battle scars. She brought him Sleepy Time tea and rubbed his temples and had him breathe while focusing on the pattern, and later in the morning, she convinced him to go on a long hike along Hawley Brook because she'd read that rhythmic exercise engaging both the arms and legs released endorphins. She played uplifting music in the house and had the private chef prepare an evening meal that contained flaxseed and walnuts because Omega 3s play a vital role in emotional health. She convinced him to turn off his cell phone, because she knew that above all, he must avoid trauma triggers. She allowed him to take the lead in their conversations, but pointedly steered them away from reminders of Keway Solutions. She offered cues to talk about the upcoming trip they had planned to Tahiti, and provided supported and companionship all through the day.

And the next morning, for the third day in a row, Robert Edelman woke up screaming. The snake was still in the cockpit. This time, he volunteered his own proposal, that a long drive in the country might help. Since Alma had her thrice weekly session at Artists for World Peace booth at the Simsbury Farmer's Market, she gauged any need or desire he might have for her to go along, and when such a need proved slim to none, Alma figured that some alone time in the pretty autumn countryside might be balm for his troubled spirit.

Indeed, when he returned, he was noticeably calmer, and he'd worked out an equitable plan: They should move the Tahiti trip forward and leave as soon as could be arranged. That suited Alma fine—whatever helped. She made the requisite calls that afternoon; Dorrie Cliburn at the travel agency changed their flights and bookings, the domestics were informed, including those who would maintain the place; their mail was stopped; the Artists for World Peace would cover for her at the market. She had people to help them pack, and the task was completed before they retired.

And the following morning, Robert Edelman woke up with a serene smile on his face—there was no screaming at all.

Alma—bless her soul—had managed to misinterpret a key component of his dilemma, as profoundly as it was possible for someone to do. She saw the world's victims with 20/20 vision, but the gumption of the victimizers was a blur. Even worse, she saw people like Robert as equal victims. It was her loss, ultimately, Edelman understood, not his and not her silly, loopy father's who had probably suffered more guilt over the citizens he'd missed than the ones he'd shot. Eliminate them all, you leave nobody to tell the tale.

He didn't like to wake up screaming, of course—for one thing, it made his throat sore. He lay awake in the predawn hours and considered brain chemistry. Those who put all their ingenuity and energy into fooling the people around them may have different wiring, but they were usually successful. Barclay Howe's speech before the board still rang in his ears: "Bob's expertise, enthusiasm, and exceptional generosity to the shareholders have been very much the stuff of legend..."

So had his facility for firing people, *en masse* or as individuals, but Howe failed to bring it up, though in truth it was far closer to Edelman's genuine legacy that the wad of visionary leadership the high-stakes negotiation that had increased sales at Keway Solutions from $100 million to well over a billion during the course of his tenure. He shit-canned with impunity, with delight, with vigor and without regret, and it amused him to consider the reasons why.

Decreased connectivity between the amygdala, the part of the brain that processes negative stimuli? Mania without delirium? So they said. Heritable condition? Witness Daphne—he guessed than neither of them could actually testify to an understanding of the 'thing' that made people want to be friends, made them attractive to one another or what underlay their social interactions. It was all illusion, everything elaborately staged. Everyone adapts to moral rules to some extent, just as most people holding up hymnals on Sunday morning figure out how hit a few notes. Very, very few are opera divas, and a Robert understood it, he was the Enrico Caruso of sociopaths.

Alma didn't get it because he didn't want her to get it. He never showed that side to anyone but the casualties. Not that it mattered—she'd played her own part in the melodrama well enough and had been rewarded accordingly. She'd come from a family of perpetual losers—her father couldn't hold a job, and growing up she'd never had a bedroom she hadn't shared, nor clothing not handed down, and here she was, living in the most exclusive zip code in the state, spending her hours enriching the community through the arts. No blood on her paws, only fleece—'Hats for a Cause' was her latest artistic quest for world peace, where all the other equally bored, similarly clueless wives in the neighborhood designed and sold fleece hats. They called 'functional art pieces beyond their imaginings'—a bravura performance.

It had been theater of the absurd, to be sure. Even though he'd been yanking Logan Montgomery's chain at the transitional meeting, trying to goad a little shock from him, the idea that technology was barreling toward a post-human era was obvious. Certainly, Edelman predicted a future where the limits of the mortality were transcended, where people cheat death by uploading their minds into computers and replace themselves with artificial intelligences. He doubted he'd live that long, which was a shame: He'd be first in line.

It was easy for him to say—he'd been raised by old money held in safe and profitable syndicates, and with every opportunity available. As an adolescent, when the other boys were playing lacrosse and squash and other contact sports, he'd prowled junkyards and collected magnets and wires to build radios and wild electronic contraptions, preferring mechanics to interaction but otherwise, he'd conformed to family traditions, attending the obvious schools, obtaining the correct degrees and excelling in business. He'd done what was expected of his tribe's male progeny. Marrying Alma at twenty had not gone down altogether well, but they'd gotten over it—she was pretty, polite, respectful and quiet, and his tribe's repressed female progeny admired her flair for arts and crafts.

His difficulties in life were few—he suffered little about anything ever, which is one of this recent bout of troubles had been unprecedented—the onset of night terrors so inexplicably profound that he'd been wrenched to consciousness on three consecutive mornings with his throat constricted, his eyeballs bulging, clutching bedclothes, heart clobbering his ribs like a pile-driver, and screaming, screaming, screaming...

It had taken him many miles on that long drive through the calming countryside, hours beneath ocher-tinted leaves far from the civilized façade to finally work his problem out:

After a long career in positions where subordinates lived in perpetual fear that he might fire them, he was handing over those reins, leaving his cherished vocation, his *raison d'être*, his craft:

Destroying lives was the only sense of empowerment he'd ever felt.

He'd rationalized it every step of the way, and every board he'd reported to had been delighted enablers. In fact, they'd nurtured the affliction: The removal of imperfect operatives was vital to the winner-takes-all culture, and as a team, they'd developed rituals as fervently as any cult. It was rule-governed and filled with symbolism; the secluded office, door closed, the exit interview with meaningless luck wishing when 'And may God have mercy on your soul' might have been more appropriate. It was a purification rite meant to alleviate executioner's guilt, on par with feeding the condemned a last meal.

The truth was, for Edelman, and those who shared his dais, corporate officers in droves without number, there was no guilt— but there was considerable satisfaction. There was beauty in the beheading, fulfillment in the finale—it was mania without delirium. And now, since he faced a future where he could yet transform his self-awareness into logic gates or his synapses into silicon, he had to come to terms with giving up his sense of ultimate control, or find another outlet.

Of course, screaming didn't cut it. Being an extremely bright fellow when it came to his own interests, on his long, secluded drive down the New England back roads, he'd come upon another avenue that did.

The following morning, when Robert Edelman woke up smiling—and decidedly not screaming—he rolled over in the Monarch Vi-spring bed, wrapped his fingers around Alma's artsy neck and strangled her to death. It was still dark out, so he was able to carry her corpse, wrapped in bedsheets, to the Range Rover unseen and drive it fifty miles to the hole he'd pre-dug the day before in a far corner of a state park. On the way back, he stopped at a rural dump frequented by black bears and got rid of all of her luggage. He kept his own, and at the airport, canceled the trip to Tahiti, booked another flight to Thailand and made reservations under an assumed name at the Mandarin Oriental Hotel in Bangkok, and once there, waited until his wire transfer of millions of dollars began to come through, in increments of course. It was amazing what a fortune could accomplish.

He purchased an immaculate villa in Phuket province with incredible views of the headland along Nai Thon Beach, and lived quietly for the next twenty years, hiring strings of impoverished Thai gardeners, housekeepers, pool boys, mechanics and drivers, dispatching them regularly whenever he saw fit, disposing of the remains from his yacht into the depths of the Andaman Sea.

The provincial police force was corrupt beyond measure, and easily dealt with, and it's fair to say that for the rest of his life, Robert Edelman never again woke up screaming.

Not even once.

TIME ENOUGH AT LAST
(PART TWO)

"Imagine, if you will, what took place immediately after Henry Bemis broke his glasses in the classic short story 'Time Enough At Last' by Marilyn Venable, later translated into everybody's favorite episode on *The Twilight Zone*..."

"There was the rumble of complaining stone. Minute in comparison which the epic complaints following the fall of the bomb. This one occurred under one corner of the shelf upon which Henry sat. The shelf moved; threw him off balance. The glasses slipped from his nose and fell with a tinkle.

He bent down, clawing blindly and found, finally, their smashed remains. A minor, indirect destruction stemming from the sudden, wholesale smashing of a city. But the only one that greatly interested Henry Bemis.

He stared down at the blurred page before him.

He began to cry."

Henry Bemis cried until exhaustion overcame him. And shortly, in a world filled with tragedies beyond measure, he began to feel a little silly over his outburst. After all, this was Armageddon, and he had survived it—him, Henry Bemis, former subservient of his wife Agnes and drudge to his employer Mr. Carsville, now unexpectedly liberated and finally, for the first time in his life, his own man.

That was worth better than sniveling over a pair of broken glasses.

He was severely myopic, it was true. Unable to see his hand in front of his face. But it was *his* face and *his* hand, and didn't need visual confirmation to understand that. And fate was now entirely his as well, to live or die as he saw fit, and if he chose the latter, he might end it quickly without hearing Agnes' screeching voice upbraiding him, 'Henreee, you can't slit your wrists today; this is the Smith's canasta night. They'll be here in thirty minutes and I'm not dressed yet, and here you are… contemplating suicide!"

But then again, the thought of slitting his wrists made him physically ill. The means lay at his feet, of course—the shards from his ruined spectacles. How fitting it would be to destroy himself using the very object that had thwarted his stroke of fortune! Yet, when he ran his fingers along a broken edge of glass, he realized that the act would be closer to sawing open an artery, and he doubted he had the stomach for that. Plus, the ache from the wound on his leg, where he'd accidentally cut himself on the jagged remnant of an automobile fender, made further bloodshed unthinkable. Some of the old, pre-Apocalypse Henry Bemis slipped through: Maybe he'd get lucky and bleed to death from a gash he'd already administered.

In fact, focusing again on the leg made him feel woozy. He wondered if he'd already lost so much blood he was beyond saving. Then it would hardly be a choice, would it?—that would be like a blooper from his former existence, where life happened to Henry Bemis. This was the brave new world, where Henry

Bemis happened to life! Where everything was a choice!

Suddenly, the survival instinct kicked in. He felt around the rubble until he came into contact with the book he'd been holding prior to losing his glasses, *The Collected Works of William Shakespeare*. He tore out a page to stuff into his torn trousers to staunch the flow of blood. He couldn't see that he'd ended up with 'Merchant of Venice', in particular the passage where Shylock says, 'If you prick us, do we not bleed?'.

His myopia was such that he missed this post-modern irony.

Gradually, his blurred vision grew blurrier. The pain in his leg swelled up until it engulfed him, and he slid into a deep, dull swoon as the fever came on him, and for a long, blank period, he was as insensible as he had been inside the bank vault.

And yet, without medical attention, without antibiotics, without… *Agnes*, he managed to survive it. The fever broke and gangrene did not set in. Henry Bemis was the master of the universe, and he had outlasted the human race—he wasn't about to let a flesh wound take him down.

How long he'd lain there, insensate and febrile, he couldn't say. Days, anyway. It had rained, and he'd surfaced from the delirium long enough to suck trickles of water running along the collapsed marble walls of the library. Now, he was fully back into his senses, and ravenously hungry. Hungrier than he'd ever been in his life. And all around him… food for thought, but nothing more.

His leg looked bad, but no worse. Perhaps even a little better. It was healing. He weighed his options, felt his stomach gnawing holes in him, and in a burst of inspiration, he recalled that across the street from the library, there had been a small food market. Even without vision he could crawl that distance—he was certain of it. So far, he'd heard no signs of life in the gaping world around him, not the howl of a dog or the caw of a crow, and he assumed that if the store had survived the blast, neither man nor beast was around to loot it.

To determine his next move, he decided, he must find food, and that was the incentive that impelled him through the first, grueling motions. Cautiously, not wanting to re-open his leg wound or dislodge debris, he began to navigate the through the rubble, hand over hand, and in an hour, he had cleared the collapsed dome, the fallen wings, and was out on the library's front lawn. It was still green and lush beneath him, and he took this as a positive sign; had the rain contained anything toxic, by now, it surely would have killed the grass. He filled his pockets with small fragments of the shattered marble bust of Edgar Allan Poe that had stood on at the library's gateway, and tossed them, listening to the sounds they made as they struck whatever lay in front of him, an upturned automobile here, a fire hydrant there. Slowly, carefully, he traced his way across the street and to the market.

Although Bemis couldn't see it, a huge portion of the roof had collapsed onto the register area where Raheed had stood for many years and who probably now lay underneath it. It was no matter to Henry Bemis; as the sole survivor of the human species, he had not intended to pay anyhow.

Much of the contents of the store shelves lay crushed and scattered across the floor. In the summer heat, it was beginning to spoil, and the odor was foul, although Bemis could not be certain if it was ravioli or Raheed he smelled. He overcame his nausea—if he was to make any sort of headway as a blind man in a upturned city, he would have to put his gag reflexes on hold. In fact, hunger proved greater than disgust, and, using a piece of window frame to clear the space in front of him, he felt around until he found some intact containers. He didn't care what they were, of course—by then, he was famished. He tore open whatever he could find and inhaled it as only a desperate hungry man can do, not even taking time to enjoy it. Not that what he found was particularly enjoyable in the first place—chopped garlic in oil, canned cheese sauce, chili peppers, tomatoes, carrot juice, and a baked potato wrapped in foil that had rolled over from the chicken rotisserie. Fermented carp was not among his favorites, but to a starving man, it was manna from heaven, and he scarfed down an entire jar of Manischewitz Sweet Gefilte Fish.

Finally stuffed, he lay in a satisfied heap upon the market floor, feeling the nourishment push strength into his limbs and sharpness to his thinking. He became clear-headed for the first time since the disaster. He considered his options through a much keener sense of purpose, and tried to reconstruct a mental map of the neighborhood so that he could form a plan.

In doing so, he had the most encouraging eureka moment of his entire life. Down the block from the mini market, no more than a shop or two away, he recalled that there was an optometrist's office.

Why he hadn't thought of it before was clear: He had never been a customer of local eyeglass shops; he trusted no one but Dr. Torrance to grind his thick lenses into his own complicated prescription, and Torrance was on the other side of town. He might crawl there in time, but Torrance was certainly dead and…

Surely there were pairs of unclaimed glasses there that he could use. If not to correct his vision to 20/20, at least to make life more functional. If he was to live in such a crazy world, he'd have to get used to the idea that certain creature comforts would be a curtailed. So excited did he become at the now obvious solution to his most pressing dilemma that he undertook the trip with all the glee could muster, feeling his way quickly down the demolished concrete sidewalk, past one imploded storefront, then another… and there it was, and with even less damage than the mini mart!

Amid the overturned counters he found spectacles by the dozens. It was mere seconds before he'd found a pair that stripped way some of the fog he'd been staring into, and that allowed him to find still stronger prescriptions amid the chaos. In the end, he lit upon the technique of wearing two, then three pair of glasses at the same time so that the combined lenses worked in tandem. He found a combination that was nearly perfect, and he caught a glimpse of himself in the remains of a mirror that hung on the far side of the shop, and burst out laughing.

He looked like a clown, but in a world without circus goers, who cared?

He found the optometrist's case and loaded it up with glasses, then returned to the store and filled it up with everything edible he could find, including more gefilte fish. With time enough again, he might even learn to like minced-fish forcemeat stuffed inside fish skin.

For now, he had everything he could want. He could break any number of pairs of glasses—he had reams of them. And across the street, the library was knee-deep in books. All sorts of books, philosophy books, history books—the collected fiction of all the masters. He need only settle in and begin.

Finding a comfortable spot amid a pyramid of fallen shelves, he sighed in satisfaction and chose a book at random—scattershot reading would be half the fun. It was a collection of O. Henry short stories, and he began to read, blissfully, intently, happily.

Midway through the witty wordplay of 'The Gift of the Magi', a peculiar thing happened. Despite his new, nearly perfect vision, the page he was reading grew a little blurry. This was accompanied by a rumbling in his gut, and quickly, sharp pains begin to shoot darts into his side. Swallowing became difficult. With a start, he noticed that the sack he'd filled with food was leaking at the edges, some foamy, whitish gunk trickling onto the library floor. He pulled out the culprit jar—the gefilte fish has a hairline crack along the side and pus-colored ooze was dribbling from it as if the fermented fish was… re-fermenting.

Suddenly, his body convulsed and he upchucked onto the O. Henry collection. That purge allowed him to rally long enough to stagger over to the section on foodborne illnesses, and he scrambled through the scattered volumes until he found one on botulism.

There is was, in lurid, graphic detail in the chapter headed 'Causes and Symptoms'. His volleyball match with good luck vs. bad had made a final spike into the latter court: Individually, in unsanitary conditions, every single food item he'd wolfed down at the corner market—garlic in oil, peppers, unrefrigerated baked potatoes, gefilte fish—was susceptible to infection the deadly bacterium, and he'd stacked the deck by eating them all in the space of about twenty minutes.

He body was racked with such seizures of agony that all three pairs of glasses he was wearing fell from his nose and smashed with a tinkle.

Henry Bemis wanted to cry, but he was too busy dying.

FATHER DEATH

I never learned his real name—never asked, never cared, and he never volunteered it. To his face, like I always did with men of his generation, I called him 'Sir', and with my friends—on the fleeting occasions we mentioned the man with the house beneath the bridge trestle—I called him Father Death.

And that house, my God: Amid a maze of old tires and derelict mattresses, among the casually lethal knots of homeless, dope-sick addicts casting off their sour and grimy smells, the house was a tiny one-room cottage, not much bigger than a tool shed. It was backed into a huge, crumbling concrete pylon and it had neither electricity nor plumbing, yet Father Death maintained it immaculately, with a garden in front where he grew collards and tomatoes, a miniature picket fence draped with brilliant roses, and, maybe most striking of all—in a land where everything wore graffiti tags or the flakes and peels of neglect—his tiny house was untouched by the vandals and painted brilliant white.

I discovered Father Death's house one balmy, seductive early autumn afternoon when I was fourteen; one of many days I skipped classes at Ruby Bridges Academy. I loved to trot down to the river and hang around with the older dudes who fished for carp and walleye and drank from paper bags and generally had already lived so much life that they preferred to spend the rest of it casting reels into murky river water. I've always had a feel for these edge people, more than the rest of my crew, and I loved listening to them chat and bullshit and I recognized style behind their mutilated spirits and resilient strengths.

On that particular day I took a different path along the river course, wandering near a low wall that had once served some now-forgotten purpose and had been neglected so long that trees grew through right the concrete. The few businesses that had ever existed here had closed before I was born and remained as red brick husks with the names of what they'd been entirely faded away. Where the wall ended, a pile of railroad ties turned grey and festooned in silvery spider webs, and behind this stood Father Death's house.

Except that it didn't stand so much as it nestled and banked; such a breath of wholesomeness amid the self-perpetuating pathology of the city was even stranger than the witch's gingerbread hut in that savage storybook forest, and like Hansel, I stepped near and touched it to see if it was even real.

It was: I ran my finger along the miniature picket fence, the delicate latch on the gate; I squatted by the garden where fat red tomatoes hung obediently and leafy beets plants seemed to be seeping gently into the ground. I stroked the clapboards and felt the silky warmth of the paint in the morning sunlight, and when I tried to peer inside, I was startled to see Father Death standing on the other side of the window pane, observing me with profound and silent intensity.

But for the eyes, he was not remarkable—a cocoa-colored man with a neat white beard and tight white curls; he was dressed in a brown sweater and looked to me like a retired school teacher. But for his eyes—even through the window glass they were unsettling and shone with something like cold green fire. It wasn't the expression, and it may not even have been the pale olive hue, which was not only the same color as the river, but seemed somehow linked to its sluggish implacability and ominous depth, where people swam and drowned and sometimes their corpses were never found.

And the gaze fell directly over me, because there was nobody else there, and I held it for as long as I could before I needed to turn and run. At which point, a gnarled black finger came up in beckoning gesture. It struck me as neither threatening nor compulsory, and I could have run all the same, but I didn't, and in another moment I had passed through the white door—without a lock or a bolt—and stood in the middle of a solitary, spotless room.

Not that there was much to spot up—there was a cot spread with a blanket, a small table and chair and in a corner, incongruously, was a gigantic stuffed gorilla. My eyes darted around but his remained fixed. Finally, sounding softly puzzled, he said, "I thought I knew why you'd come out here, but now I think it's something else."

Since I didn't know why myself—whether it was fate or coincidence or something more significant that had tugged me along the crumbled concrete wall—I sputtered dumbly, "Why you think I was here?"

"Because you knew that I could tell you things about your death. The circumstances. I can do that. The reason. The hour. But that isn't what you want, is it?"

It wasn't. Of course not—"Why would I want anyone to tell me that?"

"Because someone can. No other reason, son. Knowing that I know and you don't? It plagues certain people. It infests them. It gestates—it festers inside. If they don't take the information the first time around, they come again. Three times. Sometimes four. But they always come back. You will too."

"But… how? How can anybody know that?"

Remember, I was fourteen. Callow. Credulous. I'd seen my share of life already, of course—by that age, all of us from the projects had. Enough life to know that the world was filled with cold-blooded insanity that crossed thresholds sooner than you could set them. And that didn't even take into account the social chasms that lay just beyond our hood—the massive, world-defining dynamics we'd have to learn to navigate one way or the other, or die in the attempt. The real world was indomitable; it was out there and waiting. Among the people who inhabited it I assumed that there might be folks who could foresee your death. Why not? In truth, at that point, I was more intrigued with the mechanics than the possibility, so I repeated the question: "How could you know?"

He approached me, resolutely, entering my space; he took

my head in his hands, he pressed his face close to mine and scrutinized me for a long, long time–as though he was after something deeper than my shaken expression, something behind it. I was mesmerized. I looked back and saw eternity twinkling in the watery green.

He released my head. "Like that," he answered.

I remained still, trembling slightly, otherwise inert. "Did you see me die?" I asked.

"I did," he answered.

There was a small Formica table with a couple backless stools in the corner by the stuffed gorilla, and he indicated that I could— not necessarily that I should—sit down.

"But that's not what your came out here for, is it? I know what you're after, son—I saw that too. What you came out here looking for today. Yesterday. And maybe tomorrow."

"What's that?" I answered, an edge of defiance mingled with my interest.

It didn't seem to put him off in the slightest. He said, gently, "Your father."

I was a small kid, but I thought of myself as intellectually powerful, even then. You had to be a special kind of broke to live in the projects, and most of us came from haunted lineages. I hadn't seen my father since I was five, and I certainly wasn't searching for him out here in the dust and degradation and desolation of edge-city dumps—my father was long gone and not coming back; of that I was sure. He was dead or in jail, not to be found in these dark landscapes.

"Not in the flesh, maybe," he said. "In the essence. You find some in this man, some in that. Some in me. But you never find a single one complete, with all the good and the bad, all the insignificance and omnipotence. You're here because your father disappeared, and there is no fear that consumes you more completely than fellow human beings disappearing, accounted for or not. Because if your father can do it, on a whim, without a trace, maybe without even wanting to, so can you."

Within this there was so much truth that I couldn't listen any more. It took my breath away. I fled; I ran back to Ruby Bridges Academy, and after that, I went home to a dysfunctional incubator of neurosis and hopelessness and tried to keep myself from evaporating.

I might have left it that way, maybe forever—I'm not sure. But everything changed with Allen and Marcus Hughes, a couple of my boys from 6E. They were urgent kids who never did anything with a grasp of proportion and they had no patience whatsoever—they were the sort of street toughs who succumb early to damaged programming, who start fires for fun, out of boredom, then simply flee when they get out of hand. To them, the humiliations and compromises of life had already offered a workable balm: Having the most bitches, stomping the most brothers, talking the most shit.

They were my crew only by default; they lived across the hall from me. And also by default, I became their leader, because I had learned early to diffuse certain life-altering situations beyond their violent instincts to do so. Thug life sounds good in rap songs, but in real time survival, if the dude you accidentally bump into isn't packing, he might not care about catching an aggravated assault charge for beating you down with a tire iron. Instinctively, I knew how to dial those situations down, and they occasionally saw the value in that. Not that they needed my temper-cooling skills often: Allen was a year older than me and twice as big, while Marcus, only twelve, was already a bruising behemoth with more bulk than either of us.

In general, they both took cues from me, at least until I told them about the white cottage beneath the trestle, where Father Death claimed he could see your fate, detail by detail.

In hindsight, I should never have mentioned it, because once I did, we were off the bridge with nowhere to go but down. Naturally, they wanted to check it out—prudence was not their terrain and this was the sort of beast they liked to poke, the kind of cage into which they wanted to stick their hands. I couldn't dissuade them, although in the end, I didn't even want to: As I said, at fourteen, I had no ability to be skeptical of Father Death's claims; to imagine he might be a fraud, like the fortune tellers at the fair. I truly believed he had looked into my eyes and extracted details of my death, and although I didn't want to hear about them, it was hard to mount a credible argument against the Hughes brothers' justification for wanting to:

"If you know when the doom hand is coming, you can avoid it. You just plan on being somewhere else that day."

So the following morning, we skipped school and made the trek down the pock-marked road that ran along the river bank. As we walked, Marcus, who had wanted to be a rap star since he was five, started popping off whack hip-hop rhymes and electric phrases about living large and slaughtering rivals. Allen, in his expansive pants, gold-framed tooth, fitted baseball cap and Air Jordans, was similarly light-hearted, bobbing his head to his brother's beat, jostling me and throwing stones at the pheasants that had begun to repopulate these open places. They were of a like mind: This was a fun day trip; at the end, they were going to learn how and when they would die, but to watch them, you'd think they were going to the State Fair to ride the Kamikaze and hit on girls.

I suppose I had my own revelation about them that morning, and about the strange pyroclastic flow of fatalism that ran through my streets, where death was not a predator lurking in the shadows, but another pesky companion on the life stroll. Somehow, I didn't feel this way, which made me an anomaly in the hood, and as we walked by the painted, crumbling wall, the shuttered Shrimp Shack, the sumac trees overgrowing everything, I recognized that about myself for the first time ever.

The Hughes brothers were intrinsically different creatures: They had no expectation of fruitful lives, and as such, any expository information about the end made their current images complete

160

and whole. Amid the cycle of drugs and AIDS and omnipresent warfare along with a general mission statement stating, 'If you want the last word in a violent place, you got to be the most violent,' to them, the more complete the picture, the better.

It was not my place to argue. I did, however, worry that their edges were too rough: When we approached the house beneath the trestle, I was overwhelmed with its pristine and isolated sense of beauty; it was an idyll, an awesome beacon in the shadows. Instinctively, I put on my respectful face, but I wasn't sure they had one.

It didn't matter, of course—that was another lesson I learned that day. Father Death did not require mollycoddling—he provided it. He had known that my needs were unique and individual, and he saw the same thing instantly when it came to the brothers. He came outside to greet us, and his damp green eyes were wide with welcome—his people came back, as he had promised, and I was now his people.

Allen and Marcus filled up nearly the entire interior space of the cottage; they were crude and inappropriate, cantering though a range of expression, pointing to the stuffed gorilla and laughing., "That the guard dog, Pops?"

Father Death replied, "That belonged to my daughter Lucinda. Fifty years gone this April. Cancer of the marrow, she was only five years old. So yes, the gorilla is a talisman. It makes my home holy, and people respect it as an asylum—a place of sanctuary."

That sapped some the brothers' hulking comic hustle. With them, in Father Death's summation, there was no equivocation—he knew why they'd come. I know he knew because when I started to explain it, he held up his crooked black finger to quiet me: "No need," he said. "I recognize these young brothers, rising spiritually toward manhood. I know these works-in-progress; I've known them always, boasting and taunting their way through brief lives. I knew them before they were knit within their mothers' wombs. I used to preach to them on street corners, but now I wait until they come to me. You can see the value in that, especially since in the end, they always come to me."

I could see the value in that, indeed, and what he'd told me as well, and I understood that Father Death might have other equally appropriate names; he could read through the swagger and the pride and the chaos we all slide through, haplessly or by choice. Calling him 'Father Essence' ultimately made more sense to me, but today it was Father Death because the Hughes brothers were not here to listen to street corner lectures about redirecting their lives; they wanted to read their stories in a single, finished volume.

When Allen said, "You tell me how I'm gonna die?" Father Death replied, "In technicolor, son, if that's what you want to hear."

It was, so Father Death took Allen's big, buffalo head between his tapered fingers and like he'd done with me, focused raptly on Allen's gaping glare, seeing far away, past the game, past the seething, past the now. The things he saw were as personal as things could be, and Father Death said we might want to wait outside as he shared the vision, but Allen would have no part of it: "Naw, that's cool. We blood. This is fun—let 'em stay."

At that, Father Death had Allen sit at the Formica table gave him a date and an hour that was less than a year away.

It would come down like this: Allen was sleeping with a girl called Luck—that was true and everybody in the small white room knew it—even, apparently, Father Death. But what we didn't know—couldn't know—is that sometime in December she'd start getting bold with Bink Dog from another click. Apparently, the mutual girlfriend passes along some of Allen's smack talk and on January 15 of the year coming up, at 2:17 AM, at a red light, a Chevy Blazer pulls up beside the car in which Allen is riding and people inside open fire with an Uzi, hitting him four times in the chest and killing him instantly.

Through the small window where I'd first seen Father Death, oblique September light filtered and briefly turned everything in the tiny, whitewashed room into a golden dreamscape. There was pure, unsullied silence, then, far off, the sound of a tug on the river. Finally, Allen hoarsed out a guttural sigh and said, "That's some shit there, huh, my brothers? Luck gonna burn me."

Suddenly, Marcus in his silly break braids and canary-yellow t shirt from Spoonie G looked like he'd rather back out of the whole deal than take his turn at the Formica table. I have no doubt he'd have jumped at a chance to slip quietly from pretty cottage and run back to 6E, lock himself in and spend the next twelve hours watching low-impact, mind-melding tv shows. But he couldn't do it—that's not how street life works, not how family dynamics work, and Marcus knew he had an obligation to keep up with the challenge, to leap from one rooftop to the other if his brother did it first, to let an even bigger firecracker go off in his hand.

I certainly didn't want to be here. I didn't want to hear the bones break or smell the blood, even in narration. It's why I hated to fight—the first sucker punch takes you unaware, but the second one you wait for, steel for, tremble over—and that's what we were doing as Father Death took Marcus' gigantic head between his nimble fingers and did the death watch. As much as I cared about these mammoth, intimidating babies, and as little as I had envisioned for their futures, this was invading the most private space they had. This was rubbernecking at a car accident where they were the victims—you didn't want to look, but you did, and once you did, you never got the gore out of your head.

Marcus got the Cliff's Notes version, but that was fine: Context wasn't needed. He had fifteen years to live, but you got the impression they wouldn't be pleasant years. After Allen's murder he hunts down Bink Dog and immolates him, lands in state-run juvenile justice facility where, lacking filter or tether, he attacks and kills a supervisor. On turning twenty-one, he's transferred to the prison in Bellamy Creek where at noon on May 4, a decade and a half from now, he's beaten to death by a gang of inmates carrying socks filled with batteries.

My role in these brutal conclusions—if any—lingered somewhere behind the cryptic green gaze of Father Death, and I suspected that the more significant it was, the less I wanted to know about it. For all knew, I might not even live to see these big, sad boys die. As for the old black gentleman in the whitewashed cottage beneath the bridge trestle, I believed sincerely that what he said was what he saw.

Why he shared it with us, for the time being, eluded me.

There was nothing more for us in the house, and I expected at least some introspective silence on the walk back, but there was nothing but defiance and bravado. "I remember that day," Allen blustered, "I get that day tattooed on my forehead so I don't forget. January 15."

"Do it. Or I will. You don't get taken out in a drive-by, I don't go to jail. I tag the whole house with it so I don't forget."

Changing the subject was useless, of course—I tried, even understanding that they'd be fixated for a while, but I was hoping they wouldn't stumble across an obvious solution, which they shortly did, of course: "Let's go find Bink Dog tonight and put a cap in his ass and be done with it. Let's take down that bitch Luck to pay her back for something she ain't done yet."

And instantaneously, that was their plan. Fortunately, as I mentioned, the Hughes brothers were jitterbugs without the organizational skills to arrange a milk run to 7-Eleven let alone a gang hit, so I tried to re-focus their energy in a different direction: Maybe they'd been given this information as a sacred and supernatural gift, perhaps directly from God. Maybe it was a sign and they could, in fact, change these timelines, not by blowing away Bink Dog, but by getting their shit together and becoming productive people who would neither find themselves riding in hoopties at two in the morning nor killing guards at P.T. Riley Boys Training School.

I don't know if I myself believed that one could change what was preordained, but for me, these strange encounters were bookended by the idea that my own fate might also be in some cosmic balance, and they became my wake-up dispensation. My minimal obligations seemed clear and going forward, I began to apply myself. I stopped taking afternoons off to shoot breeze with derelicts and instead, spent them inside classrooms paying attention; I cracked the books and found teachers willing to put in extra time after school to drag me back up to speed. An upshot of this, obviously, was that I spend less time with the boys in 6E, and by January, when I was scholastically solvent, I hardly saw them at all. They'd fallen in with other homies in the meantime, meaner kids, scary kids, sordid kids who shot the eyes out of rivals and pretty much played for keeps. I'd been their leader by default, and now they had a leader by predilection.

I hadn't been back to see Father Death in those months, but neither had I forgotten about him, and now, with the date he'd given for Allen's end approaching, I felt a tug of duty since I had instigated things in the first place by having opened my mouth. I caught Allen in the dingy hall at Christmas time, and again on

New Year's Eve, when he nodded at me with a quizzical smirk, like he'd processed that morning by the bridge trestle so long ago that it was non-existent in his current world. The night before the night, though, I saw him in Popeye's with the girl Luck who was supposed to orchestrate the drive-by, and I felt like a trifling punk for giving it a final go.

But he wrapped his arm around me, took me aside and assured me that he had it well under control: "Luck cool," he said. "That old cat in the white house scamarama for sure, but just to be safe, don't worry—I'm taking her to Chicago for a few days, we leaving tonight and it all gonna blow over, you'll see…"

I even went so far as to knock on the door of 6E on the night of the night, and big, bleary Marcus assured me that his brother had indeed gone to Chicago for the weekend, and I slept a little easier—at least until four in the morning when their mother woke up the whole sixth floor with her screaming.

At the funeral, I learned that the whole thing had been a set-up, with Luck pretending to get a call in Chicago saying her mother was ill; Allen had fallen for it and rushed her home and paid the price for dropping his guard, and now the rules of war were clear, and Marcus—thirteen and explosive with rage beyond his years, beyond his coping skills—was not to be restrained by me, by his mother, by the handful of people who knew what was street-code inevitable and knew it without a mystic in a whitewashed cottage by the bridge trestle.

And the rest of this story played out exactly as Father Death said

167

it would. Even the part about me coming back in the end to hear him tell me about my death.

It was many, many years later, however—decades after Marcus was beaten to death in Bellamy Creek Correctional Facility. By then, I was on the tail end of a reasonably wholesome life—I'd married a decent young lady from the neighborhood and our kids were grown and moved on; she'd passed in March and I was living alone in the brick house on Outer Drive we'd shared for forty years. I'd gone being from a wiry young scholar to an old dude with ragged teeth and a paunch, but I'd retired from the city water department with a pension and was reasonably content with how I'd played my cards. I had no doubt that my death, however it was to come down, would not be attended by many regrets.

Still, I was nagged with the knowledge that Father Death could fill in the blanks. Blanks that, for a multitude of reasons, finally interested me. Back on that warm September morning, he had phrased it perfectly: For these intervening years, it had gestated within me.

In the meantime, I'd grown comfortable enough in my own skin that nothing he'd say held any particular dread to me. But I was getting on, and now—like Allen and Marcus had all those years earlier—I saw some personal, private value in reading my biography complete. So on another bright September morning, when many things had changed and all things remained unchangeable, I made the trip again, down by the low concrete wall, out into the barren terrain beneath the bridge.

Common sense told me that Father Death was dead himself by then; that couldn't have survived all these years—he'd been an old man when I was an adolescent. But nothing about Father Death—not the miniature house, not the picket fence, not the clairvoyance, not the luminous, river-green eyes set like gems into a coal-black façade—operated by reason. None of it was chartered in logic and none of it followed prescription—except for his omens.

So I was not in the least bit doubtful that I'd find him there, at his window, waiting for my arrival.

Which he was. Neither did I have to remind him who *I* was—he remembered me immediately and nodded at the notion that he'd been expecting me, tomorrow if not today, or in another month if not then. Or the following month. He received me with respect and civility in the small, pristine room with the cot and the Formica table and Lucinda's stuffed gorilla.

This time, we talked in grown-up terms, about the years sandwiched between this visit and the last, about all the fatherless brothers and motherless sons who'd turned up in the interim, looking for various bits of wisdom, where those who wanted to know their fates were told, either on the spot, or later when they changed their minds. Those who'd wanted to know something more complex about surviving life—like I had—had been given the insight of his lofty overview. We talked about young bloods like Marcus and Allen Hughes, trying to breast a world of cultural disconnects, of a vulgar ideology of alienation, and most of all, how faith in silly dreams can overshadow a sane view of most situations. These were the identical challenges I'd faced, and the same ones my sons had been braced to expect while they were still in Pampers, and which they'd overcome as efficiently as I had—they were both successful, professional men.

Many of the kids who'd found Father Death were like the Hughes brother, of course; they had remained defiantly unaltered, scarred and scowling, and had succumbed early to the shitstorm.

But not all of them. I was living proof. So, the conversation was long and convoluted and it lasted all day, and in the last part of the afternoon, when the sun made sharp, savage slashes in the sky, I was ready to know, and this time, when Father Death took my face between his nimble black fingers, my head was thatched with thin gray tufts. I sensed it was ritual: He remembered what he'd seen the first time.

And indeed, it proved to be so, but there was more: I returned the scrutiny, looking deeply into the translucent green eyes of Father Death, this time from the perspective of a man who had seen his own share of tragedy and triumph, and what I saw amazed me, but in the end, it didn't surprise me.

Afterward, we did not take seats at the Formica table; Father Death led me through a small rear door, into a patch of lawn behind the cottage where there stood an exquisitely carved cross, painted white, now tinted with rays from the dying sun.

"Lucinda?" I asked and he smiled.

Behind the cross, a path fell away through a maelstrom of tall weeds and piles of broken concrete and trailed all the way down to the river. Father Death asked me if I was sure, and when I said I was, he pointed to the dunnish current spreading a slow, half mile toward Canada.

He said, "You will fill your pockets with debris from those piles and walk into the river."

And he gave me the time and date.

There was a folded lawn chair leaning against the clapboards of the house, and I opened it up and sat down quietly, opposite Lucinda's grave. As I watched, Father Death filled his pockets with debris from the concrete pile, and walked slowly, deliberately, confidently, into the river.

As I knew he would: I'd seen it.

And since the date that Father Death gave me that afternoon has not yet come, I am there in the tiny cottage beneath the bridge trestle now, tending tomatoes, standing at the window; patient, taciturn and utterly content, waiting for your visit.

COSTELLO & ABBOTT

Two in the morning had always been a tough go for him, even as a success story. Success being a relative term, and in this case perhaps even a modest one. Nevertheless, he was surrounded by the sort of trappings that measure the word in its New Economy interpretation, from the Bose Wave Radio on his stereo shelf to the Porche Boxter in the exclusive, underground parking lot two blocks from his apartment house. Though he hadn't yet stumbled over any truly serious coin, at thirty-one, he'd settled into a comfortably upscale GQ existence, an interesting career, a productive options contract portfolio, and, as of three weeks ago Friday, he was regularly doing hip-hugger Monica; a woman from his office who, though no member of the municipal brain trust, was both excruciatingly sexy and well-educated... all in all, not too bad for a guy who at the age of seven had been judged to suffer both symbiotic psychosis and mild autism.

That particular diagnosis stemmed from a couple of isolated events from his childhood, hallucinations, each of which he could recall with crystal clarity... though as a rule, he chose not to. As you can imagine, they were profoundly disturbing memories, and as far as he'd come to understand schizophrenia, there was no associated neurological or brain damage, and plenty of kids outgrew it. Since he had suffered no real symptoms since the age of seven (except, possibly, on the night his mother passed away), he figured he had his dragons licked, and didn't have a whole lot

"Yeah! And the tall one with the 'stache, he was like, the straight man, wasn't he? Abbott...?"

"I guess. Really, Monica, I'm up to my ass in alligators right now. Is this going somewhere?"

"Well... it's only that I saw this special last night, a retrospective of all these Forties comedies, you know? And during the Abbott & Costello routines, for some reason, they had the roles turned around. Costello was acting like the serious one, and Abbott was the goof..."

He'd been growing more annoyed by the second, and now, he began to show it: "So what? Monica, come on. Maybe it was supposed to be experimental, a joke or something. Maybe it was supposed to be funny. They were comedians, weren't they?"

"Yeah, but, I don't know. It wasn't even sort of funny. It was just weird, that's all. It's really been bothering me. I taped part of it and I wish you'd watch it for me and see if you can figure out what's going on." Her voice took on a coyness that was, suddenly, overtly sexual. "Come on. For me? Honey? Please. I can't stop thinking about it."

"Sure. Cool, fine..." he'd exhaled, taking the tape as she thrust at him. "Sorry I'm such a..." The right noun eluded him. It was the first time she'd called him 'honey', and for some reason, that was important to him; he'd said, simply, "I'll take a look." ...anything to slither by, to avoid the gathering squalls of argument, which would have been their first.

By eight in the evening he'd forgotten all about it. A blowout round of squash at the health club, a couple of beers at Lannigan's with the guys from Conceptual Design, and he was ready for an early night. At home, he found two messages on his machine from Monica, wondering if he'd formed an opinion on the videotape yet. Two messages! Jesus Christ, he'd thought to himself; maybe it made sense to rethink the relationship. Dizzy was one thing, but this girl might seriously have a screw loose. He tried to call her but found that her line wasn't working. Predictable glitch in a plugged-in reality; the hyper-connection gone disconnected. A computer voice apologized to him. Heartwarming. He'd shaken his head in disgust and resigned himself to being a trifle pussy-whipped as he plugged the tape into the machine. He'd even glanced at it from time to time as he went through his weeknight bachelor bedtime routine.

From what he could see, the clip appeared to be of a typically vaudevillian, dialogue-heavy burlesque, like the duo's tiresome "Ya gotta pitcher on that team?" sketch. Only sure enough, now it was Costello who appeared to be the smooth-talking, officious city slicker, while Abbott played the mischievous bumbler, the pie-in-the-face buffoon continually suffering from conniptions of frustration. He'd listened intermittently as he moved through the apartment. The skit was called 'The Telephone Salesman' and, between the bathroom and the bedroom, he picked up on a portion of it that had gone something like this:

Costello: Didn't I just tell you? We're not hiring!

of incentive to dwell on them.

In fact, he resented reminders of them, which leads to two AM. At two AM, even a co-op jewel of a life tended to suck. Minor stuff blew up all out of proportion. Little things. Take tonight, for instance. Take the *Abbott & Costello* tape...

It had gone down like this: that morning, at work, with fifteen separate logs on his fires, he'd been approached by Monica, who'd looked uncustomarily distressed. "Can I ask you a question and you won't think I'm stupid?"

"Go ahead," he'd replied quickly. Three weeks of her somewhat limited mental gymnastics, and he was prepared for anything; on their first date they'd wound up at a neighborhood tavern playing along with a rerun of *Family Feud*, during which she'd volunteered Omaha as a Middle Atlantic state.

"Remember that old group *Abbott & Costello*?"

"Yeah..." he'd answered uncertainly, somewhat distracted by paperwork.

"Which was which again?"

"What?" His testiness, a trifle too evident, didn't stop her from blithering on. Her tone climbed higher and took on a strangely urgent edge: "The fat one was Costello, right? He was usually the clown, the butt of the jokes, right?"

"I don't know. Costello was the dark one, I suppose".

Abbott: I don't care if you're hiring or not!

Costello: Then why did you ask me for a job?

Abbott: I didn't.

Costello: Wait a minute. Didn't you just walk in here and tell me you wanted to sell phones? ·

Abbott: Yes.

Costello: And like I told you, we're not hiring!

... to tell the truth, he couldn't watch it very long. There was something tremendously disturbing to him within the reversed nuances of the Abbott $ Costello characters; the switched facial expressions, the inverted delivery... The voices were right, but here, Costello was the patronizing joke-feeder while Abbott wore you down with his overbearing physical schtick. The humor was wincingly unfunny, as always, but beyond that, it just didn't work. The chemistry was way off. If it was an early misstep on the part of the pair, or a late attempt to revive their careers, it had been a big mistake. Which is probably why the clip was sufficiently noteworthy to have been included in this phantom retrospective. No big deal. Except that, for visceral and private reasons, he'd taken it very personally...

And six hours later, he was unable to sleep, hideously troubled, and he lay tossing and turning in a damp wad of Calvin Klein sweats, nursing irrational anger toward Monica for having subjected him to these unwelcome emotions. Unwittingly, of

course. After all, there's no way she could have known that at
the age of seven, he'd awoken one night in the small hours,
needing to take a pee, reached for the night light and found, to
his confusion, that there was a wall where the dresser should
have been, that the lamp had somehow moved to the other
side of the bed; and when he switched it on, he discovered that
his entire bedroom, in fact, had been transposed, turned back
on itself, like a reflection in a mirror. Potentially, some bizarre
practical joke, except that every single color within the room was
a chromatic opposite as well; the walls which had been powder
blue had turned a pale tangerine, the deep navy shag rug was now
vivid orange, the toys, the posters, everything was a diametrical
opposite, even his sheets, which were white when he'd gone to
bed, and had now changed to black. It looked like a photographic
negative. He'd begun to scream, scream, scream, and couldn't
stop; his parents had rushed to his bedside, and from there to the
diagnostic unit at the city hospital where they'd readily agreed to
a three-day evaluation by a team of psychiatric specialists. They
were simple people; his father, already an old man, retired from
the railroad, his mother, a church secretary; they couldn't so much
as pronounce the term infantile schizophrenia as comprehend
it, and when he was released, his system clogged with Librium
and a psychic badge which incorporated the phrase 'inability
to integrate sources of sensory input', they'd led him carefully,
tremulously, gingerly, back home, where he'd been persuaded to
peek within his bedroom. To him, it smelled somewhat weird,
but otherwise, appeared to be fine again, and they figured that he
was cured, though at two AM, he found that he needed to prove

himself by reaching for the night light, which was where it should have been, and when he switched it on, everything was still okay and he was contented and relieved, but a minute before he fell asleep, the smell suddenly started to get to him, especially when he realized that the smell was new paint, and then, it occurred to him that the walls must have been painted, and he got up and made a scratch mark by the outlet cover near the heating duct and saw that there was a substratum of orange color beneath the powder blue, He'd kept his wits long enough to check on the secret burn he'd accidentally administered to the rug behind the closet door while goofing with his dad's lighter, and sure enough, it was gone. The navy carpeting was evidently brand new; you could smell that, too. In fact, the entire room appeared to have been redone; all the furniture was closely styled to the original stuff, but it was different, most of his toys looked the same, but they were new, though a few were merely approximations, not identical, and once he figured out that his parents were in on it, it was over for him; he tore from the room, hitting out, screaming again; screaming, screaming, and was thereupon subjected to a much longer stint in the lockup ward, six months this time, and when he was finally cut loose, his parents had moved from the house altogether, and settled him into a new bedroom. Following which he'd never had another problem with his perceptions until the night twelve years later when his 67-year old mother had died. And even then, he was half-convinced that the psychotic episode had been hers, not his.

She'd been subsumed into Brookstone Memorial with an

impossibly high fever. Brookstone was where his father had
passed away five years earlier; an impenetrable institution
vibrating with tension and pain, a succession of long, mazy
corridors, mysterious machines, foreign lingo, an impenetrable
hierarchy... Bivacqua, her doctor, was a recessive little man with
a pre-cancerous pallor; he'd called her condition pancreatitis
and respiratory failure. The dutiful son had remained within
the ICU, hovering, holding her hand, listening to the rasping
progress of her death trajectory. In the wee hours she'd regained
consciousness, briefly, barely, long enough to clutch back at him
with sincere, terminal gratitude. Who knows what occurs to a
person during these intractable bonds of finality? She seemed
driven to unburden herself of inner malignancies, certain secrets.
In a faltering voice she'd said, "Remember when you were seven
and you were treated at the mental hospital? Remember your
bedroom... remember what you said about it...?"

"Of course I remember," he'd replied gently. He would have
preferred some other subject, but there didn't appear to be much
space in that particular moment to bring one up.

"Honey, it was true... Everything about what you said, every word
of it. Your room really was backward like that..."

"...what...?" he'd whispered, weakly.

"We lied to you, to everyone, to the doctors.... to Gran and
Gramps.... while you were hospitalized in those first few days,
we did everything we could to put it all back together again;
we gutted the room, burned everything, bought new furniture,

painted the walls, replaced the rug, your things..."

"Why... didn't you tell me?" His murmur was numbed by sudden, almost psychic pain. He felt as if someone had clumped him rather pointedly in the testicles.

Feeble sobs began to rack her frame: "We were frightened, honey. So terribly frightened. Your father and I, we thought it was you. We'd checked the entire house, even the attic, even the crawl space, and it was only your room that was turned around like that... We were afraid that somehow, you'd been possessed by the ability to will such things to happen with your mind. Besides..." she said, growing suddenly more intense and fairly barking out words, which were dazzling in their vigor and clarity: "Besides, besides, besides... There wasn't a god damn thing we could do about it!"

In twenty years, he'd never heard his mother swear, not once; a fact which his expression doubtlessly betrayed, for she made sudden, direct, conspicuous eye contact with him and held it. Her face broke into a broad grin that appeared to him to be almost self-satisfied. All symptoms of infirmary seemed to melt away from her ravaged form, and she sat bolt upright, returning his puzzled glance for so many seconds that he grew uneasy... returning his attention to her withered hands, he'd continued to stroke them in rapid, nervous circles... and when he'd dared look back he found that she still had him transfixed, resolutely, within her glittery stare. The smile became positively creepy, as it was utterly incompatible with her previous state. He'd risen up, intending to ring for the nurse, and as he did, he'd found that her focus didn't follow him, but rather, remained directed upon the point on the chair where he had been sitting. He realized that she was dead. A week later, Dr. Bivacqua had informed him that her blood culture had contained a strain of staph bacteria called klebsiella; when pressed, he'd confessed that it could occasionally trigger what he, in the profession, referred to as 'false memories'. There were worse things in this world, he'd pointed out, than to die with a smile on your face, but his choice words of solace had been unaccountably spooky: Mom's 'super-bug' infection had ultimately proven resistant to every form of antibiotic administered, and as Bivacqua placed his left arm around his shoulder, he'd whispered in his ear: "There wasn't a god damned thing we could do about it..."

In the years since, he'd often wondered if that night and the follow-up session had unfolded exactly the way he recalled it, or if he'd been suffering from latent psychotic flashbacks. As with the rest of his nightmares, however, he preferred to relegate these thoughts to the dusty pigeonholes of consciousness.

Still, that particular night, a world of justification wouldn't help him fall asleep. He toyed with the idea of phoning up Monica, since if he had to be awake, he couldn't see any reason why she should be allowed to sleep. However innocent she might be, his insomnia was her fault. Wasn't it? In the end, he desisted, recalling her screwed-up phone service, though he preferred to consider that it was a conscience pang that had stopped him. He considered that a more prudent and satisfactory plan might be to leave a message, a curt one, on her machine at work. He rolled it around in his mind, figuring that he could express himself in such a way that she'd get the point without being too offended. After all, why mess with a perfectly good lay? He arose and undertook the wordsmithing over a couple of fingers of Talisker, and as it took a certain amount of concentration, it proved to be a good prescription. When he placed the call to the office switchboard, he found that her extension was not hooked up, and that the automated recording did not seem to recognize the spelling of her name. Another bugbear, he figured, within the frustrating links of modernity. Oh well. He gave it up before it pissed him off. At any rate, the exercise of composing his thoughts had somewhat calmed him, and he found himself, behind the bolts of malt whisky, quite exhausted.

He was nearly back to sleep, hovering in a semi-REM fog, when it came back to him. Like an anvil to his metatarsus. The tape! The gist of the *Abbott & Costello* sketch, which he'd picked up almost subconsciously. Talk about eerie. Beyond that, it was fucking impossible. He must have misheard it. Or misinterpreted it, or something. But then again, if he had, the whole stupid routine wouldn't have made any sense. Now, he was upset beyond the pale of the cause, totally out of the sleep fix, and in another moment, he was gulping more scotch, pacing in front of the VCR, tape inserted, watching as the voltaic snow of nascent television swirled into view once again.

There was Costello, standing behind a set-piece counter, surrounded by a number of boxy, prehistoric-looking telephones.

The acetate-over titles came on: '*THE TELEPHONE SALESMAN, Colgate Comedy Hour, debuted December 5, 1954. With Joe Besser and Dorothy Granger*'.

In sauntered Abbott, and the conversation progressed this way:

Abbott: I want two cell phones.

Costello: I'm sorry, we're not hiring.

Abbott: Whadda I care; I need two cell phones.

Costello: Didn't I just tell you? We're not hiring!

Abbott: I don't care if you're hiring or not!

Costello: Then why did you ask me for a job?

Abbott: I didn't.

Costello: Wait a minute. Didn't you just walk in here and tell me you wanted to sell phones?

Abbott: Yes.

Costello: And like I told you, we're not hiring!

Abbott: Lemme get this straight. You carry telephones here, right?

Costello: Oh yes, certainly, all kinds of phones. Big phones, small phones, black phones, blue phones...

Abbott: Cell phones, right?

Costello: That's right. We sell phones.

Abbott: And that's why I'm here! I work for a major mainframe corporation, and I need two cell phones for my job... (stops Costello mid-sentence)... And I'll break your arm if you say you ain't hirin'!

Costello: (Exasperated) Very well, then, I'll have to have my supervisor contact you. Where are you going when you leave here?

Abbott: IBM.

Costello: Well, you're welcome to use our lavatory.

(audience guffaws)

Abbott: Why would I need your lavatory? I said, IBM.

Costello: Well, you're not going to do it in the middle of the floor, are you?

The studio audience roared as the tape faded back into a blizzard of static.

He coughed and glanced around. Cell phone jokes in 1954? What, precisely, was the deal here? Might Alan Funt leap gleefully from the closet at any moment? He moved to an equally absurd, though more scientific bent: Might Monica have somehow picked up stray signals from a rogue dimension? A parallel universe? According to everything he'd seen on PBS, there was such a thing out there, distant and nearby simultaneously, shimmering and glittering within some all-encompassing Stephen Hawking orbit. Aren't television waves supposed to travel on indefinitely into outer space? Maybe they could pass through the continuums as well. Or was this all

linked to his previous episodes of psychosis? How did Monica
fit in? And his parents? And by default, Dr. Bivacqua? And the
switchboard operators? Naw, it was all too insane, too *Twilight
Zone*; he shouldn't let his mind wander like that, especially after
a lot of whisky; it was beginning to get away from him. This was
the kind of stuff that made you lose control, miss work in the
morning. The true explanation was undoubtedly simple; it was
some video trick, some special effect, a techno-manipulation of
an old film clip or else a couple of lookalikes acting like assholes.
Why dredge for madness in the cistern of day-to-day stupidity?
Still, as he turned off the set, he felt jittery and ill, like after you've
found a major spider inside the shower stall. Despite the hour, he
didn't want to hang around the apartment. It seemed close and
depressing. It gave him the creeps, actually, to be alone. The night
was already shot, he was half in the bag, and he figured that he
might be better off finding a cafe and slugging down coffee until
it was time for work. He tossed on some clothes, phoned down to
the front desk and scared up Louis, the Moroccan doorman, who
generally worked the twelve-to-eight shift.

"You want I should get somebody to bring your car around?"
asked Louis, in his unaccountable, French-Arabic accent.

"No, I'm sorta drunk, just get me a cab."

"Haven't seen any cabs go by in a long time tonight, mister. Half
hour, more..."

"Just buzz me when you find one, okay, Louis?"

As he hung up the phone, however, he realized that he didn't care to remain upstairs even long enough to wait for Louis' return call. Even shooting the breeze with the doorman and his bizarre Moroccan breath would be better than pacing furrows in the carpet within the oppressive apartment. He grabbed his coat, and tugged open the door and there stood Monica, an inch away from his peephole, beaming broadly. He nearly went into cardiac arrest.

"Christ, you scared the shit out of me!" he said. "How'd you get in here?"

"The front door, goofy. How else?"

"The doorman let you in? Just now?"

"Sure..."

"Louis? Nappy-haired guy with a funky accent?"

"I dunno; I guess. Why? Is it a problem?"

"No, of course not... it's just that... Jeez, you musta made it up here in about fifteen seconds. You don't even look out of breath..."

"So, I'm in shape. That's one of the reasons you love me.." She pushed out her breasts, which were restrained by an exquisitely revealing black sweater. "Aren't you gonna say I can come in...?"

"Well..."

"The tape!"

Once inside, she settled comfortably into his low-key écru sofa as they exchanged explanations for the peculiar encounter; he told her that he'd been unable to sleep, and had been on his way out to a bar or an all-nighter, that he was currently in the process of trying to track himself down a cab.

"Yeah, it took me almost twenty minutes to find one," she said. "I almost gave up, you know, but I couldn't sleep either. You weren't returning my phone calls, and... I had to know."

"Know what?"

"If you watched it. The tape! That's why I'm here, silly. Did you see it?

"Yeah, I saw it." For some reason, he really didn't feel like dealing with her. He moved into the kitchen, where he began to fiddle with his coffee maker.

"Is it a trip, or what?" she called out to him. "I mean, what's up with that? Man, I can't figure out what they were trying to prove..."

"If it's so important to you, why don't you just look it up?"

"I did, but it wasn't listed anywhere. I even called the cable company, but I couldn't get anybody to answer at the front desk..."

"There's a lot of that going around. By the way, your voice mail is on the fritz at work. You want coffee?"

"If you have any Bailey's. So, what about the tape? I mean, it's obviously been bothering me to the point where I decided to come over and bug you about it... I mean, you know a lot about trivia and stuff, don't you? What in the fuck was Abbott doing playing Costello?"

He didn't have a clue as to why she was carrying on so. He dumped water into in the reservoir of the coffee machine. It made its usual power-surge implosion and he jerked back his hand to avoid being electrocuted. "Relax, already. It probably wasn't even really them."

"Oh, it was really them, all right."

"Yeah? You seem pretty positive about that for somebody who didn't even know which was which this morning. Besides, that wasn't even the weird part. The weird part was that they were making cracks about cell phones..."

"What's so weird about that?"

"Cellular phones. Didn't you pay attention to the routine? They were making up moronic puns about the difference between 'selling phones' and 'cell phones'."

"Yeah? So what?"

"Well, the thing was supposed to come out of the Fifties, wasn't it? They didn't have cell phones in the goddamn Fifties..."

"They didn't?"

"Oh come on, Monica. That's sixty years ago. You mean to tell me that you think they had cell phones sixty years ago?" He shook his head in amazement. "Didn't you graduate from Bryn Mawr?"

"Excuse me," she said with a righteous huff. "I was a B.A. You think that taught me anything useful? Anyway, maybe it was like, topical humor. Maybe it was a sort of a really brand new invention back then, that's why they used it for the skit."

"It was not a sort of brand new invention back then, Monica; give me a break. Besides, they mentioned IBM mainframes, too. You're telling me you think they had mainframes back in 1954?"

"Oh. Well. How should I know? Hey, buddy, don't jump down my throat, I told you that the tape was strange. That something didn't seem one hundred per cent kosher about it. Now you know what I'm talking about..."

"Frankly, I'm not sure what you're talking about, Monica. It's really no biggie. It was just a couple of modern guys doing an impersonation of Abbott and Costello. It was... I don't know, *Saturday Night Live...*"

"On *Wednesday* night?" she asked in a you-think-you're-so-smart voice.

"Oh, Christ, it was a rerun, for crying out loud. Or some other show. My point is, it wasn't Abbott and Costello, it was probably just actors portraying Abbott and Costello, trying to update the old 'Who's On First' routine..."

"Well, it didn't look like actors to me," she pouted.

Actually, it didn't look like actors to him, either. It looked like the genuine duo. But, who knew what kind of magic they could weave inside the Hollywood studios these days? If they could make Forrest Gump talk to LBJ, couldn't they make Abbott & Costello talk about IBM? He was about to end the conversation altogether. It wasn't progressing too well, and the more he thought about it, there was something about her own story that didn't make a heck of a lot of sense, either. He'd just gotten off the phone with the doorman when she'd showed up, and it really defied imagination that she'd been able to make it up five floors in the time it took him to grab his coat. Besides, she didn't appear to have just turned up at his doorstep grinning. He'd gotten the impression that she'd been standing there awhile. And if she'd come earlier, why wouldn't Louis have mentioned it when he called? Not only that, but by her own admission, she'd arrived in a cab, and Louis had clearly stated that he hadn't seen any cabs in at least a half an hour. The other explanation, therefore, was that she'd arrived before Louis came on shift, a few hours back. Why'd she'd been inside his apartment building for a number of hours, he couldn't begin to deduce, but suddenly, he was rather uncomfortable in her presence.

The phone trilled. Only once; Monica dived for it. "Oh," she said into the mouthpiece. "I'll tell him."

He stood at the kitchen door. "It's your doorman," said Monica. "He says he's got a cab waiting for you. I'll tell him to let it go..."

"Hang on," he replied. "Lemme talk to him." It occurred to him that he wanted to be removed from the situation. Desperately, and he wasn't about to let the only cab on duty in the city fade back into the night. Crossing the room gave him enough time to come up with an excuse. He took the phone, and listened to Louis babble in rapid-fire patois, then said, "Hang on, I'll be right down." He turned to Monica. "Look, the poor schmuck busted a nut for me finding that cab, I got to give him ten bucks or something. I'll just run down; it won't take me a second."

He headed for the door. "Have some coffee; there's Bailey's in the cupboard over by the microwave. I'll be right back up, honey."

"I doubt it," she said.

He didn't even bother to ask what she meant by her last remark. He closed the door behind him, sprung toward the elevator, and nearly collided with Louis as the gate skidded open. His heart made another obscene palpitation. Louis remained on the elevator, and the prospect of breathing five stories worth of garlic breath was not particularly thrilling. "Don't you usually use the service elevator?" he asked the Moroccan sharply.

"It no work tonight," Louis replied with a defiant shrug that clearly said 'life is such a pain in the ass, why even bring it up?' "Mister, I just wanted to tell you, I had to get you one of those English cabs, it's all I can find this time so late, hope it's okay..."

The elevator began its decent to the lobby. "It's fine, it's perfect. Look, did you let anybody up to my apartment tonight? Some whacked out blonde in a tight sweater?"

"Nobody, mister. Woulda noticed that one. Been real quiet

downstairs."

"That's what I thought. Okay, I need you to do me a favor, right?" He dug in his pocket for the requisite favor tariff. "In a few minutes, this chick is probably gonna come looking for me. I want you to tell her that I had an emergency, that I'll talk to her at work. Whatever you do, don't let her back upstairs. Call the cops if you have to..."

"Sure, sure," said the doorman, stuffing the bill inside his uniform. "Don't mind call no cops."

"You're a good man, Louis; thanks."

The doorman grinned and nodded; he was evidently in concord about his goodness. "So, you don't mind no English cab, huh?"

The elevator had reached its destination. "No, I don't mind, Lou... Say, what in the fuck is an English cab anyway?"

"Oh, you know, it gots the steering wheel over on the other side, and the brakes, and the clutch, and the ashtray... just like a regular car, only everything look backwards..."

The gate opened, and Louis jostled forward, intending to reach the front door first in order to perform his duties. "I ask the driver, only he say there ain't a god damn thing we can do 'bout it."

Louis held the door with an elegant flourish, his smile grown so prominent that it looked like his face was bisected by a tooth railroad. He had a piece of something foul and Moroccan wedged between his two front incisors.

"And by the way, mister. My name ain't Lou. It's Bud."

A brilliant purple cab with white tires waited beyond the apartment awning. It's 'for hire' sign read 'IXAT'; the last detail he noticed before the screaming started up again.

GIFT HORSE

The painting was by the nineteenth century Czech art theorist Pankrác Brada and was titled *Improvisation IV*. Although it was filled with broken brushstrokes, incongruent dabs of paint and bold, jarringly bright splashes of primary color, Brada had confronted his subject—a galloping horse—with freshness and immediacy. Done in the mid-1890s, the day's academics had argued that such works, painted hastily in an attempt to capture essences of form and movement rather than composition, were the scribblings of amateurs without the talent to create classic art. Critics, at the time, seconded the motion, although there was a group of perceptive collectors who'd wisely snapped up the works of artists like Brada, the painters of 'mere impressions'.

In the current day, what everyone agreed upon—Olivier Cromer and his children Marcel and Jocelyn especially—was that the painting, available for purchase at the Galerie Didier Mitxel, was the ideal gift for Mme. Cromer's 70th birthday Not only had she been a beloved patron of the Société des Beaux-Arts since her eighteenth birthday, not only did she particularly love *fin de siècle* impressionists, but her family had made its fortune breeding Anglo-Normand cavalry horses and had been responsible for some of the country's greatest jumping horses, including the Olympic star Algernon by the Trotter stallion, Cendrillon II.

The Brada painting managed to combine the first two adroitly, and the third—the fortune—by extension.

197

Because... *the price!*

Having originally sold in Brussels in 1898 for around 700 francs, Didier Mitxel wanted a €2.3 million for *Improvisation IV* and seemed confident he'd get it. He'd been in business on the Marché Berliet for over twenty years, and was a flagship among the eleven other antiques markets in the Saint-Petronilla square. When Olivier Cromer's came into his gallery, his reputation preceded him—dropping big sums of cash on artwork was something Cromer did on a regular basis. He had never before made a purchase at the Galerie Didier Mitxel, however, so when Didier—a dapper, exquisitely coiffed fellow in his mid-forties— saw that the elderly gentleman had fixated upon the Brada, he moved in for the kill.

"Let me set the painting up in the viewing room so you can appreciate it under better light."

Naturally, Cromer was wise to such tricks—the light in the main gallery was perfectly adequate. It was a commercial ploy intended to convince a potential customer that he was worth the special treatment and extra attention; it made them feel important. In fact, Cromer was important and he did deserve special treatment, but that did not necessarily require comfortable Savonburg sofas and cups of St. Helena coffee—Cromer deserved to know the painting's pedigree.

"No need for the hard-sell, M. Mitxel," Cromer replied. "I've quite settled on the idea of it. My wife will adore it; it's perfect. What remains is the authentication and the negotiation."

198

"Of course," said Mitxel, his tone shifting seamlessly from that of a high-pressure sales consultant to a fawning and deferential minion. "We would expect to produce a COA prior to any purchase; the original documents for this one are hand-signed by the two surviving Brada grandchildren, Oldrich and Ondrej, who run the Brada Foundation. They each issue certificates of authenticity independent of one another. On the price, alas, I am quite firm."

Cromer was an elegant, silver-haired gentleman with the sort of kindly demeanor that made him instantly endearing; a quality that was useful in such dealings when he thought someone might be trying to take advantage of him. His own fortune had been made in merchant banking; he was a descendant of the French/British Cromers, one of the most ennobled families in Europe. He was, in addition, a lawyer, a political scientist and an art historian with a collection of contemporary and Fauvist art, including works by Gauguin, Rouault and Paul Cézanne— but so far, nothing by Brada. In part that was because Brada was conventionally regarded as a minor painter, known to have produced fewer than a hundred paintings in his lifetime—he died at the age of 35 in 1910. Had this been a Henri Matisse, it might have sold for €12 million. But *Innovation IV*, the fourth and final in a series of zoological impressions—as Brada himself stated, 'a largely unconscious, spontaneous expression of inner character or non-material, spiritual nature'—was worth more emotionally to him than a Matisse in this instance, since it so perfectly aligned with his wife's non-material, spiritual nature.

He might have purchased it regardless of provenance.

But Cromer was no fool, and with superior forgeries deluging the market, generally coming complete with appropriate soilage, wormholes and even *craquelure*—the network of fine cracks that appears in old paint—he was not willing to trust a couple of Brada brats to authenticate the painting. With the money they'd ultimately suck in from the sale, it seemed perfectly reasonable to think that they might not be above the bogus COA or two. The problem with forgeries is that everyone wanted them to be real, and the new breed of copycat was as good or better than the original masters themselves. Henri LaChapelle, from Lille, had served a dozen years in prison after his forgeries fooled both Christie's Paris and the Musée National d'art Moderne, and Han van Meegeren's *The Supper at Emmaus* had been declared 'the masterpiece of Johannes Vermeer' before it was revealed to be fake.

Beside, Cromer had his own right-hand-man in these matters, Jacques Soustelle, a member of the CNES and an expert in Morellian analysis—to art authenticators what fingerprints are to the General Directorate. He was the expert who had finally busted LaChapelle, and he considered that all art forgers, infamous and unknown, were the destroyers not only of the credibility of taste, but of the credibility of faith.

"Certainly your man can perform whatever analysis he chooses, M. Cromer," said Mitxel, adjusting his cravat. "One cannot be too careful in this age—I'd be a fool to deny that superb fakes

have been piloted into the mainstream of respectable commerce.
Not in this shop, of course—I'm obsessive about it. I have
full confidence in my Brada, and I can have it sent round to
Soustelle's offices this afternoon—and no, I wouldn't think of
requiring collateral—to a man of your stature, that would be like
charging ransom if you volunteered to babysit my children."

So, Soustelle got the painting and worked his hoo-doo: He
examined the workmanship of the brush strokes, the stylistic
detail of the subject, the paper trail of the ownership, and
then he brought out the heavy guns: Forensics. He ran gas
chromatography tests to analyze the paint-binding medium,
atomic absorption spectrophotometry to be sure that all materials
were contemporary to the work's date and he used X-ray
diffraction to look for *pentimenti*. In the end, his attribution was
absolute; he pronounced everything about the painting authentic
and acceptable…

…except the price.

"Oh, never. Not at a thousand auctions. Not at ten thousand
antique markets. For a Brada from this period, €700 to 900
thousand, tops. Plus, it is a part of a set. Without the others, it
has less value. No, if you were to offer more than a million—
because it is for your wife—you'd be silly, but I promise you, €2.3
is an astronomically absurd sum."

That left Cromer in a quandary, and in admitting the quandary
to himself, quite embarrassed. He knew he had succumbed to
the fancy of the most desperate novice in the art business: He'd

become a touch. He'd brainwashed himself into believing that *Improvisation IV* was the one and only one painting for him; that he was in love with it and had to have it, and what's more, he knew that Mitxel had sussed him out.

It wound up being a duel of wills, an affair of honor. Cromer returned the painting to the Galerie Didier Mitxel with his appraiser's COA and suggested that he might be convinced to go as high as € 1.5 million, nearly twice the painting's actual worth, since it was intended to be a sentimental gift. But Mitxel didn't blink; he was, as Cromer's uncle Conall would have said, 'too clever by half'. Mitxel countered with €2 million, and vowed he couldn't possibly accept a penny less. He declared his willingness to wait two days for Cromer to make a counter offer, and if one was not received, he'd put the painting back on the market at full price, and ultimately, he was sure, fetch it.

Certainly, he intended to display it in the meantime.

That's when Cromer phoned his children. He sent them photographs of the work, explained the situation in detail, and—being a wise, if slightly art-besotted fellow—he solicited their advice. And they agreed, *Improvisation IV* was absolutely perfect—it would crown their mother's personal art collection at a time in her life when she'd be better off enjoying art that fretting over money. But, they could certainly see that asking €2 million was little more than highway robbery. They were not without funds themselves, and each volunteered to ante up €100,000 to sweeten the pot. In the meantime, they advised that their father to wait the full two days before adding their dose of sugar, just to see if a chink appeared in Mitxel's scalper's armor.

Didier Mitxel was indeed too clever by half, and the unclever half generally involved pretty women. Like Cromer and his Brada painting, once Mitxel fixated upon a certain young lady, he had to have her, married or single, old or young, Vogue fashionista or barista in some random café, and compulsively—if briefly—she became the one and only girl for him.

He was very nearly charmed off his Salvatore Ferraro footwear when DeeDee Fleetwood came into his shop late the following afternoon. She was clearly no random barista, but rather, a delightfully overboard, obviously wealthy American woman in her middle twenties. He swooned over her short, inspired, Right Bank-chic dress and her MM6 Maison Margiela leather boots, but most of all, over her accent, which had the lilt and sexiness of a Southern drawl. She introduced herself as the wife of Kentucky real estate magnate J. Thomas Fleetwood, and the 'trophy' part of 'wife' was understood—J. Thomas Fleetwood was in his middle sixties. Mitxel recognized the name, because a few years earlier, one of Fleetwood's thoroughbreds had won the Prix de l'Arc de Triomphe, France's richest and most prestigious horse race.

"Oh, he does love his ponies," DeeDee drawled, "And I cain't think of a better present to bring him back from Paris than that little ol' horse picture. I just adore it. How much is it?"

Mitxel bowed slightly from the waist in a way he assumed a nouveau-riche Kentucky cracker BF—beau femme—might find debonair. He said, "€2.3."

"Thousand?" she asked, fluttering her lashes.

"Alas, mademoiselle; millions."

"Oh, well I surely cain't spend that much. Tommy would massacre me and sow my grave with salt."

"What figure would Tommy not commit murder over?" Mitxel asked. "I mean, it is the work of a renowned artist after all, highly regarded by scholars of Modernism. Plus, of course, I have a Certificate of Authenticity from the famous appraiser Jacques Soustelle."

DeeDee gnawed her inner lip and pouted. "I do like totally like it, though. I s'pose I could go up another couple-a thou, but no higher."

"Ah," answered Mitxel, clasping his hands in front of his Façonnable blazer and considered.

There was more to consider than simply the money, of course. There was the throbbing morsel before him, chewing on pieces of her anatomy he wouldn't spurn a mouthful of if offered. He snapped a pair of manicured fingers, and an assistant trotted up. "Beppo, please set up the Brada in the viewing room so that Mlle. Fleetwood can appreciate the painting under better light…"

A moment later, DeeDee Fleetwood had slid her bumptious

derriere into the dusky taupe of Savonburg sofa silk and was blowing the steam off her demitasse of Napoléon-approved espresso.

"Dunno, Mr. Mixtel," she frowned, inverting the letters in his surname and pronouncing 'tel' like 'tail'. "See nothin' in this light that I didn't see in t'other. Maybe you could try to convince me over a glass of wine—Chablis is the big thing over here, right? That is, unless you can rustle us up some bourbon..."

Bourbon. How delightfully gauche, Mitxel thought as he bowed, and shortly, they were sitting together in the 18th arrondissement's go-to wine bar, L'Entreprise, nibbling cheese and charcuterie and drinking Les Folatières Puligny-Montrachet—Mitxel didn't care for the vintage of the Chablis.

As to discussing the price, a few other negotiations first needed to be established. He said, "If I ever find myself on your side of the water—and I do, frequently, with business in St. Louis, which I think is not far from Kentucky—would it be possible that you would join me for dinner? Where you could introduce me to the voluptuous and fleshy glories of... bourbon?"

"Why, I think that might just be more that possible, Deeder!" she answered, mangling his first name worse than his last. "Mr. Fleetwood, God bless his soul, doesn't always get around the old clubhouse turn as quickly as he usedta. I'd be proud to squire a dapper Parisian around St. Louis."

That settled the first part. They polished off the entire bottle of wine and DeeDee Fleetwood ended up buying *Improvisation IV* for € 1 million and a card on which she'd written her private number in case—she drawled—Tommy's private investigators happened to be more nimble during the home stretch than he was.

"I shall have the painting delivered to your hotel by La Poste— my private couriers," said Mitxel with a flourish.

Jocelyn Cromer didn't bother to change out of her short dress and MM6 Maison Margiela leather boots; she went immediately to the Le Royal Monceau Hotel and sat in the lounge sipping a superb vintage of Dauvissat Les Clos Chablis, and when the courier showed up, she intercepted him at the concierge desk and tipped him handsomely when he handed over the package.

That evening, Oliver Cromer had mixed reactions when learned of how Jocelyn had come by the Brada painting, because however diabolically clever her ruse had been, however well-planned and ingeniously executed—she couldn't stop repeating 'Mistuh Mix-tail'—it was not, in his world, an acceptable method of doing commercial transactions. But his son got such a kick out of it that he was forced to see the humorous side, and despite himself, Oliver started saying 'Mix-tail' himself, and 'Deeder', and although on some visceral level he might have enjoyed hearing Didier Mitxel's squirming explanation of what had happened to the Brada, as a gentleman he had too much class to give it another thought and blocked his number and warned his children never to do business at Galerie Didier Mitxel again.

Mme. Cromer's 70th birthday was a tremendous success, and indeed, Pankrác Brada's stylized horse, *Improvisation IV*, with all its vibrant, basic colors and simple, confident brushwork became her favorite piece in an extensive art collection; she never even thought to ask about the price.

As for Mitxel, he tried to contact Olivier Cromer one last time on Thursday evening, then wrote the experience off to the odds and the understanding that some closers, however deft, were not successful 100% of the time. It made no real difference to him anyway; he had Beppo rehang the original Brada, and delivered a handsome commission to Henri LaChapelle, who was just getting back into the swing of things. He'd already forged half of the gallery's collection on Mitxel's request and was raring to do more.

The genuine *Improvisation IV* is hanging in the Galerie Didier Mitxel in Marché Berliet at this moment. If you are interested in it, I suggest you have it appraised on the spot and don't let it out of your sight until the transaction is completed; take it with you when you leave.

My recommendation is that you wear a short skirt and don't, under any circumstances, offer more than €700,000.

O'MANCY

They came for Goody O'Mancy before midnight—that was, in their simple, credulous, violent minds, of paramount importance. At midnight, they reckoned, the old woman would fly off to the Autumnal Sabbat to rejuvenate her infernal powers and renew her pact of fidelity to the Devil.

At least, they had been assured this much by Phelim Stearnes, the Witchfinder General and Father Brogan, SJ, who had also told them:

"Women are the Devil's preferred target; by nature they are weaker than men and therefore have a greater capacity to fall; they cannot grasp spiritual matters easily and are impressionable in their beliefs; at the same time they are resentful of authority and discipline and their carnal appetites are great."

Phelim Stearnes, to whom the Eastern Conference paid the princely sum of £20 for every witch he dispatched, had carnal appetites that were not above an easy, buxom Irish lass or two, although in general, his opinion of Hibernia was less than favorable: "Nothing but bogs and marshes and Catholics who speak no human tongue."

He had been summoned to the small village of Goughal in the parish of Feakle by Father Wolfe following an outbreak of convulsive ergotism near harvest time. The disorder was alkaloid poisoning caused by the fungus *Claviceps purpurea*, which had affected the rye crop that year, but since that year was 1644, nobody connected the affliction with biology. Rather, the symptoms—those infected suffered bodily contortions, trembling and shaking while experiencing delusions and hallucinations—were clear evidence of demonic possession. And, having no one else expendable to whom to assign blame, Father Wolfe had settled upon Goody O'Mancy before the Witchfinder General even arrived.

Goody O'Mancy lived on the village's far periphery, beyond the high ash tree by the highway, down a lane that contained a single human habitation—a wretched hovel built of wattle and daub with a stone flue emerging from a gable wall so covered in moss and lichen that looked like it was growing from the landscape. She had never married, lived alone, and there was an uncanny something about her abode, as though it contained secrets not for the outside world. Contrary to custom, her door never stood open, and she kept her windows closely curtained. When she was seen, she was always alone, foraging in the fields and forests, gathering reeds and rushes. She was better versed in herbcraft than anyone in the parish, and a daring few consulted her for medical advice, and in her hoarse old voice, she'd prescribe heated corn in a pouch for the earache, foxglove for the heartache, and for the headache, a rowan branch worn in hair.

She might have known that the ergot convulsions were caused by the rye, not the Devil, but most of the villagers avoided her, believing she possessed an Evil Eye and knew hypnotic arts. To deny the existence of witches was heresy, and if anyone fit the witch profile in the village of Goughal, it was Goody O'Mancy.

To Father Wolfe, she represented an annoyance, nothing more. Wolfe was barely into middle age, but he was already bent with bone disease. He had a nose like a hawk's beak and wore the customary garb of his order—a long black cassock tied with a cincture. Wolfe was no profound cleric, but he was a man of shrewd observation. He was angular and awkward in his movements, but effective in his utterances, and in this, but for his gender and his scapular, he resembled an archetypal witch nearly as perfectly as Goody O'Mancy.

He may have had private doubts as to the old woman's Devil-granted powers, but he wouldn't let that stand in the way of appeasing a witchoholic Pope or the Witchfinder General's £20 fee. As far as any of them were concerned, the purpose of women was to bring forth babies and lay out the dead, and Goody O'Mancy engaged in neither practice. According to Father Wolfe, she knew more than she needed to know, and she did not genuflect to his niggling authority in the niggling village in a niggling county that had yet to be dragged, kicking and screaming, into the 17th century.

To him, this was sufficient sacrilege to warrant her elimination.

Moreover, Phelim Stearnes did not haggle over details. He was a tall, stately, well-proportioned man in his early forties; he was the son of a vicar, and held himself with an air of superiority before every man and woman he met in Ireland, where, he maintained, "The weather is horrible and the morals are worse."

He needed little more than a description of Goody O'Mancy—no history, no interview, no torturous inquisition—to determine that it was she responsible for the outbreak of madness among several of the town's citizens.

As to her age, according to Father Wolfe, it was not to be determined; no record existed in the parish, and this only further fueled suspicions:

"Fourscore and ten, at least. She was old when I was a boy—a woman who was passed to us from preceding generations. To this very day she carries her own wood upon her back for her wicked hearth —it is impossible that a woman of these advanced years could be engaged in such strenuous activity without diabolical intervention. Am I not right? Who attains such an age without allegiance to the demons? She has been known to bury ashes and bones and toads, and once, the entire rotting head of a mare. I can offer as proof the opinion of every single person in the barony: Goody O'Mancy is a witch."

"That is highly probable," replied Phelim Stearnes, unwilling to give this dirty, hunchbacked priest the satisfaction of the final determination. "But a few basic legal procedures must be followed when we execute a witch. They are outlined in detail in *Malleus Maleficarum*."

Stearnes held up a leather-bound volume, his favorite resource and the best known of the witch-hunter manuals—it was a book that, in the era, was outsold only by the Bible. "This is hardly my first trial, but each heretic is unique in her malice, rancor and vindictiveness—so it has gone so through all the generations born since the first and most malevolent witch of them all: Eve, partner to God's holy creation, Adam."

This was a little extreme even for Father Wolfe, but he thought better of mentioning the fact that not only was Eve also created by God, she was formed of Adam's own rib. Rather, he bowed elegantly, although his posture was such that it didn't require much effort. "Inconsistency is a trait that women and devils have in common."

"And the Jesuits are especially zealous in launching prosecutions."

They stood before the manor house attached to the small chapel-of-ease that Father Wolfe oversaw. The baron had long since perished and his property seized by the church, and this is where Wolfe lived. It was a fine stone structure overlooking a rolling landscape dotted with thatched huts, corn mills, barns, stables and pigeon coops; the view revealed hedgeless fields, a pond and a ruined monastic sanctuary embedded into a distant hilltop.

Within the manor house, the parlor room was referred to as the 'good room'. It stood behind the hearth with another fireplace opening into it and was maintained meticulously for visiting dignitaries. The Witchfinder General was certainly that, and he now prepared to retire until ten o'clock—the hour they had set to fetch their prey.

"In any case," he said, "the Lord's reckoning is clear enough. Exodus 18:22. Be it Eve or the Medium of Endor or Goody

O'Mancy, 'Thou shalt not suffer a witch to live'."

By ten, Father Wolfe had gathered a contingency of local men, dairiers and peat-cutters, tiller and tanners, some of whom with kin who had succumbed to the mad humors of the ergot poisoning, other with wives and mothers who'd come to Goody O'Mancy for her esoteric healing skills. Each of them had known the old woman since childhood and had a dread of her so superior that they had never deemed to call her anything but Mrs. O'Mancy. Now they cried out "Spirit Incubus" and "Satan's whore", as they descended the lane, passed the rabbit warren and toward the crude hut enveloped in shadowy, bog-rich forest and told themselves that spiritual warfare is the Lord's work. They were emboldened by the nearness of others they had known since childhood, and although their target on that frosted September evening was a frail old crone, and although they had behind them the strength of the church and the Witchfinder General, they were cowardly men equally convinced that Goody O'Mancy had the powers of darkness behind her.

And yet, when they burst through the door, battering it from the hinges, they saw no heretical depravity, no skulls, no crossbones, no talismans, no paraphernalia of the black arts; rather, the interior was appointed like any room of a poor, lonely woman—there was a pot suspended by a chain, rope fastened in chimney, pile of wood on one side, a broom on the other. Above a worm eaten dresser were suspended wares of bygone days, some old china stood on the mantelpiece. And there, steeped in dignity, having donned her woolen shawl in preparation for the ordeal that awaited her, was Goody O'Mancy. The appearance of the Witchfinder General in the village of Goughal was an event of such import that news of it had even trickled to her rude hovel on the edge of the vast forest.

She was ready, and by the sheer force of the numbers she faced, amenable, but she was by no means serene nor ready to go quietly into the night. She glared at the intruders with a countenance long set—her eyes were deep and glittered with ferocious defiance. If there was evil there, it was primitive evil, and when they fixed upon Father Wolfe, it was more frightful than any spell, because he knew she saw through his masquerade and all the way through to his barren soul.

But the authority of the Parliament was not as easily intimidated, and Phelim Stearnes was quick to remind them that this was not his first arrest. He barked his orders, gestured with his oaken staff, and within seconds, Goody O'Mancy was bound up and hauled away, leaving the rush candle lighted and the gorse fire burning.

The door hung from its moorings, but the hut was not deserted—there was life within. When the ruckus faded, a small, gaunt child of eleven or twelve slipped from the alcove built into the cabin wall near the hearth. The room's offshoot had been curtained from view, and in it, a girl from the forest who had been ill with bronchitis had been sleeping. Over the past week, Goody O'Mancy had tended to her with a concoction made from bilberries and milk vetch, and she was on the mend—so much so that earlier that night, the old woman had brought her to sit in front of the fireplace.

There, the child sat perfectly still, staring intently into the flames that lapped the fieldstones until the crone asked her, "What do you see there, my child?"

"I see a tiny figure standing in the fire, Granny. No bigger than the mandrake roots that grow in the circle by the quarry."

"And who is the person you see, child?"

"Why, it is as like to you as possible."

"Are you sure?"

"As sure as if I were looking in a glass."

The old woman came behind her, placed gnarled fingers on her shoulders and leered over them: "Ha, ha, so, you are blessed with *An da shealladh*, the foreteller's sight. This is good. Tell me what you see…"

The young girl squinted, and in the hearth, the flames licked, the smoke swirled, the gorse crackled and the scene changed. "Why, now I see other people, men from the village—they have tied you to a stick. And now a hue is raised, and now they light the fire… and now… and now…"

"Now, what?" the hag screeched. "Don't be a child, be a woman. Tell me what you see…"

The young girl covered her eyes with dirty fingers and began to cry. "I cannot, Granny… I see no more, the fire has swallowed

216

everything…"

Goody O'Mancy's tone grew gentler. She turned the child around, pushed her bushy brows close and peered into her wide eyes, which were luminous, terrified and ice-grey. "Be calm, daughter; it is nothing. You are graced with sight beyond the shroud—it is a good thing. May it never fail you: You have seen me snagged and throttled, but you have not seen the blaze devour me. Fire cannot hurt me, child. I am born unto the flames of harrowed spirits."

With that, she sent the child to bed in the alcove by the hearth, donned her shawl, drew herself up as much as her twisted frame allowed and waited for the men that the young girl had divined in her vision.

And now, after the woman had been taken away by angry men, the young girl rushed headlong back into the dark forest, back to the ragged knot of orphaned children in the deep dell where she lived. There were a dozen of them—they had come from all across the barony, their parents lost to famine or disease, and (unwilling to be consigned to the workhouse) they survived together, in a commonage, by their wits. They pilfered salmon weirs and granaries for food, and when one fell ill, they counted on Goody O'Mancy's skills to repair them. As to her heresy, they made no judgement: Belief in magic underscored their society, and the causation and healing of injuries and illnesses were intertwined. But they could not allow mortal men to interrupt their secret flow of living, and so—intent on setting the old woman free—

they crept as a tiny, tattered army to the outskirts of Goughal.

"No further proof is required," announced the Witchfinder General to those who assembled in Hogges Green the following morning. "She hath already been detected."

He held aloft his stick to quash the grumbling—detection was part of the ritual, part of the fun. Harvest was in, and the time was idle.

"The Reverend Father has declared that she was seen by a witness in the electoral council-room of a witch's sabbat. You would not call his testimony into question?"

They would not, but they wanted the dramatics.

"Father Wolfe knows of other witnesses who swear she was on Brosna moor at a witch-dance where the holy wafer was desecrated. Would you doubt this?"

They wouldn't, but they wanted more.

"Still others vow that they have seen her change into a goat and declare that all mankind must renounce God in Heaven and all his host and henceforward recognize the Devil as God. Is this not sufficient proof of guilt?"

It was, but they wanted something for their own consciences, something tangible, something nasty, so the Witchfinder General sighed, lowered his staff, saw Goody O'Mancy trundled up in a donkey cart, whereupon he peeled away her upper garment, and repeating the experiment from the night before. He pointed to a

218

bluish mark on her shoulder than resembled a cloverleaf and with a needle, he picked it thrice. Goody O'Mancy appeared to feel no pain, nor did any blood flow out.

So, she stood convicted beyond any question. While the proper authorities tied her to the stake beside the pond and the cheering citizens of Goughal gathered piles of broom and bramble to lie beneath it, Father Wolfe mounted an old millstone and addressed the ravenous group:

"The many lusts of men lead them into one sin, but the one lust of women leads them into all sins; for the root of all women's vices is the thirst for knowledge beyond her station. The tears of womanhood are a deception, for they may spring from true grief or they may be a snare. When a woman thinks alone, she thinks evil."

Whereupon, he himself lit the tinder beneath Goody O'Mancy, and the flames charged and boiled and rose up to quickly engulf her stooped figure.

The fire slathered and the fire screamed and the flames devoured the kindling, and now the scruffy, unkempt children poured forth upon Hogges Green armed with sticks and stolen farmer's implements, but they stopped short as they saw the same thing that the awestruck villagers saw:

Although the flames were huge and violent, and the wood incinerated, and although she stood upon burning logs in the hottest part of the blaze, Goody O'Mancy was herself untouched—in fact, her mouth was twisted into the purest expression of glee, and she taunted and mocked her accusers, crying out, "Beelzebub has shown himself and said expressly to my face we shall all be burned together in the end of days! But that is not today, you craven wretches; today your God forsakes you and today the fire shall not trouble me, it shall not…"

With that, unharried by the children, the villagers, the priest, and even the Witchfinder General scattered in fear for their souls. Meanwhile, the young girl from the alcove ran to fetch water from the nearby millpond and rushed back to the conflagration, where she flung it upon the flames that tickled O'Mancy's garments to douse them.

But of course, water, not fire, has ever been the scourge of the true witch, so through the sizzling of the wood, she listened in horror to Goody O'Mancy's final words:

"You cursed brat! Look what you've done! I'm melting! Melting! Oh, what a world! What a world! Who would have thought a good little girl like you could destroy my beautiful wickedness?! Ohhh! Look out! Look out! I'm going! Ohhhh – Ohhhhhhhhhh…"

THE NOUMENON

The community theater was the pride of Andover's performing elite, the locus of the local intellectual set and a bastion for Andover thought and expression, even though it was inside an old barn.

The theater's history was as interesting as the plays it featured: In the 1970s, Agneta Bjornborg –the drama teacher at Andover High School—identified an effusion of talent in the area, believing it needed a performance space. Her uncle owned a homestead a mile outside of town, and generously donated his barn, which Agneta and her lover Birgit power-washed free of eighty years of grime, poured a concrete floor, lay water lines, wired the place for electricity and built a stage and balcony. They were handy, those two.

The theater's first performance was 'Godspell', and for opening night, Bjornborg borrowed folding chairs from the local funeral home and relied on theater lights made of light bulbs inside coffee cans. The show was such a hit that they added two melodramas that year, and they too were so successful that it became obvious that the little theater must continue.

This launched a beloved community tradition of using crews, musicians and casts comprised entirely of Andoverians (or Andoverites, depending on which community newspaper you read, the Andover Sentinel or the Andover Herald). Members ranged in age from grade school students to senior citizens, because the theater project was meant appeal to all demographics, all economic levels and all employment backgrounds.

Agneta Bjornborg passed away in 2006, with Birgit following shortly afterward, whereupon, the rather matrilineal role of directing the plays and managing the Born-In-A Barn Players fell to Ellen Ruby, the current drama teacher at Andover High School. She'd seen the theater expand its repertoire to four regular season performances, plus a Labor Day show with a more mature theme for the adults while a children's theater workshop was offered in the post-and-beam addition. She was firmly indoctrinated in the all-inclusive policy of the Born-In-A-Barn players, committed to see that local theater did not go the way of the black rhino, and she did her own sort of community outreach whenever a new family moved into the community.

That's how she came to be standing beneath the hibiscus-lined portico on the front steps of her new neighbors, the Ogburns.

She rang the bell twice, and with unaccountable trepidation—she was a spunky, self-confident theater arts instructor with a proven track record of appealing to strangers, but the Ogburn story was not one with which she, nor anyone else in Andover, had any experience.

As a result, she had no idea of what to expect.

From the rumor mill came first the hearsay, which the internet promptly confirmed: Four years earlier, fourteen-year-old

Ryan Ogburn had disappeared from his home in Westchester County, a hundred miles north, and despite an extensive search by police, the FBI and volunteers, despite his parents pounding the pavement week after week and readily agreeing to polygraph examinations, despite a $25,000 reward for his safe return, Ryan had never been found.

These were the tragic circumstances that ran through Ellen's mind as she stood on the Ogburn's new porch, and moment after she ran a second time, she thought seriously of retreating. But just then, the door opened and a sallow, middle-aged woman appeared. Mrs. Ogburn was statuesque in appearance, and Ellen's initial assessment was that she must have been quite beautiful as a girl. The hollow face that gazed from behind the screen door was no longer attractive however, and Ellen thought—with her keen theatrical eye—that it was a face deluged by complex layers of despair; the sort of the expression worn by survivors who have not yet found their foothold back in the world of mundane routine.

The tragedy would never be behind her, obviously; the rent in her fabric could never stitched up, and Ellen Ruby made allowances for that. But she had come on a mission and was determined to see it through. With palpable reluctance, Mrs. Ogburn invited her inside, and gently, and earnestly, Ellen presented the housewarming gift she'd been carrying—a swiveling Swiss cheese board with little knives she purchased at the Bed, Bath & Beyond in nearby Fullerton. She made some welcome-wagon small talk, and it when it went nowhere, she passed along a heartfelt invitation to the Ogburns to visit the Andover Community Theater in the hope that young Gracie might be interested becoming involved.

Getting to know Gracie, of course, had been the true aim of the visit. Local scuttlebutt maintained that, as often happens in the wake of unfathomable family loss, the Ogburn's marriage had dissolved and only the mother and daughter had moved to town. According to the stories Ellen accessed in the Westchester Tribune, Gracie Ogburn had been eleven years old when her brother vanished, which meant that more than likely, she'd be enrolling at Andover High School in the fall. Ellen thought that the girl might enjoy a chance to meet some of her future teachers and classmates in the social setting of her community theater.

"There's lots of interesting folks there!" Ellen gushed. "Of all ages! Our actors dance and our dancers act! We are a warm, inviting gang of talented individuals who simply love to meet new faces!"

Mrs. Ogburn looked at her with a passive frown. Behind her was a living room filled with heavy, unremarkable furniture and strewn with shipping boxes—Mrs. Ogden had been unpacking some delicate Lladro figurines when the doorbell rang. "Thank you for the gift," he said tentatively. "And for the invitation. I hope you understand, but Gracie won't be attending high school in town. Since we… lost Ryan, I've preferred to home school her. The risks, the… you know…"

"Oh, don't get me wrong; I can't pretend to understand what you've endured. Are enduring. No idea at all. But I promise you,

226

Andover is a tight and mindful community. No way of knowing what it was like in West…" Ellen paused, not wanting to come across as an internet stalker: "…where you came from, but, in Andover, we all use the same dry cleaners, visit the same bank—heck, our front yards are filled with the same jade plants and plastic toys!"

Mrs. Ogburn shifted her angular form in such a way that was unmistakably dismissive. "Thank you again," she said. "I'm sure Andover is a lovely town… it's more like an old-fashioned village, really—that's what Gracie and I said when we first saw it; it's quaint as a Rockwell painting. But Gracie is more of a shy, homebody type. She's more into her history books than anything else. You probably have a lovely group, but Gracie?. She'd rather read than perform."

"I can answer for myself," came a sharp, tissue-thin voice from the alcove by the hallway. Ellen wasn't sure how long Gracie had been standing here, and realized instantly that the girl possessed an unsettling ability to be present and absent simultaneously. She had her mother's wide-set grey eyes and reedy figure, but behind the stiff posture was something poised, attentive and intense.

And she sounded anything but shy: "What sort of dramas do you produce?"

"Why, all sorts, dear! Enriching dramas, and musicals and comedies too! We just finished a scrappy, charming run of Colin Quinn's Long Story Short, and we are beginning to cast Agrippina, by Giovanni Affanito. If you like history, this would be an ideal way to get your feet wet with the Born-In-A Barn Players! It takes place in the days of Nero!"

"Thank you," said Gracie's mother quickly, with her face down, returned to unwrapping porcelain ballerinas. Ellen realized that the room's entire dynamic had suddenly changed, and inexplicably, it reminded her of a passage in the Bhagavad Gita where Kali, the Hindu goddess of preservation and destruction, recedes and draws near in psychic tidal waves.

But that was ridiculous—this distant young girl was nobody's deity; she was a waif who'd lost her home and half her family and who now displayed the sort of guileless curiosity about the world that home schooled kids often did. Ellen hoped the mother would see the value in allowing the girl, homeschool or not, to establish a social life in Andover. Yet simultaneously, she had the feeling the mother's hold on the domestic shot-calling was losing steam.

"We're casting all week" Ellen said hopefully, stepping backward toward the door. "As the director, I am portraying our Agrippina as rather Medea-esque, if you understand me—not exactly heroic, but sympathetic enough to root for. Perhaps you'll reconsider!"

The moment was briefly awkward. In Andover, when a guest left, the door was generally held open for them; it was the gracious thing to do. Now, Mrs. Ogburn smiled wanly from her china but she did not get up and Gracie did not move from the half-shadows of the alcove.

228

But Gracie spoke: "I believe we might," she said.

And apparently, she did. Two days later, the principal Born-In-A Barn Players were gathered around a card table in the theater discussing the finer points of Agrippina's character. The senior member of the troupe—the patriarch to Ellen's matriarchy— was Dr. Wolcott, a retired history professor from the nearby community college. He loved it when the group did period plays because his mind was eternally on tour in one historical era or another and his knack for instant trivia recall helped the little group add an authentic edge to their phrasing and fascinating nuances to their stage sets.

The group was not above a little gentle interpersonal teasing, and they often joked that if they had a nickel for every time Wolcott had sighed wistfully and said, "There were better epochs in which to have been born," they wouldn't have to charge admission.

Wolcott was indeed a worldly man—perhaps a bit of a luddite with technical things, but with a progressive viewpoint on sexual politics and gender roles that Ellen Ruby adored. The rest of the group found him to be a delightful old curmudgeon, and were happy to give him space when he lectured, and even when he grew a bit long-winded, like was doing when Gracie came into the theater:

"Agrippina had the unique distinction of being the sister, wife, and mother of three different Roman emperors, Caligula,

Claudius, and Nero respectively. This allows her character to portray all aspects of Freud's rubric about feminine identity, and so the audience should see her as all three at once—saintly Madonna, vulnerable sibling and debased wh... harlot."

He was going to say 'whore', but then he realized that the amorphous presence had slipped into the barn. "I'm sorry, young lady—I didn't see you standing there. I'm afraid Agrippina has rather more adult themes than some of our other works."

Gracie Ogburn hovered in shadows behind the last row of funeral chairs, which the theater had since purchased. "That's okay," she said. "I've heard of harlots. In fact, my father married one."

In another place, Ellen might have pursued a line of inquiry—she fancied that her years in the dramatic arts made her something of an armchair psychoanalyst. Was Gracie referring to her mother, or to the woman her father had subsequently married? Being as fond of gossip as the most bored biddy at the Andover Senior Center, Ellen had devoured the buzz that after the Ogburns split, Mr. Ogburn had married an old high school booty-call.

But it wasn't the time or place, of course, so instead she said, "Wonderful! I'm so glad your mother changed her mind!"

"I know the buttons to push," Gracie replied confidently.

Ellen introduced her with pride—Gracie was, in ways, her personal conquest: "Troupers, meet Gracie Ogburn! As most of you probably know, she's an Andover newbie, and I'm so pleased she's decided to check us out! Let's give her a real Born-In-A-

Barn welcome!"

There was a cheerful round of applause from the Born-In-A-Barn Players, many well wishes and small town niceties as Ellen chirped, "And Gracie's mother tells us she is a history buff! Isn't that so, dear?"

"I read a ton of books," Gracie shrugged.

"Well, anything about ancient Rome? We'd love your insight into our proposed set design for Agrippina, wouldn't we, Players?"

Now, the antiphon was less effusive—Dr. Wolcott, the resident set insight giver, remained subdued, and his mood didn't improve when Gracie sort of sniffed over the drawings.

Ellen said, "See? We're going minimalist; nothing but a throne, a couple of benches, some pillows—but we're moving them around, so every scene looks like it's somewhere different. We want the audience comfortable even if they don't know a lot about Roman history. With the costumes too. Familiar, but not cliché. Right Dr. Wolcott?"

Even though his first name was Yancy, everybody called Dr. Wolcott by his title. He was the breed of scholar who expected formality, even from friends. His late wife had never referred to him as anything but 'The Doctor', despite the fact that his Ph.D. was in nothing sexier than the Humanities and his career trajectory had never included a single tenured position.

"We're imagining a gladiator theme for the men rather than an all-around toga party." Ellen went on. "What do you think?"

"I hate gladiators," Gracie said. "They remind me of my brother. He loved that stupid movie."

Since everybody knew what had happened with Gracie's brother, there followed a brutal, ticklish silence where the group sort of yawped at each other like gaffed tuna, but Jillian Woodbury, who owned Pounce n' Play Pet Shop, saved the day: "We could maybe call them Centurion outfits instead, couldn't we?"

"Why, we could!" sparkled Ellen. "Would that be better, dear? How about it, Dr. Walcott?"

Dr. Wolcott scowled. "I never called them gladiator costumes in the first place—you did. I said they were called dalmaticas, with a lorica around the neck. I had no problem with us wearing togas anyway—no self-respecting citizen of Rome would have dared appear in public without one."

"Yeah, but then everyone looks like John Belushi," said Brayden Guppy of Guppy & Sons Hardware. "I mean, speaking of stupid movies."

"Well, then," Ellen interrupted, "Maybe in honor of the Ogburns, and our new theater member, going forward we could simply refer to them as Praetorian Guard-style dalmaticas, not gladiator suits. And heck, maybe the women should wear togas after all. Those slinky gowns Brayden picked out look like they came from a Victoria's Secret catalogue anyway. Everyone happy?"

Everyone was, except Gracie, who asked why the throne in the set design was so elaborate, with winged lions and a fancy footstool and the name 'Nero' in glittery gilt letters above the crest. "In the paintings," she said, "Nero's throne look simple and boxy. Probably made of wood."

"This is theater, darling," said Joshua Champney, stylist at Color Me Crazy Salon. "Flamboyance over minutia every time."

But quietly, Dr. Walcott stewed—the girl was right, and minutia was his stock-in-trade. Ultimately, Gracie herself defused the situation by shrugging, "Oh, I really don't care. I was just saying, that's all."

The theatrical season wore on, and Gracie stuck around the barn to say many other things as well. She didn't formally join the Born-In-A-Barn Players—it was sort of like the Hell's Angels, where they made new recruits wait awhile before giving them their colors—but she certainly insinuated herself into the fold and made her nebulous presence known. She took a minor, non-speaking role in the production—a consequence of her apparent inability to project her voice above a low-key mutter—but it happened that the low-key stuff she muttered was devastatingly accurate, and when they passed through her dour lips, they seemed an intriguing blend of classical tragedy and contemporary satire; just like Agrippina itself.

Unless the zinger was aimed in your particular direction—then it was a bitter pill to swallow. And it seemed like an inordinate number of her zingers were cast toward Dr. Walcott. That put them at odds, of course, since Dr. Wolcott was used to his historical perspectives being the final word.

During the play's opening sequence, for example—an interpretive dance sequence that portrayed the poisoning of Claudius, Dr. Wolcott had offered some unique (everyone thought) and symbolic (extremely acute, it was agreed) suggestions; he though the dancer's movements should be staccato and jittery, representing Claudius' legendary stutter, and gracefully clumsy—a phenomenal oxymoronic challenge that lead dancer Joshua Champney loved—in order to embody his club-footed limp.

But Gracie Ogburn, hovering in the wings with a notepad, said, "You know that poor Claudius suffered cerebral palsy, right? I mean, it makes no difference to me if you rig up a sump pump to make him drool buckets of saliva between lines, but anyone with a spastic kid might figure you're making fun of him."

Nobody wanted that—not even a hint of it, so they restaged the dance. Then, the scene where Nero is crowned, the Emperor— portrayed by Dr. Walcott—a tremendous visual was achieved as the spotlight illuminated Dr. Walcott's shiny bald head. He'd explained that it was a metaphor for the wannabe Emperor's naked grab for power, fulfilled as Agrippina—played by Ellen's sister Audrey—triumphantly crowns him. But Gracie Ogburn moved in from the background with her notes and said, "Bald is beautiful, I get it, but wasn't Nero crowned when he was like, seventeen years old? He may have had CP, but I seriously doubt he had alopecia."

It was true, and flustered, Dr. Walcott found a wig among the props and condescended to wear it during the Young Nero days, even though it made him look idiotic, like Uncle Fester dressed up as one of the Beatles.

Although Gracie's interjections were subtle, they were fired from a laser-beam wit, and in time, that they began to wobble the close, fruitful collaborations that the players had enjoyed for years. She corrected a pronunciation here, a line of script there, and once, following a 'fiddle' pun made by Dr. Wolcott that drew a chuckle from everyone except Gracie, she pointed out that the violin wasn't invented until the 11th century and that Nero had actually played a cithara. After that, in a huff, Dr. Wolcott disappeared.

Ellen found him in the parking lot, simmering inside his Honda Insight (literally as well as figuratively since he had his windows rolled up and it was eight-five degrees outside) and finally convinced him to open the passenger door. She slipped inside through billows of Gauloise smoke from his little French cigarettes and had him crank down the volume of the Berlioz libretto he'd been listening to.

They chatted, earnestly. He knew he was being fractious and silly, but inexplicably, he was beside himself: "I don't know how much more I'm expected to take, Ellen. She's only a child, I know, but that attitude. That imperious righteousness! God, remember being her age? We weren't like that, were we? Children then knew when to pipe down; to listen. We didn't have all the answers, did we? It's all one-upmanship these days. And to what end, ultimately? Scoring points in some frivolous age war? Pulling one over on an elder? What's achieved? An instant of smug satisfaction? And then what? Every know-it-all I ever had in class wound up stocking shelves at Walmart."

Ellen had given up smoking two years earlier, but since Dr. Wolcott apparently needed more space to emote, and since they'd been close friends for decades, she was happy to lend her ear— at a small price. She borrowed one of his strong, tar-flavored Gauloises, fired it up, inhaled a lungful and hacked up a phlegm ball like it was her first cigarette ever. Dr. Wolcott didn't notice: He took his space and ran with it. His own mention of Walmart had set him off: "A century ago, imagine how pleasant this part of the state must have been? Pre-modern-mindedness and all. Before the megastores charged in to devour everything in their path, before cookie-cutter junk food places began popping up like mushrooms after a flood. Europe doesn't look like this, you know that? Architects have to plan for this sort of ugliness—lay out entire cities to center on an anchor store, like medieval towns used to do with the cathedral. Andover has been spared the worst of it maybe, but what about Fullerton? What about Pittman?"

He rattled off towns within striking distance that had not been spared the worst of it: "Hooperville, Villa Grove, Cumberland... Can you imagine how bucolic life must have been around here a hundred fifty years ago? Children didn't 'internet', they read books—a wholesome, solitary pastime that developed rational, moderate minds. I'm not talking about muzzling children, of course not or insisting that they remain silent until spoken to, but speaking up implies a certain standard of behavior..."

Dr. Wolcott unloaded a huge, body-racking sigh, and briefly, Ellen Ruby saw him through a new filter: As a small, bald, failed academic, lost in Thoreau's life of quiet desperation, trapped inside his little hybrid car, flummoxed by a teenager, smoking ludicrous French cigarettes through an un-tenured retirement while scrounging for scraps of respect from a handful of small-town yokels. For the first time, she considered his degree: What was 'Humanities' anyway, and how hard could earning a doctorate in it even be?

Suddenly, Ellen felt infinitely sad for him, then protective of him—failed self-aggrandizer or not, he was their failed self-aggrandizer—and she vowed to herself that she'd have a gentle, neighborly, even maternal (Mrs. Ogburn was a wimp, obviously) talk with Gracie. Welcoming someone into the community was one thing; giving them free rein to upset the status quo was another.

So she did. She ended the rehearsal early, sent everyone home, but kept Gracie behind for a brief one-on-one. Ellen tried to keep it gentle, honest and instructional; a love spanking without the sting. She explained that there were, in life, certain people who were sort of anachronistic dreamers—people who couldn't quite adjust to the changing mores and evolving standards of culture, people who imagine—correctly or otherwise—that life was more wholesome and innocent in the days gone by. I think he really thinks he'd have been better off born in a different century."

Gracie made one of her characteristic shrugs: "Seriously, I don't get those idiots. They love their Civil War re-enactments and their Renaissance Fairs so much they should marry them; they think the grass used to be so much greener. But I mean, come on! People used to crap in the back yard and work eighteen hours a day back then. A hundred fifty years ago, you died of basic stuff like measles or the flu. Today, bubonic plague can be cured with a shot of antibiotics, but in the day, a quarter of Europe died in two years, and in horrible agony, too, puking blood and hemorrhaging out of their eye sockets. What kind of shit lifestyle is that??"

Although she didn't approve of a fourteen year old cursing, she had to admit that there was truth in the assessment, and she tried to regain the upper hand by saying, "People tend to remember the highlights of the past, not the brutal realities."

Gracie shook her head. "I know, right? My dad was always going on and on about how much he wished he'd married that fat cracker slut Jenna Shattuck from his tenth grade biology class instead of mom. Well, now he has, and do you think he's any happier? There's a fucking joke… Dude looks like somebody rammed gun cleaning equipment up his ass."

Enough was enough, but Ellen sensed that upbraiding Gracie about her language would go nowhere, so instead, she offered a solution to the feud that had smoothed ruffled feathers in the past and had immeasurably improved the quality of the Born-In-A-Barn Players' performances:

238

"Look, we have a long-standing tradition at the theater," she announced, smiling. "One week before dress rehearsal, the entire cast gathers for sit-down pow-wow where I am not present, where all the pent-up anxieties and differing opinions about the upcoming performance can be aired without the director's input, or even my knowledge. That's a huge pressure-cock—that gives an equal voice to every member of the cast, even those like yourself without speaking roles. Many of the suggestions made during those sessions have been marvelously insightful, and were adopted readily by myself to strengthen the final product! I'm not proprietary that way! That sessions happens a week from tonight, and maybe it would be a good time to share your insights with Dr. Wolcott—to listen to him, and, perhaps even more importantly, to see if you can understand his perspective."

"Oh, I understand his perspective all right. He's looney-tunes. Plus, he's wrong half the time. Dude knows a lot less history than he thinks he does."

Ellen's voice became firm, although she tried to avoid a tone that would indicate she was pleading. "Please, Gracie," she said. "Good neighbors are willing to give each other space where necessary."

"The only space Wolcott needs has padded walls," Gracie shrugged.

If a truce was declared during the week that followed, it was a minor one. Gracie continued to point out inaccuracies in the props, oversights in the staging, bloopers in the delivery, fluffs in the pronunciations. The character of Otho, played by gravel hauler Caleb Paulsgrave, had been referred throughout his stage interactions as 'Oh-thoe', with a long vowel sound, until Gracie explained that the name was a derivation of the German 'Otto' and should instead be pronounced like a real hard-core New Englanders would say 'Arthur'. Ah-tuh.

Advantage Gracie, three sets to nil

But the week slid by without another hissy-fit from Dr. Wolcott, although on the night of the come-to-Jesus, director-free cast conclave, he brought along a huge grab-bag of grievances—a briefcase of beefs.

Meanwhile, Ellen had decided to put her spare evening to good use. She dropped by the Ogburns to let Mrs. Ogburn know what a valuable intuitive and brilliant addition Gracie had been to the Born-In-A-Barn Players team.

Mrs. Ogburn had received her, but reluctantly—there were dark clouds gathering behind her steel-gray gaze; squalls on her horizon. She had a look of anguish similar to the one that Dr. Wolcott had worn, but without the haughty amour-propre: This was closer to fear.

"She's a brilliant young lady," Ellen gushed. "So filled with knowledge and historical trivia."

"You have no idea," said Mrs. Ogburn.

"No, really, we've all been so impressed with her, especially Dr. Wolcott. And he knows whereof he speaks, I promise you—he is

Andover's leading intellect and he considers Gracie to be quite the savant."

Mrs. Ogburn grimaced slightly and in her eyes, the storm clouds roiled. "I don't know about that, but I think I have finally worked out what she is."

"Beg your pardon?" said Ellen.

"Grace. What she is. She's not a savant, like your Dr. Walcott thinks. She's a noumenon."

Ellen was momentarily poleaxed. "A what? A Newman? She's not really your daughter?"

A moment later, Ellen's poleax gave way to a broad sword of self-consciousness Was Mrs. Ogburn giving her the same look of benign pity she'd herself bestowed upon Mr. Wolcott?

"No," said Mrs. Ogden quietly. "Gracie is very much my daughter. I wish she wasn't, frankly, as awful as that is to say. She's a noumenon, and noumenons appear throughout history without warning. Without pedigree or origin. From beyond the realm of empirical realism. And they disappear without vestige."

She couldn't help but notice how far in her wake she'd left Ellen Ruby, and she dumbed it down: "Gracie is a very bright girl, very knowledgeable, I grant you. Where do you think she gets that from, Mrs. Ruby? My genetics and my home schooling. You think her father contributed anything to the between-the-ears department?"

241

"Well, I'm sure I don't…"

Mrs. Ogburn chuckled at the absurdity of the idea. "You don't, but I do. Ryan Sr. was a beefcake meathead who charmed his way into an executive position at Aetna of Hartford. What saw in him is a mystery—had more to with brawn than brilliance. But we both knew the marriage was a mistake less than a week into it."

"Yes, Gracie shared that he was… somewhat vocal about his dissatisfaction."

"Did she?" Mrs. Ogburn laughed. "Well, it's true. He made no secret of it. He reveled in it. He always went on and on about how I'd screwed up his life and how he'd missed the love-boat with some airhead cheerleader he'd had the hots for in high school."

It was delicate, and if she didn't already have the information, Ellen would have figured this was too much of it: "Gracie mentioned that your ex had remarried. And that it didn't seem to be working out…"

"Oh, that's for sure. He's fat as a breeder sow now and he looks like he's ten years older than he is. I took her to see him once…"

"Only once? That's sad. I mean, when a couple split up and the co-parenting angle doesn't work out."

Mrs. Ogburn looked at Ellen quizzically, as though the idea of trying to maintain social decorum and say 'the right thing' wasn't nonsensical when discussing a noumenon—unless the noumenon happened to be around; in which case, you tried to be on your best behavior.

"Oh, you don't understand. Gracie hardly recognized her father, but the thing is, he didn't recognize us at all. And it had only been a month since the divorce."

"I don't follow. What are you saying?"

"I already said it. It was that day with her father that I finally determined what she is: A noumenon—the opposite of a phenomenon. It's intense, I know; it's from Immanuel Kant, but they existed long before him I suspect. Look up Critique of Pure Reason, if you like—it's about the elementary categories of understanding. It's about phenomena and noumena, the plural; a phenomenon is anything that can be apprehended by the senses; a feature of matter, energy or space-time. A noumenon is not. Gracie is not of this plane of reality—well, she is, but her category—as Kant calls it, her 'predicament'—is not. What's more, she can place people... elsewhere, strictly by intuition. I have no clue how it works, but it happened with our neighbor in Hartford when Gracie was only eight years old: There was a widow next door, an old woman, half senile, always upset about some minor thing or other. You know how old people are, freaked over nothing, tantrums beyond proportion to the incident. She went out of her gourd when a kid's toy ended up in her yard by mistake. That day, I remember, Gracie was recovering from the measles, and she wasn't quite herself yet. Or, perhaps I need to rephrase that: She was herself. The widow went ballistic over a Frisbee in her delphiniums and immediately accused Gracie of having thrown it there. The old bag really blew a gasket, and naturally, I came outside to smooth the situation over; I showed up just as the widow was saying, "I wish my Maury were here! By God, he'd run you little punks right out of…" And with that, little Gracie gave her a look of such malevolent disgust that it scared the bejeebers out of me—I'd never seen anything so formidable, and I'd hoped never to see that look again, or what happened next: Maury's greenish, fetid, half-putrefied corpse suddenly appeared in the Amish porch swing, rocking with the breeze…"

Ellen tried to speak, but the words in her brain couldn't quite find her lips. She sank into the sofa, which was still festooned in bubble wrap from the move. "Nobody else was home—nobody else saw it," said Mrs. Ogburn. "Only me, only the widow, only… Gracie. I screamed, the old lady collapsed, but Gracie shrugged. Shrugged and went back inside while I called 911."

Mrs. Ogburn continued: "I didn't know… I couldn't know, but I could guess. I know what I heard, what I saw… And it didn't help when Gracie seemed surprised when the police cars pulled up. She said, and with lunar passivity: 'What's the fuss all about? I gave the bitch what she asked for…'"

Ellen caught her breath. Mrs. Ogburn remained standing, gauging Ellen's reaction, then said, "You do understand what I'm driving at, right?"

Ellen sputtered, "You're not suggesting that Gracie had anything to do with Ryan's disappearance…? Are you?"

"Which Ryan?" answered Mrs. Ogburn behind the faintest hint of a wistful smile. "Both? We moved after the incident—I insisted. I didn't have to push… as far as anyone knew, there was some psycho on the loose in the neighborhood, robbing graves and playing sick, gruesome pranks—which, in a way, was true. I know this much: The week before my son went missing, the two children were fighting constantly. Ryan Jr. was in a gladiator craze after seeing that stupid movie… and he kept bashing Gracie on the head with empty rolls of wrapping paper and things, screaming, 'We who are about to die salute you.' She told him to stop, pleaded with him to stop, threatened him if he didn't stop, but all he'd say was, 'A sister should know when she is conquered'."

Wide-eyed, Ellen clutched the sofa's arm so tightly that the little packaging bubbles began to pop.

Mrs. Ogburn went on. "It was the largest manhunt the state had ever undertaken, but nothing turned up. No clue, no lead, no evidence; nothing. Three weeks into the search, I finally steeled up enough courage to confront Gracie about it. 'Is Ryan with the gladiators now?' I asked, and she replied with that annoying, incessant, passive-aggressive shrug of hers, 'Seriously? Do you think he survived the first round?'"

It sounded exactly like Gracie, Ellen thought. And Mrs. Ogden finished: "With Ryan Sr., though, there could be no doubt. As I said, we tried to visit him at his new home, a double-wide trailer in Villa Grove, and the new wife answered the door. What a piece of work—tattoos, denim skirt, string-bikini top, something out of Jerry Springer. There was a dysfunctional brood behind her, farty little porkers, and the thing was, they were obviously Ryan's—the resemblance was not only disconcerting, it was undeniable. The same chin, the same blue eyes. It was an alternate reality—my first thought was that he'd been living a double life all these years, but when he rolled in from some rear bedroom, half-drunk, shirtless, he looked at us with such complete bafflement that it was obvious he had no idea who we were. When we left, the new wife was accusing us of being the double life…"

Somewhere in the middle of this final, fascinating, awful, disturbing chapter, Ellen had begun to shudder, and by the time the story ended, she had filled in any blanks that applied to her. With a final yip of horror, she understood the implications of having left Gracie alone with petulant, petty, pusillanimous Mr. Wolcott and his laundry list of gripes, and without the slightest shred of Andover geniality, she rose from the bubble wrap and tore from the house.

Mrs. Ogburn was not in the least bit insulted, of course—Mrs. Ogburn understood.

Ellen knew she was too late before she'd even reached her car— knew it before her phone rang and Joshua Champney shared the latest drama with exaggerated flourishes: Nobody could find Mr. Wolcott, and they were in the process of searching the barn from bottom to top. By the time she arrived at the Andover Community Theater, they'd expanded their manhunt to the parking lot and the surrounding woods.

She didn't join them, because there was no point. She understood that implicitly, viscerally, comprehensively. She went inside and found Gracie sitting in the third row of funeral home chairs, arms folded, legs splayed out in front of her, her bland smirk halfway between boredom and glee. Ellen couched the question carefully, like you'd tiptoe through a minefield. "Can you bring him back?"

"I could," shrugged Grace. But you probably don't want me to. He was born a hundred fifty years ago, remember? He died of the flu in 1918 and I imagine he's looking pretty King Tut by now."

Naturally, they canceled Agrippina—they had no leading man. The Ogburns moved away so quickly that they didn't even need to remove the bubble wrap from the sofa. In early November, the following notice appeared in both the Andover Sentinel and the Andover Herald :

'After forty glorious years, it is with bittersweet regret that we announce the disbanding of the Born-In-A-Barn Players. While cast members have opted to pursue other exciting opportunities, the beloved barn that has hosted over a thousand productions since the tenure of Agneta Bjornborg is scheduled for demolition in the spring. The land has been sold to Walton International, who plans to build a Walmart Supercenter as the anchor store of the proposed 1.5 million square foot Andover Mall.'

WHERE PEOPLE SHOULDN'T BE

Something wasn't copacetic at Hillcrest Cemetery—there was stirring among the statues, motion near the mausoleums—night was descending with fury, and there were people where people shouldn't be.

This is something you wouldn't notice from the street. To see it, you'd have to get down and dirty, hide behind a grave marker or a marble shrine and keep watch. Then, if you waited long enough, you'd see the two gaunt figures as they slunk across the grounds, winding among the headstones, furtive but clumsy, loping but languid, finally wedging open the wrought iron bars of the Ives memorial, forcing past the oaken doors and collapsing on dirty sleeping bags in a drug stew.

They were Dusty and Acorn, a pair of bright, jittery homeless kids from nearby Lincoln, and the windowless mausoleum was where they'd been crashing and chipping for the past few nights. Cemeteries were ideal places for throwaways like them to set up camp, because they were isolated and police rarely came to roust out living people like they did in city parks. Vagrancy was illegal in Lincoln, and the week before, the cops had upended the makeshift cardboard shelter under the Central Street bridge where they'd been living, and they'd loaded up on gear and taken a vacation into middle of the state, which Dusty called 'the boom-docks'.

He was a tall, rangy kid with antic blond dreadlocks spilling from his triple hoodies and a wispy yellow beard. Although disconnected from most conventional things, Dusty had somehow tapped into the style of masculinity that drives street culture. He was handsome despite a wonk eye that put some people off, but Acorn thought was he handsome because of the eye, not in spite of it.

Acorn wore a red bandanna and a loose tank top that read 'Undernourished Retards' across the front, and as they settled into their little sanctuary within the sanctuary, her eyes glittered—half with empathy for the deceased, half with the kind of voyeuristic fascination with which she viewed her new circumstances.

Telling stories was a vital thread in their squalid, gloomy, self-contained universe, and all that day, as they dove dumpsters in their new town, she'd been chattering about their fellow tenant in the Ives memorial. There was a single sarcophagus within it, and it contained the remains of Minnie Francis Ives, who had passed away only six months earlier. Wrapped together in wads of damp, dirty L.L. Bean cotton flannel, sailing through the tail end of MDMA dreamscapes, Acorn created a narrative for Minnie Ives, filled with the sort high-blown dramatics with which she embellished her own:

To anyone who would listen, and even to those who tried not to, she'd explain her homelessness like this: "When I was ten, I was molested by my dad, who was an international banker, so I ran away and became a ward of the state and everybody I lived with from that point forward gave me Seconal and raped me more, so now I live on the streets."

In fact, she had grown up a shabby apartment with her single mother, a home health aide with certificates in Parenting Skills and Basic Relapse Prevention, which was ironic since she was an oblivious parent who smoked a lot of marijuana. Acorn had hit the pavement at fifteen and not looked back.

She earned money by eating beef stew out of an empty Alpo container and soliciting donations from passersby she swindled into a combination of disgust, fascination and pity. That's where Dusty had found her, squatting in front of a Starbucks, and told her she was "profound and measured"—and that's all it had taken to win her heart.

For his part, Dusty claimed he'd come home from high school one day to find father dead, and that since they were living on social security, he was promptly thrown out of the rent-subsidized apartment. Acorn had never verified the truth of that tale because she couldn't care less; it was victimy enough to suit her sense of righteous indignation. Dusty also said that he'd taken an IQ test at fourteen and scored 140. Since then, the only job he'd ever held besides selling Newports for a dollar on the corner was a stint at a towel and linen warehouse, which he quit after two days because why would a guy with an IQ of 140 submit to menial jobs?

He stayed on the streets because the obsessive-compulsive bureaucracy of state-run shelters was more than his wise brain could handle: "One time when I had a fever of 105," he'd pronounce, "I went to a hostel and stayed three hours left with fleas. Chose the streets over those shoeboxes in a New York second. Eggbeaters, bedbugs and baloney sandwiches."

Somehow, though, these new digs had become for them a stabilized environment, and the lure of stability was a lodestar. They found immense value in a single point of unchanging of reference, and it is hard to imagine an environment more stable than a tomb. Dusty claimed that cemeteries were huge tracts of living space that mortal beings ignored, and the draw of a sepulcher so solid that you couldn't check your email messages struck him as post-modern perfection.

That night, as Dusty prepared the cut of heroin that would be their warm milk at bedtime, Acorn droned on about her imaginary companion, Minnie Ives.

"People echo," she insisted. "I see Minnie as this old classic dame like from Gone with the Wind times, a big hoop skirt and all this stuck up sort of Southern elegance. She adored handsomeness and fine manners, and I see this epic fucking scene for her as a girl, sneaking away from the big house to meet her secret black lover. Her hair curls around her shoulders while a big buck in oversized boots and a strapping chest peels off her flowered dress; they're standing by a smelly swamp underneath a tree all drippy with moss, having raunchy, angry sex in the mud…"

The interior of the mausoleum was hot and cramped; the walls were damp and in the candle light, eerie flickers bounced off the granite vaulting. There were few sounds in a rural cemetery at night, and even the booming thunder from a summer storm barely filtered through.

"She's from one of those big plantation mansions," Acorn went on, "down some pike or lane outside a snooty town like Madison; her dad was a horse breeder and she loved horses beyond what was healthy—they were big phalluses to her when she rode them and she could feel it all the way to the cock socket. She wanted to fuck horses, but the idea was too wicked, so she invented a complex, forceful personality for her own horse, called..." She paused to think of the right horse name, "...Acromantula. She hated the church where they went so she made Acromantula her pagan god and he represented triumph and understanding and was her romantic focus until she discovered black boys..."

The heroin was the same color as the polished royal-sable granite on the floor of the mausoleum, and Dusty packed it into the Stericup from the methadone clinic on E. Pearl, then squirted a syringeful of water over it. He was intent and focused, but still listening to Acorn. Her ability to spin reality out of the ether was amazing to him even when he wasn't floating through fogs of Ecstasy.

"She was eight-seven when she died. Minnie is a weird name for a white chick. Most Minnies I can think of were black."

"Only Minnie I can think of is Minnie Mouse," said Dusty. "She's pretty white."

"Naw, her and Mickey are blacker than Shaka Zulu. I think

Minnie's Mandingo was Idris Elba black, big and virile and she
was a repressed Southern belle down with jungle fever."

"Man, you are getting into this fantasy way too heavy, boo."

"What echoes do you hear?" she asked.

Dusty swished the Stericup carefully over the candle flame,
watching tiny particles rise to the surface. That's how he
measured the purity of the stuff, because he didn't always have the
hustle to score the best cuts. This stuff happened to be seriously
pure for a change. "I don't hear echoes like you do," he said.
"My world is more finding logic in the surreal. Patterns in the
structural intricacies. If I had to guess though, I'd say it's more
like she was a rich old broad whose kids stuck her in a nursing
home until she croaked."

"What kind of home?" said Acorn. "One of those swanky one,
probably. With gourmet chefs and fitness centers. God, what if
they had stables and a riding club and she was still hot for horses
after all these years…?"

"You always find art in the excrement," Dusty marveled, placing
a wadded piece of a cigarette filter into the cup, watching it poof
up. "That's noble. Me, I slip a wire inside the cracks. The nursing
home isn't swank, it's wretched. The lobby smells like piss, the
food is cold and the old people have bed sores big as golf balls
that bleed and pus. This old broad is rich alright, but her children
want every nickel of it, and she's all messed up with Alzheimer's
and doesn't know if she's sitting in shit or shinola. The staff

punches in and drinks and plays cards, and they have this one three hundred pound nurse whose ass looks like it's sculpted out of black butter, and whenever a resident complains, she points out the window to the cemetery across the street."

"That is really bleak," Acorn said with the unmistakable fetor of awe in her voice. "Your mind goes to strange places."

Dusty shrugged. "I've embalmed my brain in caustic fluid."

But that was all the talking space they had, because it was time to embalm themselves in caustic fluid.

He drew it into the syringe and dosed them both. As they drifted, Dusty said, suddenly: "Mini-Me was white."

It took Acorn a second because she'd been clocked with a velvet hammer, but then she got it and laughed until drool came out of the corner of her mouth and she fell away. In another moment, Dusty had curled into the damp sleeping bag beside her and was also incoherent, sailing off to other lands, other shores and other sanctuaries far from the tomb of Minnie Ives.

Agatha Morley all her life grumbled at dust like a good wife.

Dust on a table, dust on a chair, dust on a mantle she could not bear.

She forgave faults in man and child, but a dusty shelf would set her wild.

She bore with sin without protest, but dust thoughts preyed upon her rest.

This was a poem that Minnie Ives had read in the 1960s, and at the time, she had scoffed, because she wasn't the sort of woman who'd ever been, or ever would be, a good wife. Or any kind of wife, come to that. She was a determined spinster, and she had colored help to worry about the dust, and although she'd fire a maid if she found a dusty shelf as quick as drop a sweater in the cloying, clinging afternoon heat, neither was she the type to worry over a dusty table over the faults of men—and the faults of men were legion.

She wouldn't—as her own mother used to phrase it— strain at a gnat, then swallow a camel. Minnie Francis Ives thought very highly of herself, and she was not, nor would ever be, Agatha Morley.

Someone she thought less highly of us was her grandnephew Winfield Ives, who had been born out of wedlock to her only sister's only daughter, and Minnie had described him to one of her hired people as a boy 'ugly enough to make an atheist curse God.'

Her loyalty to her father Andrew C. Ives was unshakeable into eternity, however, and she visited his mausoleum often—it stood next to the one she had built for herself right after he died. She lived in the house where she'd always lived, just beyond shouting distance of Hillcrest then, although now, the town's residential section had usurped the woods and fields that had once surrounded the place. It was near the First Baptist Church and it was near the textile mill complex her father owned, which had once employed half the town while being purposely built outside it to dodge taxation. It had closed in 1969, not long after she'd read the Agatha Morley poem, and she had lived alone, with her handful of domestics, peering through her gold spectacles and down her long nose at the town, treating the citizens with contempt and referring to them as a parcel of boobs.

Her people died off one by one, her Negroes grew too old to be useful or moved on or, and in the end, when she herself had begun to grow feeble, she understood that however alien and repellant he was to her, she had little choice but to order her grandnephew Winfield—the last living Ives beside herself—to move in as caretaker.

To Winfield, who'd been running a failing welding business out of the back of a DuraMax shed in a vacant lot surrounded by tumble-down fences, the opportunity was quite irresistible—the realization that if he played his cards right he stood to inherit whatever was left of his grandfather's estate, or at least, the house and the property itself, came at a time when his every other option ended in a solid brick wall.

As it happened, despite the odds, despite the quirks and eccentricities of which both the Ives, senior and junior, were susceptible, Winfield was handy enough to take care of the repair work and greedy enough to play nursemaid when his old aunt demanded it.

Her biggest infirmity, however—the one of which the old

housemaid Glorietta would have most vocally warned had she
not taken another job in Lincoln the week before he hauled the
trailer over to the paddock behind the estate where cattle had
once grazed—was not physical. It was within the confines of her
mind as a damp, embracing fever; an enveloping haunt:

She saw people where people shouldn't be.

The affectation had plagued her since childhood, and it wasn't a
whim, not a sixth sense or a talent. She knew that. The people she
saw weren't there—she knew that too. It was a movement among
the peach trees, a tick of a whitetail or a flash of something
ultimately not clothed in flesh; it was trick of a moonbeam on the
window pane that looked like a face—but it was constant, and it
was endless, and it was very nearly every day.

Like everyone in town, the chief of the Hillcrest police
department had known the Ives family for decades—his daddy
had worked for Minnie's daddy, and she was 'prosperous Hillside'.
His name was Royson Skimper, and he was a slow-moving,
soft-voiced man, silver-haired and otherwise colorless except
for unnaturally pink lips, and he'd been out to the old estate so
many times that it defied counting. The visits were the same—
he'd talk to the hired hands, walk around the grounds with a
flashlight and use his slow, sweet drawl to convince Mrs. Ives that
what she'd seen was a figment of her imagination, or at worst a
passing tramp or itinerant worker who might have holed up in an
outbuilding to sleep. He would assure her that of all the terrors
that plague children, or adults who cling to childish fantasies,

none is more terrifying that the idea that there are people where they shouldn't be.

He understood that, he'd smile; he felt it himself: Who could sleep a wink without first banishing the idea that someone is there, outside the window, looking in at you? Who could fetch something from the cellar wondering if there was some strange man among the shadows? After a glass of peach sweet tea or a cup of the hot stuff on chilly nights, the spare, spectacled woman would see the logic, then they'd talk about the old times and he'd promise to send a squad car by the property throughout the night to ensure that there were no extraneous people in the yard, lurking on the wraparound porch, shuffling through the coal cellar, peering from the cupola, or any of the thousand spots she claimed to have seen them.

And a week later, he'd be summoned back again. This went on, with ebbs and flows in the intensity of the initial, panicked phone call, for the entire length of time he'd been police chief.

But now Skimper was dead, and Minnie still saw people where people shouldn't be, and the burden of rooting them out or convincing her that they were the shreds of shadows or a mirage of fancy fell to Winfield Ives.

He was a vast, balding man, by then on the downside of a squandered life. At twenty, he'd married a thirteen-year-old from Lincoln who had produced three children in three years, all of whom died. They'd spent the next two years snarling at each other like rabid dogs, and then she'd gone back to her parents and they'd never spoken again. He learned the trade of welding from the owner of a Sinclair station where he'd worked and gone into a parody of a business in the vacant lot, taking odd jobs when they came up, easy stuff like installing railings, dangerous stuff like modifying diesel tanks, scoring the occasional professional gig even though he didn't even have a license, but for the most part, he'd subsisted on food stamps, EBT cards, and a bit of judicious shoplifting at Logan's Cash Saver.

When Meridey, Miss Ives' teenage garden boy came to his trailer to fetch him, eyelids throbbing with the nervous tic that came on when dealing with vast, dumb, secretive white men, Winfield's face, which still looked like his baby face, bulged with confusion, which frightened Meridey even more. But after he passed on the summons, Meridey didn't stop to worry—he was on his way out of town to follow Glorietta, who was his mother.

Meridey was the last of Minnie's hired hands to fly the coop, and she was firm with her uncouth relative when he appeared beneath her portico in his shirtsleeves, hangdog, deferential, forcing a courteous smile while chewing gum with his mouth open—it was the best he could do. He was thus engaged as her handyman, her chauffeur and her cook—he had some rudimentary skills resulting from his life as a bachelor; she was a despot and he was mechanical enough to learn some recipes. When pressed, of course, she begrudged him the acknowledgement of his DNA, the last of her line, and he assumed that his battle for destiny had somehow been won: He'd hit the next-of-kin lottery, to be paid in full upon her demise.

Winfield Ives was not clever enough or aggressive enough to plot murder, and for the next fifteen years, the psychological climate in which Winfield Ives and his Aunt Minnie lived together was unrelenting depressed and unhealthy. She was so used to being surrounded by her social inferiors that she knew of no behavior other than hideous condescension, and Winfield was her inferior in everything but surname.

The once-stately house required mollycoddling, and Winfield did what he could in the firm expectation that it would one day be his. He drudged about the place for the same pay as Meridey, which is to say, not much. He plugged and he ground, he replaced the ornate trims to the best of his meager talents and painted the gallery; he fetched whatever needed fetching and took buckets of water from the cellar when it flooded. In truth, the old place was crumbling from its fragile foundation to the rooftop observatory, and was quite beyond Winfield's ability to restore—nonetheless, over the decade and half they shared, he was fond of reminding anyone in town, from Logan's Cash Saver to the Rexall Drugs to the Dewdrop Inn, that the Ives House had been a shambles when he'd come and was now pretty enough to be a museum.

And all the while, Minnie Frances Ives persisted in seeing people where people shouldn't be, and indeed, the more enfeebled she became, the more real her phantoms seemed. Day and night, she chimed for Winfield—there was a man in her closet, a face in the dormer, a scurrying figure on the ell. From her third story bedroom, she could see people in the yard, sitting on the veranda, prowling near the paddock, moving past the old corncrib and

261

congregating by the old carriage house. She saw Negroes dart from the chimney pent and white equestrians by the antique hitching post to which no horses had been hitched since the nineteenth century.

To Minnies Ives, they were what dust was to Agnes Morley, and when she could, she identified her people by name: Some thus identified were alive and still lived in town, others were dead and used to live in town, still others were amalgamations of people she'd known as a girl. Unlike Agnes Morley's dust, of course, ultimately, none were actually there.

Winfield Ives maintained his cool through it all, and in fact, the older his aunt got and the less likely it was that she'd survive another winter, the easier it became. He'd sniff in every corner where she'd seen her people, examine outbuildings and sweep the grounds, finally reporting back, sweat glistening on his fat bald head, trying to be accommodating: "If they was there then, Auntie, they ain't there now."

One day, when his aunt had not signaled for her tea at tea hour, he climbed to the third floor of the Ives House and found her stone cold dead. As to what killed her in the end, he had no interest, nor in attending the funeral, which like her had been spare and thin, nor had he appeared at her internment within the granite mausoleum with the iron bars and the oaken door.

The will was the only further use he had for the old woman, and the day after his aunt's remains had been sealed within the tomb, he was seen standing outside the law office of Bryson Davis, mouth open, grinning, chewing gum. Crafty old Davis was the local probate attorney; he had been in Hillcrest for half a century and now mostly played poker while practicing. a little law on the side. And he let Winfield down as gently as possible: "The testator—being your aunt—had just about run through the last of her daddy's dollars—another year, she'd have been destitute. Stopped paying her colored help, that's why they all up and left— you didn't figger that out, son?"

He hadn't, but that was only a part of the equation: "The property, though. She ain't run through that, has she?—that's a hundred acres prime oilseed land. And the house? I been punchin that joint up for fifteen years, till it looks like a goddamn museum."

"And so it shall be, my boy—sorry. Your aunt bequeathed the entire estate, lock, stock and crumbled manse, to the Hillcrest Historical Society in the memory of your uncle—great granduncle, technically—Andrew C. Ives."

That was the size of it, apparently, and according to Davis, contesting the will was pointless—there wasn't enough money left to depose witnesses, even if any could be found willing to testify to his latent devotion of the estate, to his aunt, to the family fortune. The best he might hope for is a caretaker's position once the Andrew C. Ives Museum opened—something for which, Davis noted, Winfield might be uniquely qualified.

For Winfield Ives, with the wasted years behind him, it was back to his DuraMax shed in the vacant lot surrounded by tumble-down fences on the outskirts of town, and to add further insult to injury, his trailer overlooked the Hillcrest Cemetery where Minnie's granite mausoleum shone like a polished black bijou in the dying evening sunlight

Inside the tomb, Dusty and Acorn fluttered and hovered on their dope cloud, unaware that Winfield had seen them skittering through the graveyard the night before. Blissful beneath their chemical blanket, they didn't realize that when Winfield had found their sleeping gear and detritus that day, he'd been relieved beyond measure to discover that his dead aunt's capacity to hallucinate was no more hereditary than her house had been, and when he saw people where people shouldn't be, they were actually real—even if they turned out to be nothing more than grungy squatters disturbing in the sacred rest of a mingy, stingy, dingy shrew.

Nor could Dusty and Acorn have known that the fantastic tales they'd woven about Minnie Frances Ives' life was pale in comparison to the real one, and, had they managed to remain awake, they might even have been amused by the their own role in the final chapter.

But they were completely out of it, oblivious as Winfield set up the cordless arc welder he'd dragged down from his lonely shed, nor did they smell the acrid stink of burnt argon as he fired it up and went to work on the iron bars, nor did they hear him muttering imprecations as he welded them shut, and it actually was many, many hours before they realized, to their abject and unredeemable horror, that they would remain, for measureable eternity, where they shouldn't be.

Cruel, perhaps—but subtlety was lost inside Winfield's pale, bald, stupid, vindictive head. Aunt Minnie was beyond seeing the irony in the thing, but then again, so was Agnes Morley and her plague of dust.

The final stanzas in that poem, which Minnie Frances Ives would have shared with anyone who asked, was:

Agatha Morley is sleeping sound six feet under the moldy ground.

Six feet under the earth she lies, with dust at her feet and dust in her eyes.

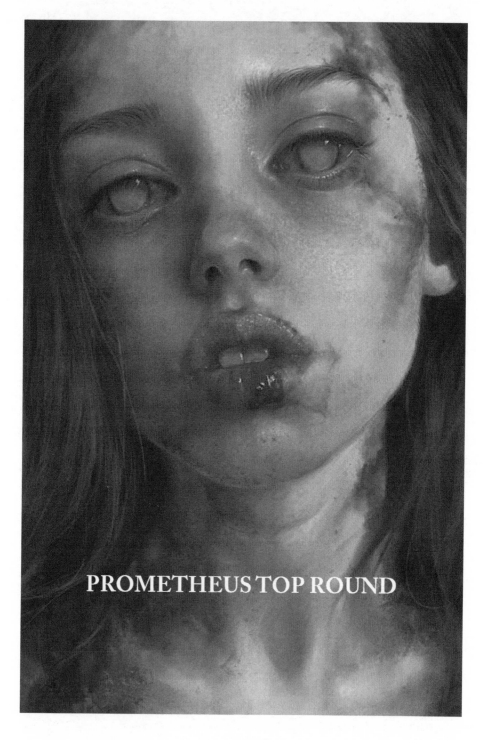

PROMETHEUS TOP ROUND

Secret societies were then in vogue in the universities of Europe, especially among students who fancied themselves part of an erotic illuminati, so it was inevitable that these three deviant fellows—students at Ingolstädter Alte Anatomie—would decide to form one too.

According to social pecking order, the least to the leader, they were Johann Georg Knigge, son of a Amtmann shoemaker, Cornelius Eck from a family of Viennese merchants and the most refined, aristocratic, clever and irreparably evil of the three, Petrus Fuchs. He was the son of the Electorate of Bavaria and an epicurean of the ghastly glories described in Milton, defended by Pliny and defined by Othello:

"I will kill thee and love thee after."

Not that the trio had the inclination to kill anybody; it was the loving afterward that interested them. And this strange hobby, they decided, should be classified and catalogued as a geheime Gesellschaft—a secret order.

In Fuchs' apartment, at midnight, with candlelight flickering on the stained window panes, they tallied a list of those clubs with which they were already familiar. There was the Hellfire Club at Oxford, the Chats-Chauds of Collège Royal Bourbon, the Mystic Order of the Veiled Virgin at Barcelona's Estudi General, the Hermetyce Society of Zamość, the Luciferians of Cambridge.

Each, in its own way, was formed to flout the repressive prudery of the times; each was a freewheeling forum for hedonism. Some held Black Masses and swore allegiance to Satan, others experimented with the outer reaches of sexuality, prowling the night streets in search of drunken Jägers to bend over in public toilets, others held lavish midnight orgies often attended by those who, by day, were members of the respectable body of students.

Upon these templates, with the winter wind howling in Ingolstadt's steeples, they formed their geheime Gesellschaft with the intention of out-debauching them all.

"You've heard the fuddled lectures of rattlebrained old professors at the pulpit, boys," Fuchs announced, his voice brimming with confidence and swagger, "—now hear mine: Our motto is from Paradise Lost, Book 9—'Defaced, deflowered, and now to death devote'. Our society is forthwith christened 'Pygmalion Unbound'."

Fuchs had long, luxuriant auburn hair he combed back from a noble forehead that spread like a vast barren above his sculpted nose—he had aristocracy in his blood, and, quite prominently, in his maxillaries. In contrast, Knigge, the shoemaker's spawn, was hunched and uncouth; his face was fat and florid as if scorched by flames and spittle bubbled eternally on his red lips—not only that, but he always smelled slightly ripe, as though he couldn't entirely bathe away whatever was contaminating him. Eck made up the middle ground: A lanky, saturnine, ash-colored scholar given to nondescript clothing, with a face you would forget five minutes after meeting him.

Physically, three more contrasting fellows you could not find assembled in any solitary room in Ingolstadt. And yet, they shared a secret pathology—a singular warped predilection, and this, in fact, was how they'd met and how they'd formed their unhallowed allegiance, first among damps of the graveyard and the charnel-houses of the Old Town, and now, in the candle-lit cell atop an otherwise respectable boarding house:

It seemed that they all shared a physical attraction to young female cadavers.

The most lyrical of them was Fuchs, of course, and he poetized the inclination like this: "The pristine stillness of death, like a shining white stone on life's throbbing shore—immobile alabaster, submissive, serene, sensual, silent…"

Verse aside, whether they'd admit it or not, all three men had been raised in loveless, violent homes and had an irrevocable dread of lust in general, and sexual women in particular. Communicating with whores were therefore out of the question, as were normal alliances made with the daughters of prominent families, as was standard for their station. They saw animate women, with daily needs, incessant entreaties and endless demands, as a rational threat to their masculinity:

"We love the dead in their utter submission and girdling vulnerability," Fuchs informed them in his most self-validating hypothesis to date, "because it arises from neither rationality nor morality."

As has been pointed out, none of them were murderers, but with the era's epidemic eruption of diseases and an outbreak of typhus then in full swing, there was no need to be. Typhus was the perfect craftsman, because not only was it not contagious, it left its victims relatively unscathed. The need for specimens for the school's anatomy lectures ensured a roaring trade in stolen corpses—it was the unspoken skeleton in the closet of every medical college of the age. So well-established was the industry in Ingolstadt that the cemetery at Church of Our Lady was protected by guards and dogs and armored man-traps, and the rich were often buried in iron coffins. The extremely poor, who were generally piled in pauper's graves, made easier pickings.

Although they'd been vaguely aware of each other's existence in school, the trio learned of their shared proclivity through mortuarial word-of-mouth: There were, among the local guild of grave robbers, certain specialists willing to accept lists of characteristics desired for your corpse, and, so long as you could afford a the extra few Kreuzers, they'd hover like vultures above neighborhoods with the highest mortality rates and swoop on those newly interred who fit your bill. The medical school was less picky about their purchases, but our three young ghouls preferred a unique type of carcass with precise attributes—hair color, body type, age and fairness of features all were vital to them and they were willing to pay for them—and occasionally, inevitably, their lists overlapped.

In this way, they met and reveled in details of their shared perversion

As morbid as thanatophilia seems, of course, their fellow student—deemed normal—also measured the desirability of Ingolstadt women based on anatomical features: The rump of one, the bosom of another; this set of juicy lips, that turn of an ankle. The only legitimate difference in these mindsets was that some men preferred their flesh on the hoof, others, on the slab.

In any case, the mission these three set for themselves that cold night in the flat above Sahlstrasse was as chilling as the gusts outside the mullion: The College would soon close for the jolly holidays, whereupon the students and professors alike would abandon the spacious offices and yawning classrooms to return to their homes for two week's respite.

If anyone chose to remain behind, they would have the baroque institution quite to themselves.

Fuchs' forceful personality ensured that Pygmalion Unbound would be among the few to forego the seasonal break, at least until they'd finished the task they'd set for themselves. This would be their defining act of depravity, their initiation ceremony to the club and their centerpiece—their chef-d'oeuvre. Until it—until she—was completed, it would be their one thought, their one conception, their one purpose.

In the truest sense of the Cypriot sculptor whose name they had purloined, they were determined to assemble the perfect

Aphrodite. Only, unlike Pygmalion, they wouldn't carve her out of marble, they'd sculpt her from human flesh.

As students at Old Anatomy, they had access to a chemistry laboratory and a two-story operating theater with a dissecting table on the ground floor, a gallery for student observers above and a glass ceiling allowing overhead illumination; it was considered to be one of the finest such classrooms in Europe. This was absolutely required for their purpose, as was ready access to the chemicals used in in the preservation of tissue: Although the science of embalming was then in its infancy, they needed their creation to withstand, entirely uncorrupted, the span of their mutual interest.

Because, the ultimate plan was to fabricate for themselves a necro-goddess; the perfect paradigm of erotic expiration—she would be, according to Fuchs, their consummate reliquiae: "Our agalma; part fantasy, part nightmare, part madhouse."

Several cadavers were at the moment being bundled up by Bienewitz, the industry's most reliable resurrection man. Upon their delivery to the medical theater, each member would choose the body he preferred, then, with the surgical tools available in the dissection room, each would remove that portion of the body he liked best—everything to be done, of course, according to their rank: Fuchs would choose the head, Eck the torso, and the poor, fat shoemaker's son, the limbs—whereupon, the latter would employ his hereditary trade with needle and thread to assemble from the severed parts into a single, transcendent, ivory-skinned

272

Aphrodite.

Then, to complete the carnal horror, each would spend an hour alone with their creation—again in order of social rank: Fuchs would go first, then Eck would be in for sloppy seconds, and finally, the poor, fat shoemaker's son would take his turn.

This would be the grand initiation ceremony to the newly-formed Order of Pygmalion Unbound, and henceforth, according to Fuchs, their motto would echo that of the great Restoration libertine, the Earl of Rochester: "Much wine has passed with grave discourse, of who does who and does it worse."

As such, in the morning, when the uncouth and fawning Bienewitz had slithered and shuffled and lumbered his way through the cobbled alleys of lower Ingolstadt, beneath the flaking stone of the damp, stark houses where shades were drawn all day, passed the spires and ducal mansions near the Cross Gate and finally turned the wrought iron knob of the medical college, they had their party girls.

Two were sisters—they had passed away within an hour of one another, said Bienewitz—and quite recently. He pried open their eyelids between a knobby thumb and crude forefinger to demonstrate, much as you might display a fish's empty orbs in a monger's stall. Indeed, the clarity of their hollow gaze, cast apparently toward the student's gallery above the theater, but in reality, toward nothing, was confirmation of the product's freshness. The sisters had been big, buxom girls and their doughy skin, stone-cold and accordioned with tactile folds and sensual

273

curves, remained pliable. Eck and Knigge lit upon them as their choices and rubbed their hands in anticipation.

As Fuchs leaned in closely to the third, the faint, damp scent of recent death—a peculiar salty smell quite unlike the rankness of decomposition—rose up to meet him. In life she'd been a curly-haired beauty with exquisitely pale lips, now gone slightly blue-grey, and could almost hear the tinkling giggles those fair lips must have loosed in life. Her arms were marred with scratches from the flea bites that had transmitted the typhus to her lithe frame, but her face remained fixed in a sort of ethereal repose suggesting complete, unassailable peace and total acquiescence to the man who hovered over her. Gently, but with a slight tug against her muscle stiffness, he slid back her lids and exposed eyes of striking cobalt blue. They were not quite as translucent as the eyes of the sisters; hers had grown slightly milky. As it happened, this was the was the stage of death that Fuchs found most compelling, and if such a thing were possible in a man of his unorthodox and outré passions, you might say it was love at first sight—his, not hers.

They paid Bienewitz eight guldens for the wares and complimented him on his duty and discretion, assuring him that they couldn't have dreamed of a more ideal ternion of carrion. Through the rest of that day, they sliced and diced, hacked and severed, chopped and amputated, then watched as Knigge— ironically, clutching a crucifix in his needle hand—began to sew them all together.

The supernal head, fringed in raven curls, had been the first appendage removed; Fuchs set it aside on a supply cupboard to prevent it from being marred accidentally. The lids only half closed, and the maiden with the ghastly gaze, obscure with blank indifference, also oversaw the operation.

And then, as the hour grew late, it was her turn—Knigge, still palming his gilded Christ, worked deftly and carefully to attach the sheaves of her neck tissue to the breast of the other, using clever, nearly invisible stitching. Eck, in the meantime, went off in to acquire bed-clothes from several chambers—Witney blankets and the finest eider-down quilt he could find—and within the office of the head surgeon, they made a nest for their apathetic, alluring Aphrodite.

"This shall be our Celestial Bed," said Fuchs, with the flourish and foppery of a true Cyprian poet. "Our bedfellow, ivory-white, brilliantly carved, shall await us on cloths dyed with Tyrian murex…"

They were by then too exhausted to consummate the initiation ceremony, but they looked upon the wonder of their creation for many minutes, doting, then retired to their own apartments to rest, secure in the knowledge that she would be there when they returned, preserved, pristine, pliant and perfect.

And she would be—although, as the corrupt cabal enjoyed the sound sleep of the unapologetically depraved, they never imagined what had happened to her in the meantime.

What they failed to realize was that, all that day, as they worked
their macabre enterprise, another set of eyes was watching them
from a corner of the student's gallery. These eyes were red and
hollow, but, like theirs, quite mortal. It was a fellow student
at the academy, oppressed by a slow fever. He had also stayed
behind over the holidays to work on his own, not dissimilar and
equally loathsome project. Indeed, he had been in the process
of purloining the very instruments they were now using—the
amputation saw, the lancets for opening veins, the crooked
scissors, the probes and forceps and anatomical textbooks—when
he'd heard them enter, and hid.

And so intrigued had he become over the talk and the tone and
the task that he'd stayed.

His name was Victor Frankenstein, and the others knew him
as a sullen, solitary scholar, a pet of the chemistry professor M.
Waldman. The trio was unaware the nature of Frankenstein's
personal experiments, of course—he was not a member of the
Bavarian elite, not part of their society, and moreover, he'd been
conducting his activities in direst secrecy in a cell above his
dormitory. For the past few months, he'd been involved in a work
of inconceivable difficulty and labor: Bestowing animation upon
lifeless matter—science that, for him, was just beginning to bear
living fruit.

Hidden amid the gallery's medical oddities—among cyclopean
and Siamese baby skeletons—Frankenstein watched the
blustering fools below as they slavered over their moribund

maiden. Without a spark of life, he scoffed, she was nothing but a passing schoolboy daydream doomed to fester and within a few days, become food for worms. As he watched, he became increasingly amused and condescending at their simplicity—they had not the slightest inkling of the minutiae of causation, the change from blooming life to the corruption of death and death to life again. And worse, they seemed to prefer the death—their brief window of physical domination over the cold flesh before the inexorable domination of nature proved the stronger foe.

He snorted quietly to himself—she'd fall apart before they'd sated half their passion.

But he gave them this much: She was blue and beautiful, a far more delightful receptacle for restored life than the hulking brute he'd been designing in his attic-room. As he crouched among the slates and iron-framed desks above the dissecting table, he conceived a strange and wonderful idea: His own being was not finished—scarcely begun, in fact; he was still collecting and arranging materials. But he had already procured the apparatus key to his goal; a galvanic battery given to him by M. Waldman. He had not yet tried the machine on anything larger than a cat, and now, it occurred to him that below, a being set tenderly within a eider-down crib, was a specimen custom-made—quite literally—for a more complex trial.

No sooner had the trio extinguished the gas lamps and secured the wrought-iron bolt than he had scurried from covert and wrapped the dead woman—women, actually—in the Witney blankets, and spirited her away to his attic-room laboratory.

Whereupon, he unpacked the battery, slipped one metallic handle into her pursed, pretty mouth and the other past her stiff maidenhead below, averting his eyes as best he could for modesty, then propelled an electrical current through her by a hand-crank attached to copper coils and iron magnets.

The smell of metal salts and singed hair filled the close, chilly cell as he regulated the current, pausing to apply sponges to the contact points and several times to examine the cadaver's matte, half-opened eyes, searching for any flicker of animation, however slight. Perhaps once or twice there appeared an ineffectual twinkle behind her milky blue gaze, perhaps there did not. What Frankenstein knew for certain is that he cranked the brass gears on the Magneto-Electric machine until his arms gave out, and in the end, could not swear that the experiment had produced the results intended. That end came near dawn with another realization: When the trio returned to find their body snatched, they might raise an alarm with the constabulary—they'd claim the corpse had been a dissection experiment condoned by the university, and with the master's office deserted for the holidays, who would testify otherwise? Frankenstein considered the likelihood that someone had seen him removing the bundle from the theater, carrying it across his back through the snowy streets of Ingolstadt, climbing with it many stories to the very top of his dormitory. If so, and if he was thus discovered, all his other work was ruined.

In the end, he carried the ashen Aphrodite back to the theater and arranged her gently, carefully, and delicately, upon her celestial bed.

An hour later, the trio returned, and several hours after that— each having each completed a tryst with the corpse and violated their violet upon that celestial bed—the newly-initiated members of Pygmalion Unbound gathered at the alehouse and, over tumblers of hot wine, discussed the grisly particulars of the experience.

As always, Fuchs took the lead: "The most dainty dumbness, the quaintest quietude. Such perfect silence imbues her every pore, from toe to tongue—she is the tomb made tactual, the demigoddess of death."

He was followed by lanky Eck, normally taciturn, suddenly driven to passionate outcry: "Her silence is encompassing, it is true; her stillness is ardor's sponge. But her perfume above all else—what words can I find to match your own, Fuchs?—you are the bard among us. But her scent, it is, it is…"

"The elixir of eternity?" Fuchs offered, and Eck said, 'Bravo!"

Through it all, Knigge, the corpulent cobbler, remained ineffably morose. He pouted into his punch, frowned and rolled his eyes at his fellows reminiscenced. Finally, when his own speech was required, he turned away entirely and faced the carved wine barrels in the corner.

"Oh, come, come, Knigge" frowned Fuchs, "Whatever is the

matter, dear boy? Are you sore at having been left for last, as usual?"

"It isn't that," he answered, poking out his lower lip like a child.

"Then what?" said Fuchs. "We have just shared the same impiety—the same frame, the identical idol, the corresponding creation—and we found her to be a consummate delight. Which of her attributes could possibly have displeased you?"

Knigge shook his head, and shuffled his feet in a pique of petulance, wiped the spittle from his lips and finally barked it out:

"She spoke," he said.

SIDE EFFECTS

In principle, Miss Tawni did not object to operating on her knees, but this particular morning, the shrink-wrap fit of her outfit—a skanky black Tadashi cocktail number and the elevation of her Dippity Do-oozing bouffant twist—made the convoluted squat required to search behind the steam register all but impossible.

Not only that, but the apartment landing was filthy, the carpet hadn't been vacuumed in decades and she had no tactile competence at the tips of her six-inch fake fingernails, shimmering like fish scales beneath the forty raw watts that struggled down from the cracked overhead fixture. Unfortunately, a rhinestone from her tiara had popped loose, rolled behind the thumping steam cock, and there was not a single gallant soul in sight, either within the vestibule, or on the frosty Detroit streets beyond. By five on a Sunday morning, even the jackers and rapists were tucked safely into bed.

Miss Tawni found that by crouching down, bracing the small of her back against a relatively unfunky patch of wall, lowering her derriere to a point several inches above the rank carpeting, she could avoid soiling or splitting her Lycra Capezios while doing a blind reconnaissance of the furry burrow behind the grate. She grunted in disgust; it was abominably hot and disgusting back there. Now, suddenly, she was grateful for the solitude, since, by necessity, she looked and sounded like she was defecating.

She snagged an artificial nail on a popped screw and swore crudely. There went the fifty dollar hot-manicure and one-tenth of a set of Donita Jones Metallic Eggplant add-ons. Gamely, Tawni grappled on. She made contact with a small, round object, but when she withdrew it, it wasn't the rhinestone after all; more like a mummified cheese ball. She wondered how the rodents had missed it... unless it had already passed through a rodent unscathed. Christ, what a thought! She crooked her head, so that the bouffant do was partially crushed by the window sill, but at least she could wedge her face behind the register. However, with forty watts to work with, it was impossible to make out much. Being six-foot-four didn't help. She'd have tossed in the proverbial towel except that the tiara had been borrowed from her cousin JayShandra, who'd been PMSing when Tawni had usurped it the previous evening and who'd be PMSing when Tawni abdicated it after church that morning. And who tended to be a nasty bitch even on in-between days.

The heavy front door opened. David Lieberwitz, who lived across the hall from Tawni, tromped in wearing a grocery apron. Thick, wet snowflakes perched obscenely on the tip of his nose. He was an oddball; slow as a zombie and about as pale, a white boy living in the middle of a predominantly non-Caucasian war zone. He'd been there at the projects for at least five years; as long as Tawni and Gran'mama had been tenants. In that time, Tawni had shared a few quick words with him, doorstep kind of pleasantries, since they both worked nights, and sometimes arrived home simultaneously, before anybody else was even awake. She'd learned a bit more about his situation from his mail, since it got accidentally jammed into her box more frequently than not. She knew that he'd arrived at the building via a halfway house for runaways. He'd probably been about eighteen at the time, which would have made him twenty-two or three now. He had a sort of downward-skid demeanor that might have made him endearing, but he was creepy and standoffish enough to counteract it.

For sure, he was the alonest motherfucker that Tawni had ever run across. She'd have been willing to bet mascara money that he'd never had a single visitor in the whole time she'd known him. Not even a hooker. He'd never once mentioned a family, never received through Tawni's overly-accommodating mail slot anything that she might have taken as a note from home. Once, on a whim, she'd even asked about it, and he'd grumbled: "Naw, my 'rents...? They're spookier than I am."

To Miss Tawni, he sounded like a suburban kid. A Pop-Tarts and Fruitopia kid from Livonia or Rochester or somewhere. Only Fruitopia kids from Rochester called their parents 'rents. Plus, he had a genuine work ethic. In five years, he'd never drawn a welfare nickel to cover his two sixty per month flat note; he'd been a janitor, a security guard, a pizza delivery boy, sometimes he'd held these jobs all at once; currently, he worked the graveyard shift at the nearby twenty-four hour Ivanhoe Market, where he bagged groceries, put away stock, and hustled along the junkie shoplifters. But strange? Some kind of misfit.

Not that Tawni saw herself much differently; for starters,

biologically, she wasn't even a woman. And not that she gave a shit to begin with. The Oxford projects, a typical, government-subsidized low-rise block of forty-nine units surrounded by gay strip joints, boarded-up buildings, and stores with iron grates, was mostly populated by strung-out losers and space cases. Isolationism was a survival technique. The projects was a good quarantine warehouse for the scum thrown off by the melting pot of society. Insanity being one of the unfortunate side effects of modernity.

David took in the scene on the landing with a puzzled scowl as his nose snow melted and trickled down his chin. Tawni showed him a self-conscious mouthful of pearls: "If you gonna wear a tiara, boyfriend, just make sure you have that bitch pinned down."

"What's the problem?" There was morbid solicitousness in his tone. Tawni explained the problem as would any demure and flirtatious damsel in distress. "David, I done searched, and searched, but lemme tell you, it's darker than Sambo's ass back here..."

David shrugged and went down on all fours, thrust his hand beneath the grate and began to fish around amid the greasy rat droppings, insect shells, spider webs, and sticky fur balls, as readily as if he'd been plucking a mint from a candy dish.

Glancing down, Tawni noticed a ferocious whitehead on the back of his neck. It was bigger than a Kennedy half-dollar. A swollen, infected Vesuvius of a zit, about ready to blow sky-high; it was surrounded by an army of satellite zits, a maroon litter of baby pimples that disappeared in pus waves beneath his apron straps. Tawni had never seen anything quite so grotesque, and she'd seen plenty; it was worse than the skin rashes you got from crystal meth. "Oh, baby, what's wrong with your neck? You got a boil there looks like Whoopee Goldberg in heat."

David glanced upwards. A lock of thinning, oily, black hair dribbled over his face. He looked as if he was considering some urgent revelation. "It hurts like hell, actually. It's a reaction to this hair growth stuff I'm using. Myrnax. Says right on the label it can cause acne." She noted that he continued to stare up at her, taking an inordinate amount of time perusing the length of her tapered leggings. "But, yeah," he frowned. "It must look pretty uncool by now."

"Myrnax is some ugly stuff, baby. Major chemistry in that jar. You outghten be messing with it."

"I guess. But I'm too young to go bald."

"Why, bald ain't so bad, child. Ain't everybody can be a pageant winner like yours truly. Besides, Lord may want you being bald; that's His business. You don't know what kinda trouble you in for if you go tampering with the Lord's business. Lissen up; I ain't just talking to y'all, David, I'm testifying..."

David's position remained fixed. He was ogling her unabashedly, all the way up to her gaff. Tawni stepped back, modestly smoothing her skirt. "Keep it platonic, baby. Remember, this chocolate motherfucking bar got nuts."

David shrugged. Tawni hadn't noticed; he was holding out the rhinestone.

Fifteen minutes later, she was rapping steadily on the door of No. 16. David appeared, still wearing his Ivanhoe apron. Possibly, he slept in it. She noted his employer's incongruous, almost ironic logo: a white knight on an armored stallion parading before a ghetto market. From behind the door chain, unidentifiable, unpleasant odors drifted out, overpowering her Yves Saint-Laurent Rive Gauche. The smells were probably the result of faulty plumbing and dirty dishes. She opted not to speculate. She thrust a tube of Tectirol-Z All-Natural Acne Cream through the gap between the door and the jamb. "Say, David, why don't y'all try this on your neck. It oughta do the job; believe me, when it comes to a peaches 'n' cream complexion, Miss Tawni Porto don't never mess around. Plus, this stuff is some kinda wholesome. Organic, baby. None of those twenty-letter chemicals, like in that damn fool Myrnax." She pointed at the label for effect. "Nothing but jojoba oil and some enzyme found in pussy-willow."

"Yeah?" he said. "I could use a little pussy-willow."

He took the tube, and she could see that he was profoundly

touched and even a little bit pleased with her unexpected succor. As far as Tawni was concerned, that settled the rhinestone-under-the-steam-cock score.

Inside the one-room shithole, David made a five-minute phone call to Candy Cookie and took care of business. He was a compulsive masturbator. Afterwards, he drank four beers, warmed up a can of Spaghettios on the jive little projects stove, flipped down on the ratty corduroy sofa and looked at the Tectirol-Z tube. Pussy-willow enzyme. Fucking jojoba oil. About what you'd expect a cross-dressing Zulu fag to rub on his face. Oh, well. He slathered a greasy handful onto the back of his neck. It stung as it dried and contracted, squeezing out a trickle of pus that ran down the inside of his sweatshirt in a slick, blood-warm rivulet.

A minute later, the back of his head began to tingle. There was an 800 number listed in fine print beneath the active ingredients. *'Toll Free! Call With Questions or Comments!'.*

Comments? What kind of lack-of-life dingledork would actually have a comment to make to a stranger in the middle of the night about some homo zit cream? He had better uses for the phone, the budget notwithstanding. Candy knew the score. Screw budgets anyway. He sucked down a couple more Millers. Only six left; maybe he should have picked up a case. Budgets were for dicks. Still, fifty hours at six twenty five only equaled three hundred twelve before taxes; goddamned camel jockey owners wouldn't pay overtime. And when you stopped and figured it out, like a responsible adult was supposed to, it was the beer and the 900 numbers that got you into trouble.

So, what the hell were you gonna do? He punched up the 800 number. The operator answered on the first ring. Pre-dawn on a Sunday morning! First ring! Imagine that, somebody with even less life than him. The operator asked him to identify the brand name that had caused him his concern, and he nearly hung up in chagrin. But he caught himself, imagining that there were probably dozens of straight guys who used jojoba oil, for any number of reasons.

Besides, there was something about this woman's voice that appealed to him. Something soothing and deliberative. Maternal almost. It was refreshing to speak to such a voice for a change. For one thing, she wasn't asking him for a credit card number or describing genitalia; she was wondering gently if he wanted to make a comment or ask a question about Tectirol-Z All-Natural Acne Cream.

"Make a comment. Well, no, ask a question, really. I mean, what's the deal, you know? It's making my head get the heebie-jeebies. Oh, and it says on the label, like, not to consume alcohol while using this goop. I drank about eight beers so far. Should I be freaked out?"

"That depends," replied the operator in her steady, accommodating tone.

"On what?"

"On whether or not you are currently on any medication for malaria"

"Malaria? What are you, bullshitting me? I'm from Detroit."

"Have you ever had an allergic reaction to Yellow Dye # 5, tartrazine?"

"Huh? What difference does it make?"

"Plenty. What about the preservatives found in fermented sausage? Any sensitivities?"

"I don't know. What's fermented sausage?"

"Salami. Bologna. Ball Park franks. Vienna mini-dogs. Bob Evans Breakfast Links..."

"I hate that kind of crap."

"Well, nitrates are the culprit. Any history of problems associated with gentamicin or tobramycin, or any other aminoglycoside antibiotic, including amikacin, kanamycin, neomycin, netilmicin, or streptomycin?"

"I dunno.... I don't think so."

"What's your name?"

He was briefly startled. "...It's David Lieberwitz..."

"Not to worry about the eight beers, David Lieberwitz, unless you're planning to drive somewhere. See, adverse reactions are often caused by cumulative drug interactions. That's the concern; most of us are walking drugstores, you know. Drug-to-drug reactivity is one of the most overlooked phenomenon in pharmaceutics, especially given the truckload of prescribed medications and the 40% of the American public that uses OTC preparations in a given twenty-four hour period."

"OTC?"

"Over the counter. Brand-namers. Like Tectirol-Z. Or Extra-Strength Hybrium, which in 25 mg doses is used to treat malaria. See, the active compound in Hybrium is hyanine, which when combined with the jojoba in Tectirol interferes with the liver's ability to metabolize alcohol, and prevents the body from eliminating it. Effectively, the combined effects of these products causes you retain and concentrate the booze in your bloodstream until it reaches a toxic level. Nitrate or yellow food coloring-sensitive individuals, making up approximately four point two percent of the population, find this reaction tripled."

"Man, how do you know all this stuff? College, or what? What's your name, lady?"

292

"Mrs. Doosenberry."

"What are you... uh, wearing?"

"A housecoat. Trust me, David; I'm old enough to be your grandmother."

"Well. So, how do you know all this stuff?"

"It's what I do for a living. I'm on call twenty-four hours a day, like it says on the Tectirol label.
All this information I'm giving you is on an FDA database. The mainframe's in my mud room, behind the clothes dryer. Know what I'm doing right now? I'm sitting in front of a CrystalScan computer screen in my den, drinking decaffeinated Folgers and entering information as you feed it to me. An instant later, the myriad potential, predictable, and preventable reactions to the smorgasbord of available medications appears in luminescent green letters."

"You have a cool voice, Mrs. Doosenberry. Know what I'm doing right now?"

"Drinking another beer and playing with yourself?"

He jerked his hand away so hard he spilled his Miller.

"For the tingly scalp, David, the safest product out there is

MiCort; the powder, not the topical salve. Mix it with a pint of lukewarm water, loosely bandage the affected area and change the dressing once every six to ten hours. Of course, excessive perspiration can result. If it does, try Dri-Zine Aerosol.... given that specific pharmaceutical cocktail, there should be no further side effects. Oh, and I nearly forgot, David. While using Tectirol-Z All-Natural Acne Cream, or any OTC product containing vermonyl... that's the clinical term for pussy-willow enzyme... in fact, it's also prescribed for menstrual cramps... you're not suffering menstrual cramps are you?"

"I... I mean, I... I, uh..."

"Gotcha! Anyway, David, if you choose to continue using Tectirol-Z, and want to remain alive, don't consume the following foods: Avocado, fava beans, canned figs, or pickled herring. Are you writing this down? Forgive me; your name...Lieberwitz... you're Jewish, right? Gefilte fish is an no-no. Those foods contain tyramine, which is totally incompatible with vermonyl. Leads to abdominal hemorrhaging and potentially lethal bleeding into the brain. Good night, David."

"Good...?"

The line went dead. He stared at the receiver. Shook his head. Gefilte fish? What the fuck was that? An ever-blinking sign for the Manhole Club, a dive across the street, filled the room with an eerie strobe effect. A patrol car passed by, languidly. He looked at his watch. Five hours till the bar opened. Wonder what Candy was doing right now? On second thought, he could imagine. He applied his twice-daily squirt of Myrnax, and thus, exhausted his roster of pastimes. He scratched his scalp. Passed wind. Smoked a Marlboro Green to kill the smell, watched a column of migrating cockroaches gathering about a tarry scab that had collected around a crack in the ceiling molding... having a fucking field day, those lucky roaches... and fell asleep.

He awoke mid-afternoon with severe, throbbing gastrointestinal pain. It felt like somebody was pile-driving I-beams into his descending colon with rhythmic abandon. Half an hour on the toilet, hunched in a fetal position, nose plugged by his knees, spewing out godawful gallons of blackish muck, led to a momentary cease-fire, allowing him to stagger over to the Ivanhoe... not, as he often did on his day off, to scam on Laquenda, the AM checkout girl with the hypnotic, emerald-colored irises, but to pick up some Lanolyte Plus Extra Strength Diarrhea Relief. Much to Laquenda's personal relief.

Evidentially, the Lanolyte contained rhyphenoxylate and xatrophine, and a supplemental portion of phenylpropagelanine, meant to replenish the electrolytes he'd necessarily flushed into the Detroit river. The label displayed a blatant, boldfaced warning against use if abdominal obstruction was suspected. As far as David was concerned, nine Millers and lukewarm Spaghettios were suspected. He downed a dose of Lanolyte like it was a schnapps slammer, then another dose for good measure, just to get him through an afternoon's worth of schnapps slammers at the Manhole Club. There was an 800 number printed above the manufacturer's address. Toll free. Comments and questions. Just in case.

Before leaving, David heisted a jar of MiCort Powder, and stashed it beneath his woolen Salvation Army pea coat. A coat that he'd been unable to wear since his neck acne had kicked in the month before. If nothing else, the Tectirol-Z had worked like a charm; within the span of a few hours, the mother zit had gathered her brood and split town.

In five years, David Lieberwitz had never once missed a day of work. Anywhere. Didn't matter; he'd limped through shifts with fevers well into three digits, with ripped tendons, fractured bones, pulled muscles, infected eyeball membranes, savagely incapacitating influenzas, bronchitises; he'd shown up grieved, bereaved, drunk, hung-over, high on acid... bosses had wondered if he'd take a day off for his own funeral.... it was little enough to be proud of, of course, but there was no one to nurse him or lay guilt trips on him inside the flat, and nothing much on TV... so an hourly pogue on a budget might just as well gut it out... That was his philosophy. Be a man. Bite the bullet. Until Monday.

By four forty on Monday afternoon, twenty minutes before his shift was supposed to start, he was curled into the tiny space beneath the cluttered counter in his kitchenette, wailing in fitful, infantile spurts, trying to lift his head out of the half-inch of perspiration which his pores had produced since he'd last been able to function. His floor looked like a pipe had burst beneath the sink. He was congested to the point where a garage-worth of cinder blocks might have been piled on top of his chest; moments before, he had hacked out a thick mucus plug, which throbbed and contracted like a tormented snail a few feet away from his face. Pink wheals were spreading across his back, down to his buttocks, as tenacious as kudzu. He was shivering like a wino with Parkinson's disease, which is why he had wedged himself beneath the counter in the first place. The uncontrollable body movement, when he pressed himself against the peeling Wal-Mart lamination, offered some relief from the itching.

Showing up for work would clearly be an obstacle. But one he intended, as always, to overcome. He took the first step. With a Herculean grunt, he rolled to the phone, managed to knock the receiver off the hook, and in several attempts, hammered out the 800 number on the Lanolyte bottle, which, he noted in disgust, bore no advisories as to mucous plugs and muscle spasms.

To his surprise, Mrs. Doosenberry answered the telephone, and on the very first ring. "Of course it's me again, you silly goose."

What were the odds of that? "David," she confided gently. "I'm it. The only operator ever on duty; the sole FDA advisor for consumer products in the United States. Perfect job for a widowed retiree with four grandchildren and a parakeet, don't you think? I work out of a two-bedroom bungalow in upstate

New York, near Buffalo. Overworked? Come on, dear, be realistic. How many people... no offense intended... do you honestly think call a phone number on the back label of diarrhea medicine? Or shampoo? Or toothpaste? I log a call about every six weeks, and usually, it's some pervert with insomnia. Again, no offense intended."

None taken. Actually, David dredged up enough positive delight to briefly counteract his symptoms. Which he then proceeded to describe in technicolor.

There was a faint, electronic clicking from Mrs. Doosenberry's computer. She went on: "I've taken the liberty to initiate a profile on you, David Lieberwitz, tracking your current roster of medications and cosmetics, and calculating the possible adverse reactions you might expect. While it's not part of the job, mind you, it's a little service I've worked up which comes in mighty handy when a concerned consumer such as yourself develops unanticipated side effects related to a specific agent, or to any combination of agents. Understand, of course, that it's a useless exercise unless you are perfectly candid with me related to your product intake. Perfectly candid. You must answer my questions honestly. Remember; I'm here not to judge, but to advise. Without specific and truthful details, including ingestion quantities and specific SOBs... strength-of-brands... forgive the shop-talk... my cross-reference is useless. It's the minor interactions that carry the punch, you understand?. Remember the story of the flapping butterfly in Brazil causing a tidal wave in

Borneo...?

The furious onset of a Richter-scale gut cramp doubled him up.
A thin stream of projectile vomit spattered against the seepy wall,
scurrying the roaches. "Help me..." he moaned.

"Of course I'll help you, David. But first, you must help yourself.
Okay, you took some Lanolyte, more than the recommended
dosage, I'll bet. That alone was unwise, what with the beer and
the Tectirol; understand, mixing alcohol and vermonyl with
phenylpropagelanine puts approximately fifty percent of the
male population at risk ten percent of the time. This particular
combination decreases the blood's ability to clot normally,
and can interfere with the kidneys ability to produce uric acid.
Obviously, you lucked out this time. Next time, who knows?
Not to belabor a point; if you would have had the insight to
ask my opinion, I'd have told you that the best thing going for
your case of the Hershey squirts is Co-Phate II, which is totally
phenylpropagelanine-free. You don't need all those electrolytes
anyway..."

Mrs. Doosenberry's voice was almost mesmerizing. David grew
faint, fixing his gaze straight ahead. As he watched, the watery
wall stain grew fuzzy and multiplied. In fact, the whole room did.
He retched again.

"Now, bleeding and urinating are not your problems," continued
Mrs. Doosenberry. "Cramping, sweating, and nausea are your

problems. Coupled with body tremors, correct? According to the spreadsheet, that reaction may be induced by a number of products, but especially by Prölong-12 Mentholated Throat Lozenges. David, do come clean now. Have you been popping Prölong-12s?"

"No. I... swear it."

"That's strange. No mentholated lozenges at all? You haven't noticed any blurred or double vision, have you? You never mentioned..."

"Yes!" he cried. "I can see four blurry pukes right now..."

"David..." she said, adopting a quiet, but scolding tone. "David, David, David. Naughty boy... you're a smoker aren't you?"

"Sometimes. But not too much, Mrs. Doosenberry. Only when I drink beer or take a dump..."

"I should have guessed. What brand do you smoke? Wait, don't tell me. Kool Mild..."

"Marlboro Green."

"Same difference. It's the menthol that got to you. Mr. Doosenberry too, God rest him. Angelosante's Disease... that's chronic pulmonemia brought on by flavored tobacco snuff...

it took him out in 1986, same day as the space shuttle blew a gasket... But that's another story. Here's yours, David: Menthol is formed of a specific amino acid chain that breaks when it contacts both rhyphenoxylate and xatrophine simultaneously, resulting in a number of chemicals whose names I wouldn't even try to pronounce... suffice to say that one of their molecular structures is similar to peptic cholera... non-lethal peptic cholera, of course... and your symptoms are a mimicry of that. Fortunately, the worst of it is probably behind you." She chuckled merrily at her own pun. "For now, a teaspoon of Arm & Hammer baking soda stirred into any commercial cola should neutralize the amino acids enough to get you on your feet and down to a pharmacy. Some symptoms will persist for a day or two; here's what I would do if I were you: For the nausea, try Nodyltone, but don't exceed 50 milligrams in four hours. If you can't live with the body tremors, get some Chlor-Olfatron, which contains a mild levodopa... used to treat delirium tremens... but which may cause heart palpitations or offensive anal odors if inhaled excessively or used in conjunction with selenium sulfide shampoos. So, be careful. Oh, if you choose to go with the Chlor-Olfatron, and if you should miss a dose, skip the missed dose and resume your regular schedule. Never 'double up'. Co-Phate for the runs, of course, and as for the excessive sweating, personally I'm still big on Dri-Zine Aerosol..."

"Aerosol...?" he countered, weakly. " Are you sure? Isn't that bad for the environment?"

"Oh, the environment will be just fine, David, like always. That fluorocarbon versus ozone layer myth was propagated by Democrats with an agenda. Dri–Zine is less an environmental threat than cow flatulence. Don't, however, be alarmed by Dri–Zine's cyoantrylic agents, which may cause temporary sexual dysfunction…"

"You're kidding…!?"

"Temporary, David; meaning a week or less. And only in about 2% of any given healthy user. Any time you're dealing with cyoantrylics, the libido may be diminished; hence, its recommendation by the Federal Penal system and the U.S. Army. Not the end of the world, David; trust me. Anyway, that's why God invented Viagra."

"What about the itching?" he replied, petulantly.

"Itching? What itching? You never mentioned any itching."

"Well, it didn't seem… Anyway, my… you know, my… my butt itches like hell."

"Hmmm…" A cyber whir, and the tick-ticking of Mrs. Doosenberry's able fingers. "That ups the ante. You've told me everything? Everything? Say! You don't have a hamster, do you?"

"No hamster."

"Well, then; I'm stumped. Unless..."

"Unless...?"

"Oh, excess sweating may foster the growth of fungal spores. Jock itch, you know, or athlete's foot. Possibly, you may have contracted ringworm as well. Safe and simple solution, based on your drug matrix, is aluminum sulfate. You've got a choice: Maxi-Strength AluGel, which contains alcohol for drying, or Seccoderm. But no more cigarettes, David; that's a prescription for disaster. Bye, now."

She was gone, her voice swallowed by electromagnetic fog. David held the receiver as his vision slowly cleared. He glanced at the clock. Five to five. Baking soda and Royal Crown, huh? Cakewalk. He might make it yet. In style, too, since he recalled having stocked the Ivanhoe shelves with both AluGel and Seccoderm.

Two months later, Tawni bumped into him in the Oxford hallway, as she was busy throwing the deadbolt to No. 18... she always threw the deadbolt exactly twenty-four times; a touch of ODC. It was nine o'clock in the evening; she was maximum vamped, from her curly gold Donita Jones fingernails to her size thirteen pumps.

David was exiting his own flat. Tawni didn't recognize him. He had a jaunty step; his hair looked full, thick, and blow-dried; he was fit and forty pounds trimmer, like he'd been hitting a gym; his complexion was toned, bronzed, and crystal-clear; his eyes filled with the lusty gleam of a healthy, horny man-child.

"Baby? Who are you, and what y'all done with that fey bubba, David Lieberwitz?"

David did a deadpan run-way whirl for the full effect. He was wearing a Paul Smith London wool suit and a stretch moleskin pea coat; he looked like he just stepped down from the showroom window at Brooks Brothers.

"Boyfriend, y'all looking so-o-o fine... Y'all got a fish on the hook tonight, or what?"

"A what?"

"A fish.. a woman... A... Never mind. You got a date?"

David nodded with shy self-satisfaction. "You know Laquenda Murrow, from the market?"

"Laquenda Murrow? Honey, Laquenda's my niece." She conjured up Laquenda's image; an anorexic, fifteen-year-old, brain-dead Rhianna wannabe with tacky green contact lenses.

"Me and her's going out tonight," David crowed. "See, the sand nig... see, my asshole bosses finally promoted me to the produce aisle week, so I do dayshift, now. Got me a real life."

"Man, I tell you what you got... you got it going on..." She retracted the dead bolt all the way... she'd lost count, anyhow... and pushed at the door to No. 18. "Come on in a sec, I want Gran'mama to see this! Child; that is if her pacemaker can handle it!"

David grinned, nodded, and passed over the tiny threshold of No. 18; the first Oxford apartment he'd ever entered beside his own. Amazing what a sense of self-respect could do for an interior, he thought. His, no doubt, could use a makeover. Tawni's apartment exuded love and tranquility; gospel music was leaking softly from the stereo, and the inner sanctum was all houseplants and pictures of Jesus. Scrumptious scents wafted over him; oxtail soup and herbal tea. He sniffed eagerly.

"Y'all want some tea, David? Gran'mama swears by it; she brews it herself outta powdered corn silk from her brother in Kentucky."

"Mize well," said David. "Seeing as I don't drink beer no more. Beer's bad for your liver. Plus, studies indicate that it can cause ankylosing spondylitis when mixed with the CBC inhibitors in Keen Antimicrobial mouthwash..."

"Beg your pardon?"

"This gargle I been using. Called Keen. Mrs. Doosenberry recommends it. You oughta try it. More'n ten million bacteria in every drop of human saliva, dude. Swear to God. Mrs. Doosenberry told me..." David stood in the doorway to the kitchenette as Tawni poured the tea. He jerked a thumb toward the plastic soap dish. "You know what else she told me? ...you leave your soap like that, all wet and shit with dish water? You support the growth of bacteria, including microbial pathogens like Homococcus and Pseudomonas..."

"Say what?"

Gran'mama padded in from the radio room, wearing a size eighteen floral nightgown, looking somewhat glassy-eyed. She surveyed David with the squinty, suspicious glare of a projects survivor. "Who you say that is, Lamarr?"

Lamarr was Tawni's real name. "Said it twice, Gran'mama; now, doll, pay attention." Tawni gently touched Gran'momma's shoulder, steering her head in the right direction. "Tonight, that ain't nothing but hottest show in the city. No, it ain't Rudolph Valentino; guess again. That's David Lieberwitz, from across the hall."

Gran'mama pushed out her lower lip and scowled. She looked like a cross between a pit bull a Jacques Cousteau mini-sub. "That fat, drunken honky in No. 16? That retarded white-trash bagboy who's always bugging Emmy's gal Laquenda? I don't believe you!"

Any broader, David's smile would have hurt. His teeth shone like gems... Oramint dentifrice and TuskLuster enamel buff... and he excused himself, somewhat grandly, so as not to be late for his tryst.

Twenty-four hours later, sashaying down the hallway, Tawni caught wind of a fierce odor emanating from David's flat. Denial and Rive Gauche might get you past a backed-up drain, but this stench wanted attention. Now. It smelled like a Mexican slaughterhouse in mid-July. David's deadbolt wasn't in place; in fact, the door was partially open.

Tawni nudged it the rest of the way with the tip of her Dolce & Gabbana sandal. The stink redoubled and smacked her in the face so hard it curdled her lip-liner. John Wayne Gacy's crawlspace couldn't have smelled that bad. If she hadn't seen David the previous night, she would have suspected that he'd been moldering inside his flat all month, like poor Mr. McGinty; a suicide on her block when she was a little boy.

But there was David, slumped into the polluted corduroy sofa, whining imprecations in staccato, throaty gasps. At least, she surmised it was David; he was wearing an Ivanhoe apron that read 'Assistant Produce Manager Trainee' on the bib. His body was swollen beyond recognition, big as a Lawnboy tractor; his face was a macerated mass of whitish, soggy tissue, and his hairless head resembled the smooth, discolored cap of a necrotic wood fungus. Draining, threadlike gashes crisscrossed his exposed arms; his eyes had shrunken into wads of bloated facial skin and looked like a puckered pair of anuses dumping out festoons of canary-yellow pus. His mouth and chin glittered with a similar, festering discharge that was sluicing from his sinuses. The cushions beneath him were slick with rank-smelling bodily fluids that erupted at intervals, in sullen burps.

Vomit caught in her throat. She was almost pleased; she didn't realize that she had any gag reflexes left.

David had seen her, and was pointing awkwardly but urgently toward a coffee table. His hand was thick and formless; it appeared that his fingers had melded together into a greasy, conical clump. The table surface was littered with bottles, tubes, tablets, jars, childproof containers, phials, capsules, ointments covering every range of ailment, malady, and indisposition known to modern hypochondria: Precyse Medicated Mist, Dri-Zine Aerosol, Sktrach-Not Topical Balm with Amylbutocin, Keen mouthwash, Liquidex Rootbeer Flavored Diet Plan, Lytzzz-Out Sleep Aid with PPH, Dr. Pran's Fistula-B-Gone, Co-Phate, Co-Phate Plus, Maximum Strength Co-Phate Plus with Oxyphylosulfactamide, Sorbatine Benzohydroxocycaline Gyrocaps, Trantralac Undiluted Cough Calmer with Effervescent Elixodyne Pain Relief...

For a moment, Tawni thought that David was prescribing; he appeared to be urging her toward a roll of Gripp-4 lozenges, which was used to control nausea. But, he was pointing at a telephone with an 800 number scrawled on a scratch-paper, moaning, "Myrnax... Myrnax..."

Tawni paced the room, wringing one hand, holding her nose with the other. "Honey, you don't need any Myrnax, believe me; you need to drag your drug-taking ass down to the clinic..."

A low roar arose from deep, desperate wells within his thorax. He gurgled and gacked out the contents of his esophagus, then spoke: "Oh God... I can't make it to any clinic! I can't move. I've got such a migraine, my head feels like it's splitting open." Literally, it was. A slow ooze of rancid juice dribbled from a rent which was forming in his forehead. "I can't dial the phone... You gotta help me. Call Mrs. Doosenberry..."

"Mrs. Whosenberry? Sugar, you don't need no Mrs. Nobody; I'm calling 911..."

"No!" he bellowed, with all the passion of which a human voice is capable. "They can't do shit for me, 'cept maybe make me worse by giving me some prescription crap that won't interact right with all the OTC's..."

"The OT...?"

"Look at me!" he shrieked. "This all happened in the last few hours, after I got home from work. One second, I was fine. Next, everything started letting go..."

A pinkish wreath of steam belched from his split brow. The sheer force of his howling caused several loose incisors to drop from his mouth like bloody, over-ripe mulberries. "You gotta get Mrs. Doosenberry on the phone," he lisped. "That's the number. She'll know what I should take. But first, I gotta come clean with her... I gotta 'fess up... I never told her about the Myrnax!"

For all her pluses, Tawni was not one for crisis management. She didn't 'do' blood, she didn't change diapers, and in a medical emergency, she was prepared to let anyone take charge, even the victim. Hastily, clumsily, she punched out the 800 number with her curling gold ad-ons.

Mrs. Doosenberry's mellifluous voice responded at a single ring; as was her routine, she asked for the specific drug about which the caller had a question.

"Oh, it ain't me I'm calling for," Tawni cried hysterically. "Miss Tawni don't never put nothing from the medicine cabinet into her holy temple, 'cept for Hysmarin..."

"Hysmarin, eh?" replied Mrs. Doosenberry sharply. "That's a very potent hormone, sir. No concern for the side effects? You should be! Bradycardia, iron-deficiency anemia, hypertension, bronchospasms, tinnitus, esophageal reflux..."

"Never mind, honey; you shoot estrogen *because* of the side effects..."

David's voice was growing weaker and more pathetic. "Myrnax... Myrnax.... Tell Mrs. Doosenberry 'bout me and the Myrnax..."

"Look," said Tawni into the phone, "I'm from across the hall. I'm over here in No. 16, David Lieberwitz place..."

"Oh, David! He's a sweetheart, isn't he? A nice Jewish boy, that's what Mother used to say. I haven't heard from David in a coon's age... almost nine hours... How is he?"

"Not so motherfucking good, miss, if y'all forgive the Ebonics. Something's happening to him... he's... falling apart!"

"No reason to panic, dear. Just describe Mr. Lieberwitz's symptoms, and we'll find something on the shelves to put him right..."

"Symptoms? Uh..." Crinkling her nose, bending a bit closer, Tawni replied, "Lord almighty... it's like his head's blowed up to the size of a disco ball; there's a big crack down the middle of his forehead, and it's jacking out some kind of nasty goo... Oh, Jesus H. Christ! Something just fell out of his head and rolled behind the cushions." She winced, glancing at down her sandal. "And there's this funky dooky all over the floor..."

"What color's the dooky?"

"Color?? Some kinda... puce, I guess. No... more like a mauve."

"Hmmm. Bloody stool... A very severe allergic reaction, no doubt... Any mucous discharge from the glands or fistula formation between the bowel and bladder?"

"...Myrnax..." groaned David.

"...any denuded flesh, draining sores, loss of nerve coordination, shortness of breath, drowsiness, disorientation as to time and space?"

"Yeah, all that shit..."

"Does the vomitus contained gastric juices or the fecal contents of the ileum...?"

Desperately, David raised a clumsy, suppurating limb. "Just tell her about the goddamned Myrnax," he croaked. "It's gotta go into my side-effects matrix before she can say what product can help me..."

Tawni didn't have a clue as to what he was talking about. "Lady," he interrupted. "David says to tell you he's been using Myrnax!"

"Come again?" replied Mrs. Doosenberry, momentarily silenced.

"Myrnax, the hair restorer? Impossible, that was taken off the market years ago... You must have misunderstood him. Anyway, as I was saying, is the poor soul showing any signs of obvious psychiatric disturbances, petit mal epilepsy, seborrhea, gastrointestinal upset, noncancerous but festering liver tumors, pulmonary embolism, digital gangrene...?"

Tawni covered the voice part of the receiver. "She says you can't buy no more Myrnax, honey..."

Mrs. Doosenberry went on. "...scaling, rupturing nodules, large, flaccid scrotal erosions...?"

The cleft in David's skull was widening, and as Tawni watched, the living bone began to decompose in spasmodic shudders. Brownish secretions were spewing from small lesions in his brow, making his head look like a molasses sprinkler. His voice was clearly failing. "At Ivanhoe... We stock it; goddamned boss buys recalled product, ten cents on the dollar..."

"...skin legions, conspicuous ulcers, patches of vitiligo, elevated or diminished calcium levels...?"

"It's Myrnax, all right, girl", Tawni howled into the phone. "He's buying it close-out at Ivanhoe..."

"Oh, my. My, My. Black market...?"

"Naw, Chaldean. So fucking what? You mean to tell me the Myrnax is doing this to him?"

"Not at all, sir. Myrnax was a consumer fraud; it was taken off the market because it was utterly useless; the active ingredient was Di-hydrogen monoxide." She chuckled conspiratorially. "Water!"

Tawni was not up to the joke. For one thing, it was over her head; for another, David's head was imploding into his shoulder blades. She gaped in horror.

Mrs. Doosenberry continued: "No, Myrnax on the scalp is as safe as a squirt of Absopure. And about as effective. David's condition is symptomatic of a total breakdown of the delicate balance we'd established within his personalized drug portfolio. You understand, the series of medications he was ingesting each can produce specific, identifiable adverse reactions, so we'd built up a menu of OTCs... over-the-counters, sorry; it's shop-talk... each remedy curing a specific side effect, forming a delicate, but perfectly symmetrical pharmaceutical circle, until he was not only perfectly healthy, but side-effect free!"

"Strangely," Mrs. Doosenberry frowned, "my database indicates that the only known chemical capable of upsetting this particular equilibrium is propoxychlorothiazine flumethicone, which is not contained in any currently available, or, for that matter, any obsolete OTC medication. In fact, it occurs naturally only in Peruvian bat guano and hybrid Kentucky corn silk. No matter.

You see, unfortunately, there's nothing available to help the poor dear. Nothing at all. Alas, these are the days I dread as a professional. According to my calculations, David will completely metastasize into side effects within half an hour. Meantime, try to make him comfortable... for the spastic rectum, try a spoonful of Co-Phate Plus... for the de-ossification, Might-E-Bone, but use the quick-acting tablets, not the gel caps... for the digital gangrene and decaying gums, try..."

Her voice faded into high-frequency static, but it didn't matter. Nobody was listening. Miss Tawni had fled the room, leaving the receiver dangling, and David had disintegrated into the sofa.

Made in the USA
Middletown, DE
09 October 2016